Her subdued elegance stood out in the crowd.

The tilt of her head, the sweep of her slender neck, bespoke a woman of grace and refinement.

Ben's heart surprised him, lurching uncomfortably in his chest. Memories, long forgotten, rose to the surface of his mind like bubbles rising in a champagne glass.

The line of passengers advanced; she drew closer. The varied colors and indeterminate scents of the waiting area dissolved into the background as his gaze homed in on her face. The confusing discord of a score of languages faded to a soft murmur.

Eight years and a divorce decree separated them; an ocean and most of a continent divided their lives. And yet, once they had been everything to each other. Everything.

Maggie was even more beautiful than he remembered.

Dear Reader,

When two people fall in love, the world is suddenly new and exciting, and it's that same excitement we bring to you in Silhouette Intimate Moments. These are stories with scope, with grandeur. These characters lead the lives we all dream of, and everything they do reflects the wonder of being in love.

Longer and more sensuous than most romances, Silhouette Intimate Moments novels take you away from everyday life and let you share the magic of love. Adventure, glamour, drama, even suspense— these are the passwords that let you into a world where love has a power beyond the ordinary, where the best authors in the field today create stories of love and commitment that will stay with you always.

This month we present three of your favorite authors: Linda Howard, Elizabeth Lowell and Erin St. Claire. To round out the month we're proud to offer the first Silhouette Intimate Moments novel by Marion Smith Collins, whose previous romances have charmed readers the world over. Then, next month, get ready to meet four new authors, all making their debut in the world of contemporary romance. Look in the back of this book for more information on just how special next month will be here at Silhouette Intimate Moments.

Leslie J. Wainger
Senior Editor
Silhouette Books

Marion Smith Collins
Another Chance

Silhouette Intimate Moments
Published by Silhouette Books New York
America's Publisher of Contemporary Romance

SILHOUETTE BOOKS
300 East 42nd St., New York, N.Y. 10017

Copyright © 1987 by Marion Smith Collins

All rights reserved, including the right to reproduce
this book or portions thereof in any form whatsoever.
For information address Silhouette Books,
300 East 42nd St., New York, N.Y. 10017

ISBN: 0-373-07179-5

First Silhouette Books printing February 1987

America's Publisher of Contemporary Romance

Printed in the U.S.A.

MARION SMITH COLLINS

has written non-fiction for years, but only recently has she tried her hand at novels. She is already the author of several contemporary romances and has no plans ever to stop.

She's a devoted traveler and has been to places as far-flung as Rome and Tahiti. Her favorite country for exploring, however, is the United States because, she says, it has everything.

In addition, she is a wife and the mother of two children. She has been a public relations director, and her love of art inspired her to run a combination gallery and restaurant for several years.

She lives with her husband of thirty years in Georgia.

This book is dedicated to my friend, Jenny Eddings, who didn't have to think twice when I suggested a trip to Rome; to our husbands, Bob and Mike, who thought several times; and . . . in Roma . . .

To Mario Loetta, our driver, who was very understanding when I wanted to wander around alone in the Colosseum at midnight;

To Pia Baldelli at the University of Rome, for being a fountain of information and a gracious hostess;

To Pier Luigi, Mario Torosantucci; and everyone at the small hotel on the Via Lombardia; and to all the warm and wonderful people of Italy who made us so very welcome.

Chapter 1

Leonardo da Vinci Airport was swarming with people despite the earliness of the hour. But Ben Altman, restless and impatient at the delay caused by the crowd, had no trouble spotting his ex-wife. Through the opening in the wall separating the international concourse from the waiting area, he caught a glimpse of Maggie's shining hair and was gratified to see that she was near the front of the line of people waiting to clear customs.

Ben's heart surprised him, lurching uncomfortably in his chest. Memories, long forgotten, rose to the surface of his mind like bubbles in a champagne glass.

The line advanced; she drew closer. The varied colors and indeterminate scents of the waiting area dissolved into the background as his gaze homed in on her face. The confusing discord of a score of languages faded to a soft murmur.

Maggie was more beautiful than he remembered. Her subdued elegance stood out in the crowd of passengers.

The tilt of her head, the exquisite shape of her small ear, the sweep of her slender neck, bespoke a woman of grace and refinement. Even when filled with fear and anxiety, her eyes were dark with a promise of unexplored depths. Wound loosely into a twist and anchored with pins at the back of her head, her golden hair was streaked with moonbeams. Eight years and a divorce decree separated them; an ocean and most of a continent divided their lives. And yet they had once been everything to each other. Everything.

Observations like that could get you into a hell of a lot of trouble, Altman. Ben smiled grimly to himself and jingled the loose change in his pants pocket with one hand. In the other a cigarette burned unnoticed. Trouble like that, he didn't need. He couldn't cope with memories, not now.

A bulky woman shifted from one foot to the other, giving him an unobstructed view of the rest of Maggie Altman. The severe cut of her black linen suit was relieved by a soft drape of white between the lapels. A jaunty red silk square protruded haphazardly from the pocket over her breast, as though it had been added at the last minute to buttress her courage.

The small sign of bravery touched Ben even more profoundly than her beauty or the memories. His grim smile altered to one of melancholy as he dropped the cigarette to the floor and ground it out with his heel.

Unquestionably they both were going to need all the courage they had. Was she up to it? Was he? Ben realized that his palms were sweating. *Get hold of yourself, Altman. If there was ever a time in your life to exercise the air-conditioned attitude you're so famous for, this is it.* Not only courage, but shrewdness and—hardest of all—patience would be essential over the next few days, or weeks, or... however long it took.

Ben took a long, deliberate breath and let it out very slowly, bringing his emotions under control, forcing his mind to function with his newsman's objectivity. In the process his eyes narrowed, his gaze sharpened. A muscle in his jaw clenched. It was time to get down to business. No one, he vowed to himself, would distract him until the job was done.

Maggie could be a help, or she could be a hindrance. Dispassionately he searched her features for a clue as to which to expect. Her appearance hadn't changed much, he thought, then immediately amended the thought. Maggie, he reminded himself, was a woman now. She wasn't going to collapse on him, weeping and hysterical.

Her anxiety must be overwhelming, but even under these nerve-racking circumstances, there was something...a quiet control about her that hadn't been there eight years ago. He could almost feel the leashed energy radiating from her slender body, the suppressed tension. He could recognize those feelings, those emotions, because they reflected his own so completely.

Margaret Anne Bentley Altman was conscious of the customs agent's careful scrutiny as she answered his questions in fluent Italian. She longed suddenly for the old diplomatic passport that had made these things so easy. *Forget it, Maggie. The man is simply doing his job,* she chided herself.

Gradually she became aware of another feeling, a sensation that she was being watched. She raised her eyes. Framed in the doorway of the wall dividing the official area from the concourse was her ex-husband.

Neither of them moved, or even breathed, for an endless moment.

As she looked straight into his wary and guarded gaze, a simple fact registered: despite the regularity of Ben's appearances on the network news, when his rugged features would be juxtaposed with the Colosseum or the Spanish Steps or St. Peter's, she'd forgotten his personal impact. She'd forgotten that no matter what the environment, he was a man in charge of his surroundings.

Tall and broad-shouldered and fit, even in wrinkled chinos and a dark sport coat, he was an impressive figure. His charcoal hair was dusted lightly with silver, but that she had known. The Italian sun had darkened his tan; the lines that radiated from his eyes were deeper than they'd been eight years ago. That she had known, too. The physical changes had registered on her easily, smoothly over the years. The impersonal eye of the camera had deluded her into complacency. But the camera could never completely register the vitality and the charisma that were so much a part of him.

Maggie realized she was staring. Unconsciously she corrected her weary slouch and acknowledged his presence with a nod. She dropped her eyes to watch the Italian finally slash a crosswise chalk mark on her umber leather suitcase. *"Grazie,"* she murmured when he returned her passport and motioned her through. Lifting the bag, she entered the wedge of passengers that shuffled with maddening slowness toward the doorway where Ben waited.

Ben moved forward to lounge with a deceptively casual stance against the wall, but inside he was a mass of conflicting feelings. He straightened as she drew near, ready to hurry her out of the airport to the car, and the traumatic events that awaited them.

Squaring her shoulders, Maggie walked toward him, meeting his gaze directly. She reminded herself that Ben was here, as she was, to deal with a terrible situation. Were it not for the crisis that had brought her to Rome, they might not have met for another eight years.

"Maggie," he said carefully when she was a few feet away. Up close, his sea-green eyes were somber and worried, and a little bloodshot.

He held out his arm, as though to draw her into an embrace. It was a natural gesture, an offer of comfort under the appalling circumstances of their reunion, but it somehow served to increase her nervousness. She couldn't surrender to the temptation of comfort in any form, not now. She repeated the words that had become a refrain in her head during the long overnight flight from Washington to Rome. *You can live through the next minute, Maggie; don't think about the one after that. Don't think about the next hour, the next day, just the next minute.*

Pretending to misunderstand Ben's gesture, she extended the hand that gripped her suitcase. "Ben. Thanks for meeting me."

Ben nodded, nonplussed for a moment by her reserve. He reached for the bag, noting with surprise that it seemed to weigh almost nothing. "Is this all?" The girl whom he once knew couldn't cross the street without a matched set of luggage filled to capacity.

Maggie smiled, correctly interpreting the reason for his surprise. "This is it," she responded. "I've learned to travel light."

Ben arched one dark brow, an engaging mannerism that had become a Ben Altman trademark. The familiar action was so much a part of her memories that Maggie felt her response immediately. This wouldn't do. This wouldn't do at all.

"Come on then," he said. "My car's not far." With his free hand at her elbow, he led her swiftly along the edge of the concourse, skirting the crowds.

Maggie lengthened her stride effortlessly to pull slightly ahead of him, her steps quick but not frantic. She didn't want him to touch her, not yet. She needed to recover from the rather surprising effects of this reunion first. "Is there any news?" she asked, amazed at how composed she sounded.

Ben hadn't missed her withdrawal. Her question jarred him back to the present, to their reason for being here, like this. He shook his head. "No, not a word. At least not one that they'll reveal to me."

"But you're Jamie's father. Surely they would keep you informed."

"I'm also a reporter," he reminded her unnecessarily. "I was allowed into the embassy for a five-minute off-the-record meeting with the deputy ambassador this morning. He says that it looks like kidnapping, but there has been no news of the car, no ransom demands, nothing."

"Damn," she muttered shakily, displaying the first crack in the facade of calm. The few bites of breakfast she'd made herself eat on the plane sat heavily in her stomach. She swallowed hard, compelling them to stay there and plunged a fist into the pocket of her jacket. "I can't believe this is really happening."

"I wish to God it weren't," he said, sweeping her with a sidewise glance. The catch in her voice, the way she was staring steadily ahead, affected him the same way the sight of the red handkerchief had. And he didn't like it one bit better. Where the hell had this ache come from? He would have sworn that the woman who could make him feel vulnerable didn't exist, but it seemed that Maggie still could. If she'd just let him take her arm, touch her in some casual way, perhaps the strange longing within him would be eased. But she didn't need his support. Moving quickly but without obvious haste, she was as graceful as a dancer. A muscle in his jaw contracted. He remembered . . . he remembered too damned much. "The people at the embassy aren't going to like your being here, either, when they find out."

Unaware of the emotion boiling inside Ben, Maggie sidestepped a portly man in a three-piece suit. *"Mi scusi,"* she said, summoning a smile when her shoulder bag clipped his elbow. The man was left behind. "I know. They'd probably rather I stayed in Washington and gave out tearful interviews." She hesitated, wanting to thank him for notifying her so quickly, for arranging everything, yet not sure how to. "Ben—thanks."

"Yeah. This is a hell of a situation, the kind of thing that happens to other people, not you."

"The area's been calm for a while. I guess I was hopeful it was all a mistake."

His sigh was audible even above the airport noise. "We have to be hopeful, Margaret Anne." The old endearing use of her full name slipped out without his noticing.

She steeled herself against the memories. "I feel so helpless. If you hadn't called, I probably wouldn't have known that my father and my son were missing until I saw it on the news."

"If I hadn't gone by the residence to pick up Jamie, I wouldn't have known, either. They're really keeping it under wraps. I can't help wondering how much more they know than they're telling me."

Maggie's gaze slid to his strong, square jaw, and away.

Ben didn't miss the quick suspicion in her brown eyes. His response was immediate and irritated. "No, I haven't blown the whistle," he snapped.

"It's your job."

The accusation was just what Ben needed to jolt him out of the sentimental reverie he'd fallen into. His brow darkened angrily. "Damn it, Maggie, Jamie is my son, too. Do you think I'd take any chance at all with his safety? What the hell kind of father do you think I am?"

As a question it was pretty much rhetorical. Ben was a good father—for two months in the summer and a week at Christmas. He would have liked more time; she knew that. Maybe when Jamie was older...the thought caused her fingers to tighten around the strap of her shoulder bag in a choke hold.

They didn't speak again until they were out of the terminal. The July heat hit Maggie a breath-stealing blow, and the bright Italian sun punished eyes sensitive from emotion and lack of sleep. She fumbled in her bag for her dark glasses, but they weren't there. "Damn," she muttered again.

The epithet, fairly mild by today's standards, sounded brash from that exquisite mouth. Ben smiled to himself. "What did you forget?"

She rezipped the bag. "My sunglasses."

"There may be an extra pair in the glove compartment of the car. Over there." He led the way to the sleek Italian sports car she'd heard so much about and opened the passenger door. Her bag was deposited in the space behind the seats.

"Mom, you should see Dad's new black Ferrari! It's really something!" She squeezed her eyes shut against the echo of Jamie's words. Excitement had glistened in the heavy lashed green eyes that were the mirror image of Ben's. After his Christmas visit Jamie had described his father's car in excruciating detail, as he did every particular of his biannual trips to Rome.

She arranged herself on the smooth leather, reaching for the seat belt as he came around to climb in beside her. He took dark glasses from behind the visor and slipped them on, started the car and flipped on the air-conditioning. "Did you check the glove compartment for sunglasses?"

She found a pair. They were smartly styled and definitely feminine, but she didn't comment on the fact. "Are we going to the chancery first, or straight to the residence?" she asked.

The official building that housed the offices of the United States Embassy was located in the heart of Rome on the Via Veneto, but the ambassador actually lived a few miles away on a broad tree-lined boulevard. The walled estate sat amidst other ambassadorial residences in the area.

Ben paid the parking fee and maneuvered smoothly into the traffic headed for Rome before he answered. "I can take you either place, but I doubt there are more than a handful of people at the chancery who even know that anything's happened."

"Let's go directly to the residence, then. Judith will know as much as anyone." Judith Ames had been her father's private secretary for fourteen years. Nothing got past Judith.

"I'm sorry, Maggie. Judith's on vacation. She left two weeks ago for her sister's place in New Hampshire. I thought about calling her, but I decided to talk to you about it first."

Maggie hid her distress at the news. She had counted heavily on her friend's support. "I guess you're right. There's no point in alarming her until we know something."

"Maybe the appointment secretary will have something to report. She shares an office with Judith."

A slight emphasis in his voice cued her. His words had significance beyond their meaning.

What was the appointment secretary's name? Maggie frowned, trying to remember. She hadn't met the woman, but she'd heard her father mention her. Lola, that was it. Lola...something...Orenda. "You suspect Lola Orenda of being involved?"

"I suspect anyone who might have had the remotest opportunity, or any information about the ambassador's movements."

Maggie half turned in the seat, another question on her lips, but before she could speak, Ben's hand went to his forehead in a familiar gesture. He raked back a lock of dark hair that, she remembered, was governed by a cowlick and resisted all attempts at discipline. His fingers remained to massage his nape in frustration. It was a move she had seen him execute a thousand times, and it told her more than any words how disturbed he was by the situation. *Dear Lord, were all her memories going to be this vivid?*

Their marriage had ended long ago, too long ago to think about. There were more important worries on her mind now, and she couldn't afford anything more than an uneasy alliance with Ben Altman. She sensed his gaze on her again.

"How was your flight?" he asked.

The mundane question provoked a bark of mirthless laughter and reinforced her opinion that her ex-husband still wasn't quite sure what to make of her. Sadness touched her heart for the two people who had once loved so wildly, so passionately. Now they sat here, unexpectedly reunited as the result of a fiendish act of terrorism, but divided by more than the width of a seat—divided by the highest barrier of all, a dead love.

"You can stop being so formal, Ben. As you said, it's a hell of a situation, but I'm not about to fall apart on you. I've changed—grown up a lot in eight years." Her voice took on a decisive timbre as she moved on to more practical matters. It was imperative that she be practical. "Now, tell me what's being done to find my father and my son."

"Our son," Ben corrected.

Maggie opened her mouth to make a caustic remark, then changed her mind. Nothing would be served if they got into an argument. "Our son," she agreed.

Ben reached into the pocket of his jacket for a cigarette and held a lighter to its tip. "Well, as you can imagine, the intelligence people have descended en masse, both military and civilian. Sorry. Cigarette?"

"I quit."

"Smart."

"Not really. Jamie bullied me into it. I'm surprised he hasn't done the same to you."

Ben's mouth lifted in a half smile. "He's progressing slowly." His eyes clouded with memory. "He coughs and carries on so much that I've quit smoking when I'm around him."

Maggie laughed gently, caught up in memories of her own. "That's the same technique he used on me. I'm warning you, it's only a matter of time."

He exhaled, sending smoke up to the roof of the car, where it hung for a moment like a thin cloud before dispersing. "Back to the subject of our friends. So far they haven't been able to come up with anything very intelligent," he informed her wryly.

"Tell me again what happened." She braced herself for his answer. When Ben had called late yesterday afternoon, she'd been too stunned to take in the details.

He attacked the cowlick again. "The Department of Antiquities has been excavating a major archaeological find near Hadrian's Villa in Tivoli. The director invited your father out to the site to have lunch and take a look at their progress."

Maggie nodded. Her father, the U.S. ambassador to Italy, was known to be a keen archaeology buff. He would have been excited by the invitation.

"He called me to ask if Jamie could go along. Of course I said yes," he added with a grin.

"How could you do otherwise?" She met his smile. Jamie was as enthusiastic about ruins as his grandfather. Two years ago, at the ripe old age of five, he'd proclaimed his desire to be an archaeologist.

"Momma, Granddad took me to see a circus. It was this big." With a five-year-old's enthusiasm, Jamie spread his arms wide to encompass all of his tiny world.

"That sounds like fun. Were there acrobats and animals? Did you see the clowns?" she asked with a grin.

He looked disgusted. "It wasn't that kind of circus, Mom. It was an old, old circus." He frowned and stumbled over the words. "Circus me-maximum."

"Circus Maximus?"

"Yeah, that's it! Granddad tells such great stories about all the dead people who used to live there. When

I grow up, I'm gonna dig under there to see if I can find any bones and stuff."

Maggie caught her lower lip between her teeth and bit down hard.

"...finished about three, according to the director. Dante was waiting outside the gates."

"Dante was with them?" she asked suddenly, picturing the burly man who had been her father's faithful bodyguard-chauffeur for years. Inside her chest her heart gave a hopeful leap. If Dante was with them...

"When I came by to pick up Jamie at five, they still hadn't returned. The police had no report of an accident; the *principale*, Luigi Alberto, is a friend of mine. He's as puzzled as the rest of us. The limo has simply disappeared. I hung around until about six-thirty. Then I drove up to Tivoli myself. I talked to the director, drove around. There was no sign of them. I got back about eight. By then we all knew something was wrong."

"You called me at four."

He stubbed out the cigarette. "Ten p.m., our time. The Italian police have been working all night. Sometimes I wish our people would leave them to it. They're the most knowledgeable—it is their country, after all—but try telling that to the fellows from Intelligence." Jerking his tie free, he opened the top button of his shirt with an angry flick. "I just hope to hell they don't screw things up by throwing their weight around," he growled. "They're being very cagey with me, of course. The special I did after the last hijacking here didn't help." He threw her a look and started to explain. "It was an..."

"In-depth study on the seeming inability of the various organizations dealing with terrorism to dovetail their efforts and information," Maggie finished for him. "I saw it. It was very good."

Ben was trained to be the impartial, unbiased eye of the public. Over the years he had learned to keep his expression neutral. He kept his eyes on the road, his hands steady on the wheel, but he was surprised at the compliment, surprised that she'd even bothered to watch. "Anyway, I'm afraid they'll start playing the same old games."

"They can't do that!" she erupted. "I'll . . ."

Ben automatically reached across to cover Maggie's clenched fist with his big warm hand. Her eyes flew to his. Even behind the shield of dark glass he could see her aversion, and he immediately withdrew, cursing himself for the careless move. She'd made it quite clear that she didn't want him to touch her. "Maggie, listen. Neither you nor I have any official capacity in this situation. Ian is the ambassador to Italy first and your father second. And Jamie is simply his grandson—another pawn, however innocent, in this nasty game."

"I realize that," Maggie snapped, and turned her head to stare blindly out the window. The views of the city that flashed by were lost to her. She knew she had no authority here, but her father and her son were missing! Surely there was *something* she could do.

Jamie, her baby, whom she loved with every fiber of her being, was in desperate danger. She smiled sadly to herself. Jamie was a clever child, bright beyond his years. He would hate it if he knew that she ever thought of him as a baby, but he was so young, only seven. She put trembling fingers to her lips and pressed hard. On top of her fear and worry, the hours of inactivity on the airplane had left her wired. She had to get control of herself.

Ben held his breath, looking for a sign of peevishness in the outburst but finding none. Maggie's expression held only frustration with a situation in which she was helpless to do anything. He empathized completely. He wasn't used to having his hands tied, either.

"Look, Maggie. I have some rather unorthodox sources, and I've put the word out. With any luck, we'll find out something privately that wouldn't be available through normal channels." He strived to keep his voice low and reassuring. "In fact, as soon as I drop you off, I'm going to talk to a man who may know something."

"I'll go with you."

"No." It was a flat declaration. No vacillating, no tentativeness.

She shot him a glare. "Now you look, Ben. We may as well get something straight from the beginning. If I had only wanted to wring my hands and pray, I could have stayed in Washington. My father and my son have disappeared. Though neither of us has put a name to their disappearance, we both know the probabilities." She paused, taking a deep breath. When she spoke again her voice was harsh. "I intend take an active part, to do anything I can do to get them back. I have a few contacts in Rome, too, you know."

Her assertiveness startled Ben. An active part? She looked so fragile. "The agent from Washington is waiting to talk to you." As bait it wasn't much, but it was all he had at the moment. Where was the old malleable Maggie? he wondered. Then he realized the incongruity of that thought. Only a short while ago he had been looking for and dreading a sign of weakness in his ex-wife. He shook his head, hardening his resolve. "And I don't have time to waste arguing. I'm to meet my contact in less than an hour."

"Where?"

He only hesitated for an instant. "By the river, at the Ponte Palatino."

Maggie closed her eyes, unwillingly picturing the area. The bridge was only two blocks from the tiny apartment where they'd lived as man and wife. Steps led down from the bridge to a walkway beside the Tiber River. The path had been one of their favorite places, particularly on hot summer nights when the breeze off the river gave some respite from the heat in their apartment. They would walk slowly, pausing in the shadows to kiss, to whisper, and then to hurry home....

She killed off the memory by forcing her thoughts back to today. "The Ponte Palatino is on our way. It's ridiculous for you to take me all the way to the residence and then backtrack."

"This man probably doesn't know a thing. I'm just putting out feelers right now."

"Then there is no reason for you not to take me along."

"Maggie, this is not a game."

"I know that," she said, hurt that he could even think he'd have to deliver a warning like that.

"You could be in danger, as well. What if they got at you, too? And used you to put pressure on your father?"

That thought hadn't occurred to her. She wasn't afraid for herself, but she could see his reasoning. "I'll be careful, Ben. I won't take any unnecessary chances, I promise, but can't you see? I have to be doing something. I have to!"

Ben sighed heavily. They were no longer talking about her accompanying him to meet a contact. Now they were discussing her full participation, and he didn't like it. He decided to relent on this point, hoping that on others he might get her to cooperate. "Okay, we'll stop on the way." His voice dropped. "I can understand your feelings, Maggie. I know you want to help, and you probably can. But you can't rush in helter-skelter. The situation is just too precarious, too fragile."

She sighed, leaning her head against the back of the seat. "Ben, I do work for the State Department. I know how precarious any situation like this is."

Ben looked at her quietly, not speaking. The fight seemed to have drained out of her all at once, leaving her limp.

He lit another cigarette and took a long drag. The acrid sting of smoke in his nostrils overrode the scent of her perfume, which he remembered so well. He found himself wondering irrelevantly why she hadn't changed to something more up-to-date, more modern. The classic fragrance still suited her classic beauty though, he admitted as his gaze traced her profile.

As he'd discovered in the airport, she was the same, yet different: as beautiful as ever, but now the beauty went deeper. The high forehead, the sweep of thick lashes shadowing her cheeks, the delicate slope of her nose, the perfect lips, rounded chin, the elegant throat—she might have modeled for one of Ancient Rome's sculptors or Paris's haute couture designers with equal ease. Her clothes were chosen for practicality rather than effect, but the effect was there.

Yes, she'd grown up. However, the maturity was flawed by something he hadn't noticed at first. She seemed to have surrounded her herself with a brittle shell that masked her feelings. The shell was as obvious as though it were painted a blinding red; he only hoped it was protective and temporary. He would hate to think of his Maggie as a hard, passionless woman. While he admired her new composure, he felt a moment's sadness for the vivacity, the animation and unguarded emotion, the self-confident spirit that had first drawn him to her.

But then, that had all been an illusion, too.

Ben had just returned from a long assignment in Beirut; he'd been feeling burned out, exhausted and bitterly disturbed over the situation there. He'd protested when the network assigned him to cover the latest meeting between the leaders of the two superpowers in Geneva, Switzerland. He'd been promised a vacation. The network bosses considered the Geneva assignment to be one.

The entire week was planned minute by minute, the social occasions being as important as the official ones. However unenthusiastically, Ben had wangled an invitation for the ball at the French embassy, for it was during the social occasions that a casually made remark often gave the other side a hint of what might be unofficially acceptable.

He had just entered the ballroom when he heard the captivating sound of her laughter, soft but slightly husky, the kind of contagious laughter that compelled one to search for the source. His gaze found her at once; she was dancing with a distinguished older man.

Though Ben hadn't been in the country long, he recognized the man as one of the representatives who would direct the negotiations. He was Ian Bentley, based in Geneva but really an ambassador-at-large, troubleshooter for the administration in Washington, better known to newsmen as the "Master Diplomat." The extravagant title had been bestowed upon him the year before by a member of the press when he'd resolved a major diplomatic crisis between France and the United States over the sale of some military hardware to Syria.

Ian was one of the few men to rise through the ranks of the State Department to his position. His expertise was too valuable for his career to be affected by the change of administrations. It was speculated that he would be a full ambassador very soon, no matter which party won the election.

Ben approved. He wished that all ambassadorships were conferred on the basis of knowledge and experience rather than political payoff.

Who was the blonde? Ian was a popular widower and known to date often. She could be anyone.

Ben accepted a glass of champagne from the tray of a passing waiter and, keeping his eyes on the couple, began to move slowly around the perimeter of the dance floor. As he watched, another man tapped Ian on the shoulder. Though he gave up his partner with good grace, Ben could see the frown on Ian's face. *I don't blame you a bit,* thought Ben. *If I had her in my arms, I wouldn't want to give her up, either.*

Suddenly, across her partner's shoulder, the woman's eyes met his, and he forgot Ian's frown, her partner, the whole damn ballroom. Nothing existed but her. Unexpected, overwhelming desire struck him like a flash of lightning, a bolt of thunder *un coup de foudre.* He reeled from it.

He'd expected blue eyes, but in contrast to her cool blond beauty, her eyes were sultry and heavy-lashed, the color of dark bittersweet chocolate. They widened slightly at the visual caress in his gaze, and color tinted her cheeks. Charming, he thought—an old-fashioned word, but appropriate. How long had it been since he'd been charmed by a woman?

She quickly mastered her expression and looked away. He was presented with her profile, exposed by hair pulled away from her face and piled on top of her head.

The man she was dancing with said something, and she smiled slightly. The fair skin of her right cheek was pierced suddenly by the most flirtatious dimple Ben had ever seen. Her partner said something else, and the dimple deepened. Ben was unable to look away.

When the song ended, she turned toward the table where Ian had joined a group. Ben watched, mesmerized, as she moved across the floor with her partner following. The long white dress might have been created for a goddess. Its soft fabric fell from one shoulder diagonally across the bodice to be caught at her tiny waist with a golden rope. Her head high, shoulders straight, bare arms relaxed, she didn't walk; she glided. Completely at ease in this gathering of jet-setters, diplomats and Swiss bankers, she must be of royal family, a princess, surely, though her bearing was more like that of a queen.

He never remembered how he got there, but he found himself by the table, looking down at her like some adoring puppy, hoping for an introduction. Ian Bentley was occupied with a firmly corseted dowager and didn't see him.

The vision smiled again—this time for him—and he almost melted at her feet. "I'm Ben Altman," he finally blurted. "Should I bow or curtsy or something?"

His memory hadn't exaggerated the beautiful melody of her laughter. "Curtsy? That would be something to see, Mr. Ben Altman."

"You're American?" he asked, delighted to hear her East Coast accent. "Where are you from?"

"Virginia. And you?"

"Baltimore. We're practically neighbors."

She nodded, and he watched her dimple, fascinated. "Then may I have this dance, neighbor? Or do I need a formal introduction?"

She glanced at Ian before answering. "I'd love to dance. There's just one small problem."

"What problem?" He looked around, ready to fight dragons if necessary.

"The orchestra is taking a break," she said calmly, but she rose, her movements gracefully fluid. "But we could get a drink or something."

Ben groaned silently. He'd never been so clumsy with a woman, he thought in chagrin, until he noticed that she was biting her cheek to keep from laughing.

What in hell was happening to him? "You have the strangest effect on me," he admitted ruefully, thinking that he wasn't telling her anything she didn't already know. He met her grin and took a firm hold on her arm. "A drink it is; then we'll dance, and then I'd like to walk in the moonlight with you . . . ?"

He'd left a blank space for her name, and she filled it in. "Margaret Anne. Maggie to my friends."

"Since I intend to be much more than a friend, I'll call you Margaret Anne," he said in a low seductive voice.

She looked at him skeptically for a minute, then leaned down to whisper something in Ian's ear. The older man nodded abstractedly. She gathered up a shawl from the chair and a white beaded bag.

You just lost, old boy. Triumphantly Ben sent the thought toward the "Master Diplomat" as he led her away.

The music had been slow and easy at the small club he'd taken her to. They'd danced on the terrace until dawn, holding each other, drunk on the scents of the night, speaking softly of nothing and everything while their bottle of champagne went flat. They'd sipped it anyway and decided that flat champagne had a lot to recommend it. As the night waned, Ben found that she was not only beautiful but intelligent and quick and fun.

That night was filled with magic, a rare interval of enchanting perfection that poets praise but few mortals ever experience. They had watched the sun rise in a crescent of mauve over the mountains above Lake Geneva.

By the time he took her home, and learned from her irate father that this glorious woman was only eighteen years old, it was too late. He was hopelessly in love.

He'd tried to break it off when he learned Maggie's age—even Ian had given him credit for that. She was too young to cope with the realities of his job or the responsibilities of marriage.

But Maggie Bentley was single-minded and more than a little spoiled. She decided that she wanted Ben Altman, and Ben Altman she got. Three weeks later they flew to Alexandria, Virginia, to be married in her family church.

The first few months of their marriage were heaven. He'd been transferred to Rome. There seemed to be a possibility that Ian would follow soon as ambassador to Italy.

And then Ben had been given an assignment in one of the worst hot spots of the region, followed by another dealing with the latest illegal arms deal in Iran. He stole into a terrorist training camp in Libya, escaping with explicit pictures and his life—barely. Under a hail of bullets, he interviewed the leader of a military coup in northern Africa.

Ben Altman was brave when it came to confronting dangerous situations and trying to understand the dark places in men's souls. But he was a coward when it came to his young wife.

She couldn't live with her anxieties about him; he couldn't live with her restrictive demands. She begged, she pleaded, and she threatened. Marriage became a prison with velvet bars. The relationship that had begun with such magic was doomed to end less than a year after that first enchanted evening in Geneva.

Chapter 2

I thought the congressman might have come with you," Ben remarked, forcing himself to return to the present and the difficult situation at hand.

Maggie met his gaze with surprise, then his eyes returned to the road, and she was left to study his profile. How had Ben known she was seeing David Gant? From Jamie, of course, the chatterbox. "I left in a hurry. I couldn't reach him."

The truth was that she hadn't attempted to reach him. After a courtship lasting almost a year, David had recently asked her to marry him. She hadn't decided how to answer. She thought she loved David. He was kind, intelligent, thoughtful. Even though he didn't inspire the passion that Ben had, he was exactly the kind of man she would choose if she married again. So why was she hesitating? What was her problem?

Marriage was. She had made such a dismal failure the first time that she wasn't sure she ever wanted to marry again. Jamie had a good relationship with both his father and his grandfather. There was no desperate need for a male influence in his life, or in hers, either.

"Would you like me to notify him? He should be here with you."

"Why?" she asked blankly.

The car was closing in on a black limousine. Ben passed it smoothly before he answered. "Well, because you need someone."

"Someone besides you, you mean," she said sharply, then regretted her harshness. She sighed. "I'm sorry, Ben. I shouldn't have said that," she went on in a milder tone of voice. "But I told you not to worry about me. I've grown up. If I decide I need David's support, I will contact him myself."

"You're very calm about all this," he accused with a spark of antagonism.

"Calm? Am I?" Turning in her seat, she fixed him with an expressionless stare. "Maybe you never realized that the families of State Department employees are indoctrinated to expect terrorist activity, even carefully educated as to how they should respond."

Embarrassed into silence after one quick glance at her face, Ben concentrated on his driving. He knew that the employees themselves were trained, but he'd never thought about that sort of pressure being brought to bear on diplomats' families.

Noting his response, Maggie gave a bitter laugh. "When I was twelve, Mother and I had to go through a training session to learn what to expect if we were kidnapped. We learned self-defense, how to discourage rape, how to survive a beating."

"Twelve years old? My God!"

The session had taken on an aspect of unreality for Maggie, but she would never forget how affected her mother had been. Christine Bentley had died soon after the training, but her death had been at the hand of the terrorist called cancer.

"I've lived all my life with the possibility of something like this happening. My father is strong and smart. If anyone on the face of this earth knows the right thing to say and do to keep Jamie safe, and himself, too, it's Daddy. If saying that makes me seem cold and uncaring, I apologize, but I have the utmost confidence in him." She shifted restlessly in her seat. "I have to," she added in a whisper.

The silence was heavy between them. Ben finally reached for her hand. "You really have grown up," he said softly.

Maggie wiggled her fingers in an attempt to free them, but this time he held fast. "No, don't fight me."

She ceased her struggle and watched the expressions that chased across his face as he gazed through the windshield. "I have confidence in Ian, too, Maggie. He'll take care of Jamie." She had the feeling he was speaking to himself rather than to her, until he met her gaze. "I hope you'll blame my lack of tact on the fact that I really care about what happens to him, as well."

It was true. Over the past eight years his reluctant friendship with his former father-in-law had developed into genuine affection. He had always respected the man's expertise in his field, as well as his rock-solid personal ethics, but with Jamie as an additional bond, they had grown very close. "I hope you'll forgive me for making such a heartless comment. I'm sorry, Margaret Anne."

Maggie relaxed for the first time since she'd left Washington. Though there was no official connection between them anymore, Ben had let her know with those few words that she wasn't alone. He did care about her father, as well as their son, and the thought gave her strength to draw on. "Thanks, Ben," she said quietly.

"We have a lot to deal with before our lives return to normal." If they ever do, he added silently. "We'll have to put our differences aside until this is over, but if I ever say anything so heartless again you have my permission to kick me."

Maggie felt a warm gratitude sweep through her at his statement. Her lips curved in a half smile. "That's quite an offer," she chided gently. "I'll forgive you if you promise not to call me Margaret Anne anymore. Jamie has picked up on it, and it doesn't bring back too many pleasant memories."

Ben felt as though she'd struck him, but he held back a retort. How could she have pleasant memories of a man, a husband, who was so wrapped up in his job, so devoid of patience with his young wife, that he'd let his marriage go down the drain? Maggie had been the teenager, but it was he who'd behaved like one. He should have shown more maturity. Anger built in him, but it was anger at circumstances and time and...himself. Mostly himself.

Moments later, Maggie's attention was caught as he turned right off the main highway. She didn't ask any questions but watched sadly and carefully, checking street signs as he swung the wheel, first left, then right. This section of the city was heartrendingly familiar. She'd forgotten what a riot of color the streets of Rome were in the summertime. On almost every corner was a flower stall. In front of apartments and shops, window boxes and planters spilled over with brilliant shades of yellow and red and orangy pinks.

Ben pulled the Ferarri into a clear spot near a small restaurant and glanced at his watch. "Maybe he'll be early." He opened his door and got out.

Maggie started to follow.

Ben bent to lean through the door. "Stay here, Maggie. I'm just going to check around."

She gave him a speaking glare and ignored the order.

Then he was facing her across the top of the car. "Damn it, Maggie. My contact won't talk in front of anyone but me. You're going to scare the man off."

"I won't go down to the river. I'll just walk along under the trees. I've been in a plane for nine hours, Ben. I really have to move around some."

Ben's jaw clenched visibly. He glanced to his right. People strolled through the tree-shaded park. Across the street to his left they wandered in and out of the stores. "Okay, but if you even *look* like you're watching us, this man will clam up, Maggie. We may need the information he has. We may need it desperately. For Jamie and Ian."

It was the only argument that could have made her agree to stay out of sight. "I promise I won't go near the river."

Ben took off his jacket, tossed it behind the front seat and rolled up his sleeves. "I won't be long." She would be safe enough with all these people around, Ben reassured himself as he headed for the bridge. She probably did need the exercise. He tried to picture himself if he'd been forced to remain buckled into an airplane seat for that many hours after the news she'd heard. He'd have been a screaming half-wit by this time.

As Maggie watched Ben walk away, she was suddenly shaken by a new fear. Ben was a big, sexy man and had always made her feel extraordinarily feminine. From the minute their eyes had met in the airport, she'd known and had tried to deny that she was still attracted to him.

On top of her fear for her father and Jamie, this additional emotion was almost more than she could handle right now. She had vowed never again to succumb to the temptation to lean on anyone, much less Ben Altman. She had recovered from the disaster of her divorce eight years ago only after searching her soul to find strengths she hadn't known she possessed. It had been a long, painful process, made longer by the complications of going through pregnancy and childbirth alone. Her independence was hard-won, and she loved it. She had made a life for herself and her son, a happy, rewarding, productive life.

Surely Ben's appeal was simply the result of worry, she thought as he disappeared down the steps to the river. There were bound to be memories, but she would have to shove them to the back of her mind, where they belonged.

Fiercely she reminded herself that she would need all the strength she could muster. Maybe more, in light of her unexpected response to her ex-husband.

At least she'd been prepared for their reunion. One of her recurring nightmares over the past eight years had been that she would come upon him unaware in Washington or Baltimore and make a fool of herself.

Wiping the light film of perspiration from her upper lip, she headed for the shade of the tall umbrella pines that lined the park. This was probably the last breathing space she would have for a long while. She'd better take advantage of it.

* * *

The man who was waiting in the shadow of the arched bridge was lean and swarthy. His hands thrust into his pockets, he leaned against the curved stone, one leg bent, his foot flattened on the wall behind him. His eyes didn't move from their contemplation of the river when Ben approached.

Ben joined him, matching his stance. He pulled out his cigarettes, offering the pack to the man. They both cupped their lighters against the breeze.

"I got your message, Pietro. Why did you call me?" Ben asked.

The lean man inhaled on the cigarette. "Word travels. I thought you might be in the market for some information."

"What word?"

Pietro's black brows rose at Ben's sharp tone, then he used his foot to lever himself away from the wall. He took a step or two. "Word that there might be some trouble at the American embassy. I hear this one is serious," he said, looking out over the river.

Ben controlled his tone. What he wanted to do was grab Pietro's skinny shoulders and shake the man until his teeth rattled and something popped out. "The embassy on Via Veneto, or the residence?"

"Nothing specific. Just the embassy," Pietro answered with a shrug.

Silence descended as they smoked. Finally Ben broke it. He spoke in a low voice. "If there were trouble at the embassy, it would be very serious indeed; would you happen to know anything about it?"

"Not me personally," the man hastened to assure Ben.

"Of course not," said Ben dryly, stabbing out his cigarette on the wall behind him.

"Maybe certain people . . . I could ask around."

"You do that," grated Ben. When he heard the harsh rasp of his own voice, he realized just how close he was to losing control again.

Pietro lived on the fringes of the Italian underworld. Publicly he was an errand boy for a major importer in Rome, a wealthy and powerful man with contacts all over Europe and the Middle East. Privately, they both walked a fine line. Ben wasn't sure what other kinds of jobs Pietro took care of for his boss, but little went on in that world that he or one of his "cousins" didn't know about. He had been a source for Ben on several stories.

Still, this situation smacked of kidnapping, and Ben had never known Pietro, or the man he worked for, to be involved in terrorism of any kind—most especially anything concerning a child. Pietro was typically Italian in his love of children and had two of his own.

"I also heard that at least one person connected with the embassy, maybe more, might be part of the plot."

Ben was barely able to disguise the disquiet he felt at having his own fears confirmed. Pietro used words like "might" and "maybe" to qualify every statement he made, but the man didn't open his mouth if he wasn't sure of his facts. "Someone undercover in the embassy?"

Pietro shook his head slowly. "I do not think so, *signore*. My information was gathered from bar talk. A man who would talk in a bar is not a pro like an undercover agent would be. A pro would keep his mouth shut, no?"

Ben felt his anger boil to the surface. He made himself stop, think for a minute. Finally he reached into his pocket for the fifty Pietro would be expecting. His green eyes took on the color of granite, giving them a dense, cruel cast. "Look, Pietro, there is a seven-year-old boy involved in this one—a boy who happens to be my son. If anything happens to him, I'll have someone's heart for breakfast, do you hear?"

"A child?" Pietro said softly, genuine horror in his expression. He shook his head at the money in Ben's extended hand. "Your son?" The man couldn't have known, Ben assured himself, not unless he was one hell of an actor.

"Don't look so surprised. 'Certain people' have been making war on children for years."

Pietro drew himself up. "Signore Altman, I cannot take your money. You know we would never be a party to anything like this."

"You'd better not be, Pietro," Ben said in a low, threatening voice. His movement as he repocketed the bill was negligent, but his expression remained like steel, hard and unrelenting, and his eyes unmistakably threatened retribution. "I want you to deliver a message to your boss. He knows everything that goes on in Rome. Tell him that I want these people. If he's not involved, he'd better give me all the help he can, and quick."

Pietro backed away from the anger in Ben. His sneakered foot turned on a stone, and he almost lost his balance. "I'll tell him, *signore*. He is out of town at the moment, but he'll be in touch with you soon—I promise."

"He won't have to. I'll contact him," Ben said, leaving no doubt that when he did, he'd want some answers.

Ben stood unmoving for a minute after Pietro had gone. The meeting had ignited some primitive element in him that he needed to master before he went back to Maggie.

Suddenly he lunged forward, slapping the ungiving wall as hard as he could with the flat of his hand, welcoming the harsh sting that shot up his arm.

The sunshine, which had enticed people out onto the street, vanished suddenly, shut off as easily as though a hand had flipped a switch. Thunderstorms, unexpected and violent, were another part of the Roman summer that Maggie had forgotten. Looking back over her shoulder, she realized she'd wandered farther than she'd intended. And most of the sun-seekers had disappeared.

As she turned to retrace her steps, a figure caught her eye: a portly man in a three-piece suit.

Where had she seen the man before? In the airport? She remembered sidestepping someone to avoid a collision.

Nonsense. It couldn't be the same man. She was imagining things. Besides, there were still a few people around; there was nothing to be afraid of. She swore softly at Ben for putting ideas into her head. Even so, she changed direction, moving diagonally toward the street.

The man changed direction, too, cutting across the lawn to intersect her path. *"Signora!"* he shouted.

Maggie's heart began to pound. She looked around, but no one else was within hailing distance. He was actually calling her! Where in God's name was Ben?

The man closed in.

Almost running now, Maggie changed direction again, circling a large tree. She risked a look over her shoulder... and ran full tilt into a broad chest.

Large hands came down on her shoulders in a hard, cruel grip...

She opened her mouth to scream.

"What the hell...?" growled a masculine voice.

Maggie looked up into Ben's face. "Ben! Oh, thank God!" Her knees buckled. She sagged against him, clinging to his shirt to keep herself upright.

Instantly Ben wrapped his arms around her trembling body. For a brief incredible moment he allowed his embrace to tighten, touched his cheek to the crown of her head and closed his eyes. His brow furrowed with emotion stronger and more painful than he'd felt for years. "What is it, babe? What's the matter?" he said in a voice that was barely audible. Then, more forcefully, he went on, "Damn it, I told you not to wander off. I was almost crazy when I couldn't find you."

Maggie spoke into his shirtfront, conscious all at once of the power and intensity in the way he held her. It was like a moment from their past. "I was just walking. I didn't realize how far I'd gone. But, Ben, there's a man..."

Instantly cautious, Ben lifted his head and loosened his hold, scanning the park over her head. His voice was as deep and savage as the rumble of thunder that accompanied his words. "A man? Where?"

The emotionally charged moment needed defusing. No longer afraid, Maggie turned in his arms to point the man out. "He's gone," she said vaguely. Gone without a trace. She shook her head. "Maybe I dreamed him; maybe it was my imagination."

"Let's go," muttered Ben, taking her hand. He headed back to where the car was parked. "The authorities will want a complete description. And you're not to go wandering off on your own again, do you hear me?"

Maggie hurried along beside him. "You've seen him, too."

"I have?"

"He was in the airport. A rather portly man in a three-piece suit. We had to step around him on the way to the main terminal."

Ben's eyes narrowed. "I remember. I doubt that I could identify him, though. It was one of those fleeting encounters."

Maggie gave a shaky laugh. "And probably didn't mean a thing. In fact, I'm not even sure it was the same man now. Let's drop it."

"Was he chasing you?"

"Not really. Please, Ben, let's drop it. I feel like such a fool." She changed the subject. "What did your contact have to say?"

"Not much that's helpful, I'm afraid. I'll tell you about it in the car."

But when they reached the car, the man was waiting for them. Ben felt Maggie hesitate. He took a step that put her behind him. "Watch it, Maggie," he said under his breath.

The little man looked nervous. He spoke in a high-pitched, uneven voice. *"Signora*, please, lose this?" He held up a square of crimson silk.

Maggie looked down at her empty pocket and wilted. "My scarf. The poor man was just trying to return my scarf." She stepped around Ben to take it with a shaky smile. *"Si. Grazie, signore. Mille grazie."* Just as she spoke, the first drops of rain fell between them, staining the pavement. She eyed the sky balefully.

The man gave them both a stiff bow. *"Prego, signora. Buon giorno."* He hurried away.

Maggie collapsed against Ben's side, laughing in relief. His arm came around to support her, and she looped her fingers in his belt. "Oh, Lord, Ben," she choked out, meeting his eyes. "The poor man must have thought I was certifiably insane."

Ben stared down at the woman under his arm. The fat raindrops were darkening her hair in spots, releasing the exotic fragrance of her shampoo. Their hips were in close contact, their thighs brushed each other, and her breast was warm against his chest. His heart accelerated in response to the amusement spilling out of her eyes, but he couldn't smile or speak. He was silenced by the heat rising in his loins.

Feelings were emerging that should have been dead along with his love for this woman. But—the realization came to him without warning—Maggie would always hold a place in his heart, and a part of him would always belong to her.

Maggie's laughter died on her lips. Her head moved quickly, sharply, a denial of what she read in his expression.

He released her rather abruptly. "He probably did," he said shortly. "Get in before you're completely soaked."

"It wasn't the man in the airport after all," she offered in a subdued voice when they were back in the car. She was pleased to see that her hands shook only minimally as she smoothed and folded the scarlet silk in her lap.

"Are you sure?" Ben switched on the windshield wipers and put the car in gear with a bit more force than was necessary. The smartest thing to do right now would be to leave her at the residence and run like hell.

Maggie was very much aware what had provoked Ben's annoyance because she'd felt the same emotions a short time ago, watching him walk away. Despite the fact that there was no love in their relationship, there were tender feelings.

And obviously the physical magnetism between them had not died for him, either. It was there, as powerful as ever, something they would have to fight, when they didn't have time or energy for another battle. All of their vigor, all of their power, would be needed in the war to save their son. "Yes. That man was thinner," she said.

The family living quarters were only slightly less formal than the receiving rooms in the mansion that served as residence and private office of the ambassador from the United States. Oriental rugs and Venetian glass chandeliers were plentiful in both places. Fine paneling and luxurious fabrics warmed the spacious high-ceilinged rooms. The works of both American and Italian artists were displayed in places of honor. The butler, James Greenwood, fit the setting like the last piece of a complicated jigsaw puzzle. He greeted them politely, offered refreshments and whisked Maggie's suitcase away.

Maggie led the way into the upstairs sitting room. She dropped her jacket and purse on a lemon-yellow moire sofa. With a sigh, she lifted her hands to tuck in strands of hair loosened by the wind and rain.

Ben had planned to drop her at the door and leave, but she'd seemed surprised when he'd hesitated about coming in. Now his face twisted at the sight of Maggie's uptilted breasts pushing against the soft damp fabric of her blouse. He plunged his fists into his pockets, rejecting the memory of her skin glowing like ivory under his darker-skinned hands. How could his mind picture her so clearly? It had been eight years. He spun away.

"What do we do next?" asked Maggie.

The meeting with Pietro had produced no concrete information except for confirming his suspicions that someone in the embassy was involved, and he'd had to tell her so. Her reaction had surprised him. Her face had crumpled for a moment, just a moment, while she struggled for composure.

Now she shook her head. "I hate to think that somebody Daddy trusts is involved. I suppose I'm still expecting a happy ending."

"There will be a happy ending," Ben said quietly. "We have to keep reminding ourselves of that."

"I know, but..." She choked slightly and chopped the air with a hand to cut off an emotional response. "But we also have to think and plan. What does...?" She turned at the sound of a knock. "Come in."

The man who entered the room brought the reality of the situation with him. Clay Marston was often sent to areas of terrorist activity as a personal troubleshooter for the president of the United States.

Grim-faced and hard-bodied, he was unknown to Maggie, but not to Ben. The tall, dusty-haired man might look as though he'd just arrived from Harvard with a MBA tucked under his arm, but Ben had had more than one run-in with him while in pursuit of a story.

Only his gray eyes revealed him to be what he was: a damned barracuda, at least in Ben's opinion. Even heavy-framed horn-rimmed glasses couldn't hide the coldness in his gaze. If Ben's past experience was anything to go on, Marston would now try to have him ousted immediately from the mansion.

"Maggie, this is Clay Marston. He arrived a couple of hours before you did, from Washington. Clay, the ambassador's daughter, Margaret Altman."

Ben's wry tone told Maggie that this was the man from the intelligence service whom he had mentioned earlier. And the slice of Marston's eyes and the disapproval in his voice as he responded to the introduction told her that he didn't like her ex-husband, not one bit. She was surprised by his antagonism; he looked like such a mild-mannered man. "Won't you have a seat, Mr. Marston?" she asked.

He hitched his trousers and took a chair at one side of the marble fireplace, looking as though he planned to stay for a while. Ben sat in the one opposite.

The butler had followed Marston into the room, bearing a tray with a silver coffee service and delicate bone china cups. He set the tray on a convenient table and left, closing the door behind him.

When the two men declined coffee, Maggie poured herself a cup, but she was too restless to remain seated.

"May we speak alone, Mrs. Altman?" asked Clay Marston stiffly.

"Why?" Her puzzled gaze met the chill behind Marston's glasses; she shivered involuntarily. Mild-mannered? Not with eyes like that.

Ben answered for the agent, earning himself another scowl. "Because I'm a reporter, Maggie."

She shook her head ruefully, and one corner of her mouth turned up. "I forgot."

"Mrs. Altman, we're ninety-nine percent sure that this is a kidnapping. Though the authorities are questioning anyone who might have seen anything either in Tivoli or on the highway, there's been no trace of the limo. The kidnappers haven't made their demands public yet, giving us some time to investigate quietly. We'd like to keep this story under wraps for as long as possible."

Carefully setting the delicate cup aside, she turned away from Clay Marston, looking toward her ex-husband. Their eyes held for a prolonged silent exchange. At one time she'd accused this man of sacrificing anything, even their marriage, for a story. Did he still have that kind of compulsive drive?

She rebuked herself for the notion. Jamie was Ben's son. Ben would never put the life of his own flesh and blood in jeopardy.

As long as he agreed that his actions would put Jamie in jeopardy, said a small devil's advocate deep inside her. Her fingers went to her forehead; she sighed, wondering if she had the right to make a decision of such critical importance.

She tried to read the answers in Ben's eyes, but he was hiding his feelings well. Or was he? He slouched in the chair with his long legs stretched out, crossed at the ankles, his fingers linked loosely over his stomach. The pose was easy, full of assurance. But the angle of his chin seemed just a tad defensive, as though he were challenging her to trust him.

Her decision came quickly and instinctively; she turned to the agent. "Mr. Marston, you know, of course, that Mr. Altman and I are divorced. We haven't even seen each other for eight years. But whatever our problems were in the past, a lack of trust was never one of them." Moving with self-assured grace, she sat on the edge of the sofa, straightening the black linen skirt over her knees, and reached for her cup. "As a matter of fact, I intend to offer him the hospitality of the residence."

When had she decided that? she asked herself. She was begging for trouble with Ben here, trouble that had nothing to do with his profession. He had not only been the source of her greatest ecstasy, but also her deepest anguish. His presence always could make her heart beat faster, she remembered, and despite her determination to remain indifferent, it still did.

At the same time, she wanted to squelch any doubts that Clay Marston might harbor. Marston appeared to be the sort of man who would only be content if a woman had a man to take care of her. She wouldn't put it past him to have her followed everywhere she went, and an escort wouldn't suit her plans at all. She wanted to be free to move about without hindrance. She knew a few people in Rome who she hoped might be helpful.

She was older, more mature, now, she declared silently, more capable of fighting the weakness of strong emotion. Ben's physical magnetism had always had a potent effect on her, but she was confident she could handle a physical attraction. As for deeper sentiments, well, there weren't any of those she couldn't handle, either.

"Ben is as concerned with the safety of my father and our son as I am. Reporting is his job. I wouldn't dream of asking him to forgo his professional responsibility, but I have every confidence in his discretion, and I will be glad of his support until this is all over," she finished, congratulating herself on the brisk, businesslike tone of the speech. "Right now, though, Mr. Marston, I would like to hear more about what is being done to find my father and son."

"Do you want him to hear everything?" asked Marston, not attempting to hide his disapproval.

Maggie's features settled into a mask; her fingers tightened on the edge of the saucer. "Everything," she informed the agent coldly. He stiffened. When she saw his response, she bit down on her tongue. It wouldn't do to antagonize the man unnecessarily. She shrugged and tried a conciliatory smile. "We need all the help we can get, don't we?"

"As long as he doesn't turn a tragic kidnapping into a media event."

"Why, you son of a..." Ben growled, sitting forward suddenly.

"Ben," Maggie cautioned.

Ben shot her a furious glare, then stopped. He wasn't a violent man, but right now he wanted to smash the supercilious expression off Marston's face more than he'd ever wanted anything in his life.

"Have you interviewed the appointment secretary?" Maggie asked Marston.

"Of course. We're interviewing everyone who might have had knowledge of the ambassador's movements. Right now she's sticking to her story that she told no one of the schedule and no one asked. I'll question her again, of course."

"I heard from a contact that someone connected with the embassy is involved," said Ben.

At Ben's words, Maggie dropped her eyes to her lap in relief. He was going to cooperate. Even so, the tension between the two men was tangible when Marston demanded, "Did they say 'the embassy'?"

Ben nodded. "No way to know whether that means the chancery or the residence."

Marston stroked his chin. "My assistant is with the chargé d'affaires at the chancery now," he mused. "By the way, who is your source?"

Ben laughed without humor. "You know better than that, Marston."

"I suppose it is too much to ask of a reporter, but a lead like that should be followed up by a professional," Marston warned.

"It will be," said Ben, stone-faced. "Me. As soon as I have more information, I'll let you in on it."

Marston snorted. "I should have you thrown in jail for obstruction of an investigation, Altman."

It was a weak threat, and Maggie recognized it as such. But it was time to bring this to a halt. "Gentlemen? Please?" she interjected. "Mr. Marston, what about the household staff?"

Slowly unclenching his fists, Marston reached for a small notebook in his jacket pocket. He flipped through a few pages and stopped. "James Greenwood, the butler, is from South Carolina, trained in London. He was checked thoroughly, as were all the staff, at the time he was hired, but we're checking again. Dante is Italian, a widower with one child. He was security trained by a private agency. They give him good marks."

"But Dante is with them. He's a victim," protested Maggie.

"That doesn't preclude his involvement. We're checking everyone. So far Dante seems to be clean, almost too clean."

"That is absurd," snapped Maggie.

Marston ignored her and went on. "The chef, Annette Cabot, I believe you know." He consulted his pad again. "She's Swiss."

"Yes, she worked for us in Geneva. When Daddy was appointed ambassador to Italy, she came along."

Ben leaned back in his chair and listened as Maggie questioned the man for the next ten minutes concerning the rest of the people attached to the embassy.

He smiled to himself, willing to bet that the intelligence agent didn't often find himself questioned in this manner, especially by a woman whose queries were so pointed and incisive. The tables had been turned very neatly on Clay Marston.

Ben's admiration for the woman Maggie had become was increasing minute by minute. Her maturity also added to her allure. That moment in the rain had opened Ben's eyes; the feel of her body molded to his had shown him that he wasn't immune to the memory of their lovemaking. That was one memory that must be banished. At the moment, though, his only weapon against it was nothing more powerful than speculation about the intervening years. More than likely there had been other men to hold her, to kiss her, to...

Ben surged to his feet and began to roam restlessly around the room. If he was honest with himself, he would have to admit that he wasn't immune to her emotionally, either. He'd never be completely free of Maggie. He would always harbor a wish that things had turned out differently. Was such a wish the reason for his being here now instead of on his way home? The thought made him pause. One couldn't go back. They had wounded each other too deeply. He sat down a cushion's length away from her and returned his attention to the conversation.

Maggie was sitting with the upper half of her body inclined forward, her hands clasped together loosely, in a position that belied her fear. In fact, if they hadn't talked earlier, if he hadn't observed how carefully she was controlling her emotions, he might doubt that she had any feelings at all.

"I have one last question, Mr. Marston. I assume all the intelligence agencies involved are cooperating with each other and with the Italian authorities. I'm sure you agree that splintering our efforts is nonproductive, but before you leave I'd like to be assured on that point." It was as neat a dismissal as Ben had ever heard.

The first time he'd seen Maggie, he'd thought she was royalty. Well, a queen couldn't have done it better. He almost grinned when Marston spit out an affirmative answer as though it tasted bad.

"Not that I agree totally with the policy, but as a matter of fact, I will be coordinating the efforts," he said, trying to regain control of the discussion.

Suddenly Maggie softened toward the intelligence agent. Her smile was warm. "That's very reassuring to me, Mr. Marston. Thank you," she said sincerely.

When Marston stood to leave, Maggie stood, too, and walked with him to the door.

"Well done, Maggie," Ben said when she came back to sink into the plush cushions next to him. "Very well done," he commented.

"Do you think so? Lord, he is a cold-blooded bastard, isn't he?" She met his grin.

"Yeah. I just hope your little speech sticks with him for a few minutes. I wouldn't hold out much hope, though."

She twisted her body to face him, tucking her feet under her. "Ben, the White House has ordered the State Department to work out and coordinate the details of a plan for cooperation in the event of an international incident. That's the policy we spoke of. I can tell you that the in-depth analysis you did for your report had a lot to do with the president's decision. That's how I happened to know so much about your work.''

His brows rose. She could tell the information was a surprise. "Is the plan operable?" he asked.

"I don't know," she admitted with a sigh. "My job isn't on a level that would make me privy to such intelligence. But they are trying, Ben. And you'll cooperate on this, won't you?"

He was suddenly resentful and defensive. "I've told you I'll be careful. Damn it, you should know I wouldn't do anything to put Jamie and Ian in danger."

"Ben, there are no absolutes," she said quietly. "Not this time."

He got slowly to his feet. "You know how I feel about this, Maggie. Freedom of the press is an absolute. As long as a reporter doesn't editorialize, as long as he's unbiased and fair, he must be allowed to tell the public the truth."

Maggie struggled to hold on to her own temper. "When it concerns your own son, Ben, when it's his life that's threatened, can you be completely unbiased?" she demanded.

The question caused him to pause. Could he? Ben asked himself. His shoulders slumped. The truth was, he didn't know. Probably not. "Okay, Maggie. You have my word that until this is over I will be a father and a friend, not a reporter."

"Thanks, Ben." She acknowledged his promise with an attempt at a smile. Ben didn't give his word lightly; she knew that. She only hoped he understood what he had promised.

"My father is nobody's fool," she went on. "He'll realize that we need time. He's smart enough to find a way to give it to us."

I hope, I pray, she added to herself.

Ian's smart, Ben silently agreed. *But is any man smart enough to overcome these odds?* "Do you really want me to stay here?" he asked.

Maggie took a long breath and looked at him out of the corner of her eye. She could get out of the invitation now, without too much fuss. She could suggest that maybe it wasn't such a good idea.

She released the breath on a sigh. "I know you live in the Tor Carboni area. That's how far? An hour anyway?"

"Almost an hour."

"If you're like I am, you'll be crazy for news, any news. It would be more convenient for you to be in town, wouldn't it?"

Ben thought it over for a minute. He wasn't sure why Maggie wanted him there, but she was right. He would be crazy for information about Jamie and Ian, and this was the place to get it. On the other hand, his freedom would be restricted, to a degree. The residence would be crawling with officials of all kinds.

He shrugged at the thought. They weren't going to put him in irons. He'd be free to come and go. Telephone kiosks were everywhere in the city if he needed to make private calls. Finally he gave a decisive nod. "Okay." She seemed relieved. "I'll run out to my place and pack a few things. Do you want to ride along?"

"I probably shouldn't. What if some word comes through while we're gone?"

"I can give Marston my telephone number in case they want us."

She stood and put a hand to the small of her back, stretching her aching muscles. She felt grubby and tired, but rest would be impossible right now.

"Then yes, I'd like to ride with you. Just let me change clothes first." She turned at the door. "Do you mind waiting while I have a shower?"

"Not at all. Take your time. I'll hunt up Marston and then meet you downstairs."

When Maggie entered the bedroom she discovered that her bag had already been unpacked. She stripped as she crossed the room, relieved to be out of the wrinkled suit, and pulled a robe from the closet.

Chapter 3

Maggie was mistaken about one thing she'd told Marston, Ben mused as he waited for her to change. He had seen her twice since their marriage had ended eight years ago. He considered himself a reasonable, level-headed man, but both occasions had had an effect on him equally as traumatic as this morning's meeting at the airport.

Seven months after Maggie had left, Ben was beginning to get his life back in order. He wasn't happy, but he had managed to regain a certain amount of contentment.

Then he had unexpectedly run into his father-in-law. They'd had a drink together. Though Ian had never blamed Ben completely for the breakup of the marriage, the meeting was only superficially cordial.

Maggie was in Washington, Ian told him, when he asked about her. She'd taken an apartment, enrolled in college, and was doing fine. When Ben mentioned that he hadn't received any divorce papers, Ian took a sip of his Scotch before he commented casually, "I'm sure she's waiting until after the baby is born."

Ben felt every muscle in his body solidify. He became utterly motionless. In the silence that followed Ian's statement Ben could hear the frivolous songs of the birds in a park nearby, a joyous sound that was almost unbearable, a sound he would never forget.

His paralyzing shock must have been evident in his expression. All at once Ian turned as white as the linen cloth between them. "God, Ben. I'm sorry. I thought you knew she was pregnant," he whispered. He seemed to be searching his memory. "The day Maggie left Rome, I'm sure she said she was stopping at—" he furrowed his brow, trying to recall the name "—that taverna just off the Via Veneto where the journalists hang out."

"The Sermona," Ben supplied. His voice echoed loudly in his head like the hollow sound of shouted words in a dark cave.

"That's it. I'm sure she said she was going there to tell you."

The Sermona. He remembered that day...too well. It was the day he'd made the biggest mistake of his life, the day he'd put one foot in hell. He closed his eyes against the pain slicing through him like a hot sword. "No, I didn't know. Tell me where she is...where she'll have the baby...everything," he begged quietly.

Ian complied, kindly, sympathetically, sadness softening his features. "The baby is due any day." Regret was palpable in his voice as he went on. "You know, Ben, you and Maggie had something good going. It was frustrating to see it begin to crumble. I can't help but feel that if I'd been any good at my job, I should have been able to help the two of you."

Ben forced a smile. "You may be the Master Diplomat, Ian, but it would have taken a hell of a lot more than diplomacy to save our marriage."

"Maggie was very young," her father observed.

"Maggie wasn't totally to blame, Ian. Our breakup was as much my fault as hers." He signaled to the waiter. "And that is absolutely *all* I intend to say on the subject."

"I wasn't prying," Ian said defensively.

"The hell you weren't. Let's have another drink."

Ian grinned unrepentantly and a close, if incongruous, friendship began.

After he left Ian, Ben took the first available flight to the States. He checked into a hotel rather than make the explanations that would be expected if he stayed with his parents in nearby Baltimore.

Unable to avoid his own self-blame for the scene in the Sermona, he was nonetheless bitter and angry that Maggie hadn't written, hadn't made sure he knew he was about to become a father. He called the hospital each day, not sure whether to ask for Margaret Anne or Maggie, Altman or Bentley. If the switchboard operator thought it strange that he was inquiring so persistently about a patient without knowing her name, she never let on. Finally on the sixth day he was informed that a Margaret Altman had been admitted.

He went to the hospital immediately. But he didn't plan to see her. At least that was what he told himself. A meeting between them would reopen wounds that had just begun to heal. On the other hand, he was still her husband, and—damn it—she should have someone with her! She shouldn't be alone. He was standing at the nurse's desk, on the point of demanding admittance, when he saw four people enter the waiting room.

The sight of the quartet relieved him slightly, even as he avoided being seen himself. Maggie had more cousins than a duck had feathers, and these four had attended their wedding. Memories of that day surfaced, a day filled with so much promise, so much love, that the whole world didn't seem big enough to contain it all.

He shook off the memory. After that he went to the hospital only during the patients' mealtimes.

His son. The first time he stood looking through the glass at the ugly, wrinkled bundle, a primitive thrill of emotion warmed his blood. He felt that his feet barely skimmed the floor of the sterile corridor. He hovered at the nursery viewing window each day for as long as he dared, hungrily relishing the sight of his son.

He learned the baby's name by calling Ian, who had returned to Rome. James Benjamin Altman III. That was a surprise. What was Maggie going to call him? Ian didn't know.

And he consulted a lawyer. Maggie might have wanted to keep this child a secret, but he had no intention of being severed from the son who bore his name. He would sue her for joint custody.

The shocks weren't over. He was approaching the entrance to the maternity ward one afternoon when he looked up to see his parents coming out. His mother was laughing and crying at the same time. His father hugged him. "Our first grandchild," his mother said, teary-eyed. "Isn't he the most beautiful baby?" It took them less than ten minutes to make him feel like a heel for his suspicions. Maggie had called to tell them about their grandchild; she wanted them to visit often.

He saw her the day she took James Benjamin home. From his vantage point across the street, he watched her being rolled out in a wheelchair to where one of the cousins waited with a car. She looked tired but ecstatic. Her dimple pierced her cheek and his heart as she smiled tenderly at the baby in her arms.

Ben clenched his hands into fists—hands that itched to touch his child and, God help him, his wife. He blinked away his tears and called off the lawyer.

When Maggie went home from the hospital, Ben returned to Rome and found a letter waiting. She had written him on the day James was born. She had written to tell him he had a son and enclosed a hospital snapshot, which, he knew, didn't do his baby justice.

"Jamie is a healthy, beautiful baby, as you can see." Jamie...he liked that, thought Ben. He had to steady the note in his hands before he could read on. "I have no desire to punish our child for the stupid mistakes we made. He'll reach a point when he'll need his father. But I think it will be better if you and I don't meet." That suited Ben fine. He didn't want to see Maggie one iota more than she wanted to see him. He had no desire to relive the devastating sense of loss he'd felt when she'd left.

He crushed the paper in his fist, then had to smooth it out again to read the last sentence. "Maybe, after Jamie's older, we can work out a way for you to see him if you want to."

If he wanted...? Ben was surprised again, this time at the maturity that had enabled her to write those words. He visited the bank that day to arrange a permanent draft on his account, a draft that had been re-routed at Maggie's insistence into a college fund for Jamie.

She had kept her word. As soon as Jamie was old enough, she'd arranged for Ben to see his son at his parents' home near Washington, and later she'd allowed the child to travel to Rome. He and Maggie had talked on the telephone; they'd written numerous letters about matters concerning their son. But through the years Maggie had remained adamant about one thing: she wouldn't meet with him face-to-face.

The butler entered the sitting room. He seemed taken aback for a moment when he saw Ben standing at the window. "Mr. Altman, may I get you something, sir? Coffee?"

Ben visited the embassy often enough for James to know his habitual yearning for a good cup of coffee, but right now he felt as though coffee or anything else would make him gag. "No, thank you, James. I'm waiting for Mrs. Altman. We'll be going out."

"Very good, sir." The man backed out of the room.

Ben watched him leave. James Greenwood. From South Carolina, huh? He'd be interested to read Mr. Greenwood's file.

Ben began to pace, his footsteps silent on the rugs. He raked a frustrated hand through his hair. Good God! He'd known the man for years, played poker with him! And if you couldn't judge a man across a card table, when could you judge him? He was getting as paranoid as Maggie.

He wandered back to the window. Propping his elbow against the frame, he stared distractedly out over the rose garden, his thoughts drawn once again to the past.

He'd seen Maggie for the second time last November. In a way, the second time was worse than the first. He had returned to New York for a meeting with the publisher of a major news weekly who was urging him to change to print journalism. He'd been offered a job writing a regular column, originating in Washington but concentrating on foreign policy.

Eight years ago a similar offer had dealt the final blow to their tottering marriage. Eight years ago he wouldn't consider the change, especially when he discovered that the offer had been engineered by his wife.

But now he was thinking about accepting. Living abroad had its advantages but lately he'd begun to long for home. It would mean more time with Jamie, and there were moments when he felt he was getting too old for the frantic-paced life he led. After the meeting he'd flown to Washington to see Jamie and interview the Secretary of State.

The lighting in the restaurant where he'd spotted her was almost nonexistent, but it was enough for him to recognize his ex-wife and the highly visible congressman from Oklahoma, David Gant.

He hadn't known she was dating Gant, who was reputed to be one of the young movers and shakers in Congress. Despite the divorce, he discovered a remnant of possessiveness inside him that he hadn't even known was there. Maybe it was because she was the mother of his son; maybe it was because there had never been another woman he could love as deeply as he'd loved her; hell, maybe it was because, at thirty-eight, he was getting uncomfortably close to middle age.

Later, as he sat in his hotel room, sipping whiskey and analyzing his response to seeing Maggie, he told himself Gant would be good for her. It hurt beyond belief to think of another man taking on the role of father to Jamie, but if someone was going to—and it seemed logical to assume Maggie would remarry someday—he supposed Gant would be a good choice.

Now he thought it strange that they hadn't married; it was even more strange that Gant wasn't here with her.

"I'm ready. Sorry it took so long."

He looked up. "No problem." She had changed into a slim white cotton skirt and white knit camisole, over which she wore an unstructured blazer in a delicate peach color. White rope-soled sandals revealed the tinted toenails of her bare feet. "More comfortable?"

"Yes. Jet lag will probably hit me in a few hours, but for now I'm itchy to do something."

"Are you sure you don't want to stay here and try to sleep for an hour or so?"

She shook her head. "On our way out let's see if Ms. Orenda is still here. I'd like to talk to her."

"I'd like to talk to her myself," Ben said.

They found Lola Orenda in the office she shared with Judith. Marston was with her. The agent settled himself in a chair off to the side of the room, indicating they should ask whatever they wanted.

As Lola answered their questions, her hands hovered over the paraphernalia on her desk. Her wide-spaced brown eyes darted from Ben to Maggie. "I swear to you, *signora*, as I told Signore Marston, no one asked about the ambassador's movements yesterday, and I volunteered no information."

She sounded sincere, and Maggie felt a certain sympathy for the young woman. Being questioned by Clay Marston must have been a dreadful experience. The secretary looked as though she hadn't slept, either. "Tell me, Lola, did you set up the appointment in Tivoli?" she asked gently.

"No, *signora*. Your father received a personal call from the director of Antiquities last week. He informed me that he would be away yesterday afternoon, and I rescheduled his appointments."

Maggie looked at Ben. He answered her unspoken question. "The director is cooperating fully with the police to discover if the information could have come from someone in his office."

She pondered for a minute before she returned her gaze to the young woman. "Can you tell me how the scheduling is normally handled?"

Lola dropped her hands in her lap. Her chin came up with a confidence she hadn't shown before. "Unless it is a personal invitation like the one from the director of Antiquities, a request for an appointment is presented to me. For some people it is simply a matter of agreeing on a convenient time. For others—the ones I do not know—I consult with Judith to make sure the matter is legitimate, and sometimes she will set things up herself, then notify me. Every evening I make up two copies of the schedule for the following day. I provide one for Judith and one for Dante. That's all."

Dante. Maggie pictured the quiet, gentle giant who had come to work for her father years ago, the man who was so kind to Jamie. She could no more put the name "monster" to Dante than she could to this frightened young woman before her. And yet who knew what drove a kidnapper, a terrorist? Who could penetrate the mask he might hide behind?

Maggie's eyes sought Ben's clear green gaze, only to find his attention fixed strangely on the nervous young woman. He stared at her for what must have been a full minute.

"Signore." Lola's whispered plea broke his concentration. He looked at Maggie and shrugged. "Are you ready to go, Maggie?" he asked.

Silently she nodded. She couldn't think of anything else to ask that might be helpful. "Thank you, Lola," she said to the young woman. Marston followed them out of the office.

Ben reached into the pocket of his jacket and handed the other man a card. "This is my telephone number. Maggie is going with me out to my place. We'll be back after lunch."

Marston nodded. "That's a good idea," he said, avoiding Maggie's eyes. "The waiting is going to be very hard, Mrs. Altman. Kidnapping is one of the most insidious forms of terrorism there is. It tests your strength and your endurance to the limit."

Ben started toward the door, but Maggie put a hand on his sleeve. "Mr. Marston, first I . . . we would like to see the rest of your operation."

Marston didn't answer for a minute. He took a clean white handkerchief from his pocket and polished his glasses. When he replaced them, he stared directly at Ben for another minute, as if in warning. Then he moved his shoulders in what was intended to be a shrug, but it didn't quite come off that way. "We've set up in the basement."

"We?" Maggie said.

"Representatives from Interpol, the Italian police and intelligence service, the embassy security people." He led the way to a door near the back of the wide central hall.

The basement he referred to was actually the ground floor of the mansion. In front, broad sweeping steps led to the formal entrance on the second level.

Fifty or so people, men and women, milled about, talking, consulting, even arguing; the large area was a wealth of reassuring activity. A number of men wore the uniform of the Italian police, but most were dressed in conservative business suits or jackets and ties, like Marston. A bank of telephones was set up along one wall, and on another two, well-lighted maps had been mounted, one of the city and one of the country. A large conference table stood in the center of the room. "How did you get organized so quickly?" she asked the agent.

Marston gave her a thoughtful look. "We have been working in Rome for several weeks, although not here in the embassy, of course. The group was set up to facilitate cooperation between our country and our allies in situations like this."

So the plan Maggie had spoken about was in effect, thought Ben. The news was reassuring. Suddenly he caught sight of someone he knew. "Excuse me, Maggie. I'll be right back." He walked down the remaining steps to greet an older man in uniform. The man put a hand on Ben's shoulder as though in sympathy. They talked earnestly in undertones.

"He seems to know the chief of police rather well," said Marston in a bad-tempered drawl.

"I'm sure he does," answered Maggie. "In the course of his job he probably has met quite a few of the people in this room." She turned to face him. "Maybe even more people than you know."

"Look here..."

Maggie interrupted. "No, you look here. The most important item on your agenda should be the return of two American citizens and one Italian who have been kidnapped. Personal ego has no more place than professional jealousy in this situation."

"I agree," snapped Marston.

"Then why aren't you willing to utilize every resource available to you, instead of wanting to run the whole show yourself?"

He snorted. "And you think your husband's a resource?"

"I know he is. He has contacts that would never in a million years be available to you."

Marston actually looked pleased. "Cooperation is a two-way street, Mrs. Altman. Will Ben Altman introduce us to those contacts? Will he bring them in, let us interrogate them?"

Maggie knew the answer to that question, of course; Marston had neatly backed her into a corner. Nevertheless, she refused to drop the subject. "Even if he did, they would be useless to you. They would dry up quicker than a terrorist's tears, Mr. Marston, and you know it." Anger brought color to her cheeks.

Marston sighed. Suddenly he looked older and very tired. "Mrs. Altman, I'm following orders. Whether I agree with them or not, I'm following them. I want you to know that I sincerely believe that bringing in all these people is a mistake. I believe the confusion will be mind-boggling, but I'll cooperate because the president has ordered me to do so. Though I have a reputation as a loner, I'm not trying to be obstructive. I want to get your father and son back, so if you think your husband—excuse me, ex-husband—can help, I'll work with him. Hell, I'd work with the devil if I thought he could get them back. Just don't encourage Altman to go off on a tangent, will you?"

It was the first sign of humanity Maggie had seen in the man, and it surprised her. She stared at him, choosing her words carefully before she spoke. "Mr. Marston, do you have any children?"

A mask came down over his face. "No, I've never been married," he answered guardedly.

"You're undoubtedly wise. Having children makes you vulnerable. Ben's vulnerable; he has to be doing something to help. And I understand how he feels. Being involved in the search is almost a compulsion. Ben is compelled, but he's not stupid. Neither am I." She turned away from the surprised comprehension on Marston's face and descended to the floor of the basement.

Ben introduced her to the chief of police. "Maggie, this is Signore Alberto, the *principale* of the police in Rome."

She held out a steady hand. "*Signore*, I appreciate your help."

The man bowed low over her fingers. "It is my pleasure, *signora*. We will do everything possible to return your loved ones to you."

"Thank you. I—we are all very grateful for your efforts. If you need anything..." She glanced around. "I'll ask the kitchen to bring down an urn of coffee and some cold drinks."

"That is very thoughtful of you, *signora*."

"Please let me know if you need anything else." Maggie excused herself and approached another group. She repeated her thanks to each cluster of people in the room. All the while she was thinking, *I've got to get out of this room, out into the air, so I can breathe.* But her movements were so instinctive, so ingrained, that she hardly thought about them.

Ben absently pulled at the loosened knot in his tie until it was completely undone. Thoughtfully he watched

Maggie shift from group to group. She was making this a personal quest for each of them, and her poise was remarkable.

"An extraordinary woman," commented Alberto.

He stuck the tie into his pocket. "Yes. Yes, she is," said Ben.

The telephone on the conference table rang, a jarring sound even in the busy atmosphere of the room.

"It is for you," said the uniformed man who answered, holding the instrument out toward Marston.

Marston took the receiver, turning half away from the people nearby who had paused to listen. "Marston," he said tersely.

Marston's side of the conversation consisted of a series of one-word comments and cryptic questions, but as Ben watched, Marston's features hardened, and his body grew taut.

Ben didn't remember going to her, but his arm was around Maggie's shoulders. "Steady," he said under his breath, but it was his voice that shook.

Slowly Marston replaced the receiver. Maggie didn't realize she was holding her breath until her lungs protested.

"They've found the limo." There was a babble of conversation as the people in the room gathered around.

"Where?" demanded Ben, his fingers digging into Maggie's upper arm.

Marston shoved his hands into his pockets and sighed, looking over the faces before him. "You aren't going to believe this. In an alley behind the Embassy of the Republic of Ireland," he answered disgustedly.

"Dear God!" said someone in the back. "The IRA? I hadn't even thought of them being involved."

"Neither had I," admitted Marston. "Not in this part of the world. But they are on the list of groups we're checking out."

Maggie was confused and filled with despair. Avoiding the unspoken question that had already been answered by omission, she asked, "Why? The IRA isn't based in the Republic of Ireland."

"No, but parking there could have been their way of sending a message," Marston explained. "If they are involved."

"They aren't particularly known for keeping their exploits quiet," mused a woman who was standing at Marston's elbow.

"They aren't particularly known for kidnapping, either," said Marston. "Bombings are more their style."

Maggie thought she was going to be sick. She felt the blood drain from her face; she remained upright only by the strongest exercise of will and Ben's support. She wanted to ask if there were bloodstains on the upholstery; she wanted to ask if they'd found fingerprints. She wanted to know where...

"I'm inclined to believe that leaving the limo there is intended as a red herring, but I'll activate the signal for our undercover agent in the IRA to contact us," said Marston. "It may take a few days."

"I understand."

"In the meantime—"

Alberto had remained quiet throughout the call and ensuing discussion. Now he interrupted. "Mrs. Altman, are you all right?"

"Yes. I'm fine," Maggie answered automatically. The unspoken question had to be asked. "My father... Jamie?"

"I'm sorry," Marston said steadily, but his gray eyes held an expression that might have been gentle. "The limo was empty."

The rain continued sporadically. One minute it seemed the sun would be successful in its attempt to break through the angry clouds, and the next, sheets of water would obscure the road. Ben had been driving for more than half an hour and was approaching the turnoff to Tor Carboni. He eased his foot off the gas.

He glanced over at Maggie, who hadn't said a word during the entire trip. Her head rested against the cushion, her eyes were half closed, but she wasn't sleeping.

"You're very quiet."

"There doesn't seem to be anything to say," she answered tonelessly.

He agreed with her, but for some reason he wanted conversation. He wanted to hear another voice, her voice. Maybe it would keep him from feeling so alone, so desolate. "You're still wearing the same perfume." Why in the world had he mentioned that?

Maggie's brown eyes opened full. "So?" she challenged, but suddenly she was grateful to him for the distraction. She needed to think of something, anything, other than the news they'd had.

Ben shrugged, wishing he'd kept his mouth shut, and concentrated on the road. "Nothing. Just an observation."

An observation about her perfume at a time like this? Straightening in her seat, Maggie recalled her response to the sweep of Ben's cowlick, to the lift of his brow.

Following closely on that recollection came a realization—she and Ben were still intensely aware of each other—and a decision. She wasn't going to marry David

Gant. She suspected the decision had been there in the back of her mind for several days, but she didn't understand why it had emerged at this particular time.

She realized that she simply didn't love David enough to change her life for him. Whatever had prompted the thought, it was one kind of relief to have the matter resolved. And she would take any relief she could get right now.

Her gaze dropped to her hands, which were linked loosely in her lap. Her physical attraction to Ben was a factor, too, and had to be faced. Not that anything would ever come of it, but its presence alone was evidence that she wasn't ready to make a commitment to another man.

"What do you think?" asked Ben.

Maggie looked up. Ben had made a left-hand turn into a packed dirt driveway that was perhaps a quarter of a mile long, ending at a small villa. Majestic old cedars lined the drive on both sides, and on a hill to the right was a small olive grove.

"It's beautiful, Ben," she said softly, leaning forward to get a better look. As they approached, she could see that the green-tiled roof delineated the L shape of the house. An outer wall, enclosing a courtyard, was topped with tiers of the same tile, its shape blurred by the bright blooms of trailing bougainvillea vines. Bright white walls sparkled under the wash of rain.

Ben touched a button on the dash, and heavy wooden gates swung back to admit them to the cobblestone courtyard. He switched off the ignition. With one hand on the handle of his door, he glanced across at her. "Do you want to come inside?"

"Yes, I'd like to. Jamie's told me so much...but he didn't do it justice." She drew in a breath. "The view must be spectacular."

He smiled. "That's one of the reasons I bought it. Come on. Let's get inside before the rain starts again." She followed him up the walk and watched as he dug a key out of his pocket.

"Make yourself at home," he offered when they were inside. "The air-conditioning's off. It's stuffy in here, but you can find cold drinks in the fridge." Stooping first to collect the mail that had been shoved through a slot, he waved at a door to her right.

Maggie nodded but didn't move. They had entered directly into a living room of enormous proportions. Or maybe it just seemed large because it was furnished so sparsely. The walls were whitewashed, the floors, terracotta tiled. She recognized the small woven rugs scattered about as being Greek. Two long saddle-leather couches faced each other in front of a rock fireplace. A low rectangular table the size of a door separated them. Three overstuffed chairs, their upholstery fabric the color of the sky at midnight, filled out the conversational grouping.

The wall opposite the fireplace was a floor-to-ceiling window flanked by glass-paneled doors. No draperies or curtains interfered with the view of the verdant rolling hills or the olive trees, their trunks blackened by age. The Spartan room was softened only by three strategically placed ficus trees with branches gracefully brushing the ceiling.

He was right, she noticed. It was stuffy. She shed her jacket on a chair and tossed the sunglasses down on top of it before crossing the room to the window. "The hills and the cedars remind me of a picture in my Latin textbook.'' During those long-ago school days she had speculated about the Roman armies, marching triumphantly along the Appian Way, maybe stopping to camp in a spot such as this, perhaps this very spot. Except for a small swimming pool, there wasn't a man-made thing in sight. She felt as though she had stepped backward into another century—or perhaps only eight years. "I'll bet Jamie loves the pool."

"Yeah. The little devil swims like a fish. Did you teach him?"

She shook her head. "You know better than that. I took him to the 'Y.' Our apartment isn't far from the Potomac. I had visions of his falling in and my not being able to save him."

"Why didn't you take lessons with him?" Ben asked off-handedly.

Maggie looked over her shoulder with a brief speaking glance, but he was engrossed in his mail. He knew very well that she was terrified of the water. An overenthusiastic friend had pushed her off a dock when she was little, and she'd come too close to drowning.

This was the kind of house they had promised themselves when they were married. Often they would escape the city on hot summer afternoons, searching for a cool breeze. They would pick a spot like this, far away from curious eyes, and plan what kind of house they would build when they moved to the country.

"And a pool," he'd said once. "I've always wanted my own pool."

She had shuddered with dread; he'd held her, speaking softly, reassuringly. "I'll teach you, love. You won't be afraid if I'm holding you." And she hadn't been afraid as long as he'd held her. It was when he stopped that her courage fled.

Maggie attempted to shake off the past. She wasn't afraid anymore. "I never found the time," she said, finally answering his question.

Ben flipped through the mail and watched Maggie's back. She had discarded the peach jacket, he noticed. The knit camisole clung to her, leaving her slender shoulders bare and vulnerable to his compassionate gaze. They were visibly tense and too delicate to bear the burden that was being placed on them. Her ivory skin was untanned, smooth and tempting. He felt the urge to go to her, to massage the tension away, to touch his lips to the seductive curve of her neck, to take her into his arms. He wanted to comfort and be comforted, no matter how wrong it would be.

Impatient with himself, he tossed the letters to a table with more violence than they deserved. One skittered to the floor, but he ignored it and headed for the hall that led to the bedrooms and his office. "I'll just throw some things in a bag," he said, hoping she wouldn't notice the huskiness in his voice.

The shrill ringing of the phone halted him in his tracks and propelled Maggie across the room to his side. "Hello!" he barked. Then his shoulders slumped. When he met Maggie's eyes, he shook his head. "Oh, hello, Linda."

Maggie turned swiftly and went back to the window. She told herself she didn't care who Linda was.

Ben murmured a few indistinct phrases before becoming impatient with the woman on the other end of the line. "Look, Linda, I'm going to be tied up for a while. I'll call you."

Maggie wished she could hear both sides of the conversation.

Finally he said an abrupt goodbye and hung up. "I'll get my things," he told Maggie.

"What? Oh, okay," she answered, determinedly studying the landscape. When she heard him leave the room, she relaxed.

No wonder Jamie loved it here. In Washington they lived in a high-rise apartment building, surrounded by other buildings and people. There was a park nearby, but the noise of traffic intruded even there. Here one could imagine there wasn't another soul on the face of the earth.

She squeezed her eyes shut. Her son's face swam before her lids. She saw the blond hair, which was hers; she saw the green eyes and stubborn jaw, which were Ben's. *"Dad's house is really neat, Mom. You can see for miles and miles. I have my own room, and he's put up a basketball net so we can shoot a few after dinner every night."*

Jamie. Had Jamie been taken out of the city to a remote area like this, or to one of the villages that dotted the countryside? Or to the shores of the Mediterranean? The sea wasn't far away, only thirty miles or so. Could he possibly be on a boat somewhere? Or a plane? He could be anywhere in the world by now. Oh, God! She could think of no explanation for the kidnappers' silence, except the worst one.

All at once the pain became a very real physical ache. Closing her eyes, she put her hands to her temples and pressed hard against the sharp distress there, fighting the shudders that seemed to have taken over her body.

No, no! Stop this, she admonished herself. Wild speculation about where Jamie was, or what was happening to him, was useless. She opened her eyes, stood straight, squared her shoulders. Not only useless, but counterproductive and harmful. She refused to succumb to it. *The next minute,* she reminded herself, *live through the next minute.*

Suddenly she turned, wanting to see the rest of Jamie's other home. The hall down which Ben had disappeared was wide and bright, filled with natural light. She could imagine how cheerful it would be on a sunny day. Her feet made no sound on the polished tiles as she confidently made her way.

Hearing Ben move about in the first room, she passed by quietly. The next door was ajar, revealing a home office. Bookshelves lined the walls. A computer setup covered the old oak desk, which she recognized as having belonged to Ben's grandfather. At one time that desk had held the place of honor in their apartment.

The third door was closed. She reached for the knob. The sight that met her eyes stopped her on the threshold, bringing her heart up to block her throat. The hand that had turned the knob dropped lifelessly to her side, then lifted to press flat against her stomach.

Ben had gone to a lot of trouble to make a comfortable niche for their son. It was a typical boy's room, and yet it was anything but typical. Here was another huge undraped window. Here, too, was a wall of bookshelves, this one containing duplicate copies of Jamie's favorite books. A baseball cap hung crookedly on the bedpost. A catcher's mitt had been tossed on the spread, as though Jamie would be back any minute, ready for a game.

Slowly she turned, until another item halted her movement and her breathing. A heavy oak desk, almost identical to Grandfather Altman's, but new, held another computer. It must have been a recent addition, for Jamie hadn't mentioned it in his letters.

He'd been begging for a computer for a year. They'd looked together, but the model he'd had his heart set on—which sat before her now—was one of the most expensive PC's on the market, and money was tight. She'd been saving with the hope of giving it to him next Christmas.

Maggie's vision blurred; she blinked staunchly against the tears that welled in her eyes. For a minute she resented her ex-husband, resented him fiercely, for giving their son things she couldn't afford.

With difficulty she tamped down the resentment. It was unfair, not only to Ben but to Jamie. Her bitter feelings were born not from Jamie's needs but from her own, and she had always promised herself that her son would never be penalized by her broken relationship with his father. She would try to be pleased for him.

She forced her gaze away from the elaborate piece of equipment and it fell on the bedside table. Her mouth dropped open.

There, in a beautiful leather frame, was a picture of herself, a picture that Jamie would have no access to. Her face, younger by years, grinned out at her. Her nose was sunburned, her hair tossed by the wind, and behind her the blue Mediterranean contrasted with the yellow sail of the boat they'd rented. She remembered the day as though it had been last week.

The short trip to Naples had been an attempt to save their crumbling marriage. Ben had called the getaway weekend a second honeymoon; as a matter of fact, they'd never had a first. They'd walked along the romantic Santa Lucia Harbor; they'd hummed Neapolitan love songs in the Villa Comunal; they'd watched the colors change over the legendary Vesuvius, from the palest pink of dawn, to the melted-silver of noon, to the rose-gold of sunset. Away from the pressure caused by Ben's job, they had communicated as easily as they had when they were first married, as lovers do, with words and without them. And they had made love. Oh, how gloriously they had made love. For a while it looked as though their marriage might work.

Chapter 4

That's Jamie's favorite picture." Ben's quiet voice spoke from behind Maggie. "We had a good time that weekend, didn't we?"

It was bad enough remembering alone. To know that Ben was in the same room, sharing the same memory, was a torment that jolted through Maggie like a volt of electricity, leaving her light-headed. She clenched her fists in a vain effort to stem the emotions that surged through her.

The pain building within her since she'd first answered Ben's call finally demanded release. Her emotions simply could not be contained any longer. They had to escape somehow, and anger was better than tears.

She whirled on him, her dark eyes spitting sparks. "Don't you think that before you give Jamie an expensive gift like that computer, you should consult with me first?" Her voice rose on the last words.

Ben backed away a few paces. He was unquestionably bewildered by the sudden attack. "What are you talking about?"

Her hand swept through the air, encompassing the whole room. "The computer," she repeated.

Ben was still bewildered. "He said he wanted one."

"So you just go out and buy it for him," she spat. "Don't you know that young boys have to be taught the value of—of—"

Stepping closer, he held out a hand. "Margaret Anne..."

"Don't *call* me that!" Spinning abruptly, she presented him with her back. She hunched her shoulders protectively as she grasped her arms. Her teeth came down hard on her lower lip. Anger wasn't going to be enough. She couldn't let him see her cry, she couldn't, but the trembling that shook her body would no longer be denied or disguised.

Ben dismissed her angry outburst, correctly recognizing that the computer had nothing to do with her distress. He watched her struggles with a mixture of admiration and misgiving. She would be better off to let out her misery in the form of tears. So would he. He never cried, but now he desperately longed for the release of tension that tears could bring.

But he also feared the aftermath. Would either of them be able to gather together their composure once they had allowed their emotions full rein? They would need that composure, that strength, in the days to come.

A rush of feeling seemed to break through the dam of control within Ben. Suddenly he didn't care. He didn't want to think about their doomed relationship, past or present, or even about the future. Suddenly he had to hold her, had to share her fear and grief.

Maggie felt the heat from his body before his hands descended onto her shoulders, slid down to her arms, urging her to face him.

"No! Please, don't."

His warm breath fanned her nape. "Maggie, he's going to be all right. We have to believe that. They'll both be all right."

Surprised by the conviction in Ben's voice, Maggie felt her raging furies and fears settle slightly. She was still afraid, but she wasn't going to scream like a mad-woman. "I really don't want comfort, Ben. Please, leave me alone," she begged.

He couldn't do that. Had his life depended on it, he could not have left her alone. Still gripping her arms, he let his head fall forward to rest on her shoulder. "Maggie, oh, Maggie—" his voice broke as he said her name "—I need *you* to comfort *me*."

Maggie turned slowly, lifting her eyes to Ben's, and was stunned by the expression there, an expression of raw, powerful, consuming emotion.

The sea-green color of his eyes had faded to the green-gray of anguish. His cheeks were wet with tears. The Ben who always had iron control over his emotions, the Ben who could report on the most terrifying events with quiet objectivity, was crying. For their child.

And then she knew. Not one other person in the whole world felt what she and Ben were feeling at this moment. And there was no consolation except in each other.

She raised a comforting hand to his cheek, curved her fingers to its shape. "Oh, Ben. Our baby..." she choked out, shaking her head slightly. Her arms reached up and locked around his neck. She was immediately engulfed in a hard embrace.

Ben rocked her in his arms. His sobs were muted in the curve of her neck, but nonetheless they were deep and terrible. They cried together, clung together, for a long, timeless interval.

The tears offered release and cleared away some of the unspoken, unbearable pessimism that plagued them both. "I'll get him back, Maggie. I promise," he murmured finally into her hair. Even knowing that eventually the words might be proven futile, he needed to say them. He needed to voice his hope in an attempt to convince himself and her that the words were true.

Maggie's lips twisted into a parody of a smile. She understood why he had to make that promise.

He lifted his head, loosened his arms. "I have contacts the government couldn't touch. I'll get him back," he said forcefully.

"We'll get him back," Maggie said, correcting him softly. "I'm not a teenager that you have to reassure anymore, Ben. I'll bear my share of our grief, and I'll help."

Ben looked down, lost in the shadowy depths of her brown velvet eyes. He felt the acceleration of her heartbeat against his chest. He was drowning in the wave of intimacy between them. One hand stoked her back, relearning the shape of the woman he held, remembering as though he had held her yesterday, and settling on her sweetly rounded derriere.

Their bodies shifted to fit together without either of them being aware of the movement. Curves met planes naturally, easily, as easily as water conforms to the riverbed, as naturally as the wind caresses the hillside. It was as instinctive as breathing.

Without warning, he was aroused. And Maggie knew it.

She leaned away far enough to look up into his face, her own features expressing shock. "Ben, we can't . . ."

Ben knew it was wrong. He couldn't explain his urgency, even to himself, but he was filled with a passionate need to recapture what they had once had. He lifted a shaky hand and smoothed it over her head. "I want you. Rather desperately and rather obviously. Maggie, I need to be a part of you again," he told her simply.

Had he demanded or pleaded, had he come to her with deliberate seduction in mind, she could have resisted. But the simple, honest declaration of need moved her more than a vow of love would have.

She felt her breasts swell, her nipples pressing against her fragile lace bra. Her pulse slowed to a lazy rhythm, echoed by a heavy throbbing deep within her. She was aroused, too. The feeling was so alien and yet so familiar that she inhaled sharply.

He groaned, pulling her back into his arms.

Maggie, too, needed this warmth, needed it desperately, in order to stave off fear and grief, in order to draw her next breath, in order to survive. Her need was elemental; she had to have him deep inside her, to feel his body infuse her empty places with life.

"Yes, Ben. Oh, yes." With the whisper of acquiescence she opened her lips to the salty taste of their tears. Her fingers plunged into his thick, dark hair, linking at the back of his head to pull him closer, fiercely, urgently. She breathed deeply of his masculine scent, filling her lungs.

Ben's lips roamed greedily over her face, then returned to her mouth. The kiss was neither tentative nor questioning. He spread his broad hand at the base of her spine, moving her against his hips. A rough sigh escaped from the back of his throat.

He lifted Maggie in his arms, never releasing her lips. Her weight was a light, blessed burden that was no burden at all. He strode out of Jamie's room, down the hall to his own. He felt suddenly strong and sure, the doubt and fear that had dragged him to the depths of despair swept away by this unexpected, unbridled passion.

They undressed each other slowly, careful not to touch too intimately lest they lose the last vestiges of control. The excitement, the anticipation, were achingly familiar. It was like coming home. The intimacy was a balm to their frayed nerves.

Maggie knew one brief moment of uneasiness—for so long her body's sensual demands had lain dormant—until Ben stretched out a trembling hand to brush the tips of his fingers lightly over her breasts, her stomach. Her muscles contracted at the contact. With a soft murmur she melted into his arms. His hands flowed over her, lifting, smoothing. His mouth followed, tasting, caressing her breasts, her stomach, her thighs, with kisses that burned and soothed, with broken phrases of desire.

And, for Maggie, it took no effort at all to remember the bunching of his muscles beneath her fingers, the pleasurable abrasion of his hair-whorled chest over her breasts, the sensuality of naked skin against naked skin, or the sweet demand of his knee between her thighs.

He threw back the covers, following her down on the bed to cover her body with his, to grasp her face in his hands, to tangle his legs with hers. When she took him into her, her body was more than ready; it was eager to meet his thrusts. Their coming together was like rivers merging, crashing together to produce a whirlpool that cast them into its vortex. Ecstasy swirled through them. And then she was a mindless sea of sensation, alive as she hadn't been alive in years, and aware only of the man who followed her into the vortex with a full-throated groan, her name a hoarse shout on his lips.

In the aftermath of their lovemaking Maggie lay curled against his side, her hand resting lightly on his bare chest. They were both silent, each lost in thought. Ben's hand stroked her soft hip while his eyes drank in the sight of her. God, it had been so good to lose himself in her again.

Gradually he became aware that she was too still. Had he hurt her? He hadn't been gentle, but her body was so ripe, so enticing.

Maggie could not believe what had just happened: in Rome less than twelve hours, and she'd fallen into her ex-husband's bed with no hesitation. And, God help her, their lovemaking was more exciting than it had been eight years ago. Her heavy lids fell shut. The physical side of their relationship had always been wonderful, but this, this had a new dimension, a depth she'd never experienced.

What was the difference? she asked herself, but she knew very well what the difference was. Ben had treated her like a woman today. Eight years ago, she had been young, and a virgin. And, even after the first night, he'd never quite stopped treating her like a virgin. He'd been gentle and tender and very loving, and it had been wonderful; but, today he had demanded a woman's response of her. His demand had thrilled and excited her; it was a challenge she was ready, even eager, to meet, without question, without hesitation.

Maggie sat up abruptly and hugged her knees. She groaned aloud and let her forehead fall forward to rest on her forearms. Like a careless teenager, she had completely ignored the fact that this sort of thing caused babies.

"Maggie." Ben spoke quietly from behind her. "Did I hurt you, sweetheart?" His broad hand left a warm imprint on her back.

Maggie shook her head, the movement brushing her hair over his fingers. "No, you didn't hurt me."

"Then why are you upset, babe?" His hand moved up her spine to her nape, gently massaging the tense muscles he found there. "If I pressured you into something you'll regret, I'm sorry."

She was afraid her laughter might have the ring of hysteria, so she swallowed it immediately. "You didn't pressure me either, Ben. I knew what I was doing. But you may regret it, too."

"I won't," he said shortly, sitting at her side. "I'll never regret what we just shared, Maggie. It was beautiful."

She rested her chin on her folded arms and gazed at the opposite wall. "You know, Ben, once a few years ago, I was having a bout with loneliness. They come around every so often."

Gently, tenderly he combed his fingers through her hair, relishing the silky feel of it. "I know what you mean," he said in an odd way.

"Well, I thought I might get over it if I could remember how it felt to be held in your arms. I tried and tried...but the memory had gone. It made me very sad."

Ben continued to stroke her hair. "Tell me the truth, Maggie, don't you think, after eight years, we're both a bit curious? Maybe each of us wants the other to feel a little regret, a little sadness, at the loss?"

She laid her cheek on her arms and looked at him. A mournful chuckle escaped her, and then she spoke. "Your damned reporter's objectivity is showing." Her smile took the sting out of the words. "That wasn't why I was upset."

"Tell me."

"Because I'm stupid, a first-class idiot, that's why."

His smile was rueful. "Making love might not have been the smartest thing we could have done, but under the circumstances it was understandable." He tucked a strand of hair behind her ear. "We needed the comfort that only we could give each other."

Maggie caught her lower lip between her teeth and lifted her head, letting it fall back. She blinked at the ceiling. Sighing heavily, she met his eyes again. "I know," she said softly. "But what if there is another little consequence?"

Ben looked puzzled for a moment. When comprehension dawned, there was a light in his eyes that she'd never thought to see there again. Just as suddenly it died to be replaced with a look of horror that she would have laughed at if she'd had the energy.

"You aren't on the pill?"

She gave a short quick shake of her head. "Sorry." She swung her legs over the side of the bed, avoiding Ben's eyes as she looked around for her scattered clothes.

Still uncertain, Ben got out of bed. "You haven't—you don't...?" he muttered, faltering like a novice broadcast student. One arm circled her waist, while his other hand smoothed her tangled hair. He wanted to see her face but was afraid to believe what she seemed to be saying.

Maggie leaned against him for a brief second before she pulled away. She gathered up her clothes and began to pull them on. Lord, had she lost her mind? She certainly hadn't been seduced or coerced into doing anything against her wishes. She'd been more than willing;

she'd been eager and hungry for the experience after eight long years. And it was so different. *He* was so different.

"No." She stepped into her skirt and buttoned the waistband, tucking the camisole in with ruthless fingers. She looked around for her scattered hairpins. Her fingers were deft from long years of habit as she twisted and pinned.

"Maggie, damn it, look at me!"

Meeting his gaze, she tried to be reassuring. "It probably isn't the right time of the month, but I'm not always that regular."

"The congressman . . . ?"

She barely spared him a glance, but it was enough to see that his stupefaction had turned to suspicion. He stood with his legs braced apart, his fists planted firmly on his hips, looking in all his naked glory like an angry Roman god bent on retaliation. He folded his arms over his chest. "It's rather hard to believe you haven't slept with him."

Her eyes widened, her nostrils flared. "My sex life, or the lack of it, isn't your concern, except as it applies to this situation. I can promise you one thing. If there is a consequence, this time you'll be a full participant. I don't intend to go through that alone again." She picked up her sandals by the straps and slung them over her shoulder. "Let's go," she said, her manner one of studied indifference.

The rain had stopped, but clouds still obscured the sun. At the door she paused to put on her shoes and grab her blazer. The rope-soled sandals squeaked on the cobblestones as she crossed the courtyard and climbed into the Ferrari, then slammed the door with a satisfying thud.

Ben had his emotions under firm control by the time he joined her. He tossed a bag into the space behind the seat and climbed in beside her. "Maggie, we have to talk about this," he said grimly.

"No," she answered, her voice firm. "There's no reason to anticipate more trouble. We have enough to cope with as it is. It probably won't happen, but if it does, there will be plenty of time to discuss what to do."

"No abortion," he said flatly.

She jerked her head around violently. "You bastard! If I had ever contemplated abortion, I think last time would have been appropriate, don't you? My circumstances were rather more desperate then."

Ben wrapped his hands around the steering wheel and stared out through the windshield. "I apologize. I shouldn't have even suggested it. Have you changed your mind about my staying at the residence?"

If he'd been watching her face, he would have seen the surprise there. Such a thought hadn't occurred to her. "Look, Ben, we needed something today—a release of sorts—that, as you said, we could only get from each other. But I don't want you to get the idea that it will be repeated. I've managed alone for a long time. I like it that way. I would like you to stay at the residence, but only if you accept the fact that we won't be sleeping together."

Ben couldn't believe his ears. "A release? Is that all it was to you?" he breathed. He had the sinking sensation that what he'd taken for maturity in Maggie was a severe hardening of her personality. The brittle shell he'd noticed earlier wasn't temporary. Had he done that to her? The thought added another oppressive load of regret to his already heavy heart.

Annoyed with herself, Maggie shook her head against the confusion she felt. "Release, comfort, call it what you will; it won't be repeated." She was handling this badly, but it had to be done. Ben, this new demanding Ben who made love to her as a woman, was much too dangerous to her peace of mind. From the moment she'd gotten off the plane, his presence had totally shaken her confidence that she could remain aloof.

Ben was equally annoyed with himself for trying to give a deeper name to their lovemaking. "Then let's get going." She was absolutely right, Ben thought. They had enough to worry about without borrowing more trouble. Physical release was one thing, but being intimate on a regular basis with this new, harder Maggie was repellent to him.

The deputy ambassador was waiting when they arrived at the residence. He met them in her father's study. "Maggie, dear." He came out from behind the desk to kiss her lightly on the cheek. "I'm sorry I wasn't here when you arrived, but I wasn't expecting you."

Maggie's annoyance with herself and Ben spilled over onto John Gandress. "Why didn't you call me immediately, John? Didn't you think I had a right to know that my father and son were missing?"

Ben hid a smile of reluctant appreciation. Leave it to Maggie to go right to the heart of the matter. She would have made a lousy ambassador.

"I wasn't sure of our situation here," Gandress hedged. "I would have called as soon as there was concrete information."

"And advised me to stay in Washington?"

"It would have been for the best, Maggie. There's nothing you can do here."

Ben braced himself for an explosion, but to his surprise it didn't come.

"That's a matter of opinion, isn't it?" she asked mildly.

"We've had more experience with this type of thing than you have, my dear." He was trying to soothe her, but all he got for his pains was a sneer.

"John, I am an employee of the State Department. An analyst, however junior, for the European desk. Didn't it occur to you that I might have something to contribute? Some little thing that might be helpful?"

It was obvious that the thought hadn't occurred to him, she thought grimly.

Gandress tried changing the subject. "I was just going through some of Ian's papers, the things he'd been working on most recently, at the request of the police." He indicated the desk, and they drew closer to look down at the scattered papers there. "There are a lot to go through. Your father wasn't sim—" He broke off, horrified.

Ben straightened slowly, but Maggie's body jerked erect; her eyes spit brown sparks. "Wasn't?" she said into the slash of quiet. "Are you so ready to take over my father's responsibilities?"

The deputy ambassador's face flamed with mortification, and she was immediately sorry for the accusation. "Certainly not! Maggie, please forgive me. What an appalling misstatement." He took a handkerchief from his pocket and mopped at his brow. "I'm sorry," he repeated. "What I meant to say was that your father isn't a figurehead ambassador, as you know."

Maggie stared at him, stone-faced, but Ben felt her body tremble. He placed his palm lightly between her shoulders, declaring an unspoken truce. He might be mad as hell at her, but he wanted to let her know without words that she had his support. "Did you find anything in the papers that might help?" he asked Gandress.

Gandress seized on the younger man's question gratefully. "Not a thing in the official documents, I'm afraid. Neither here nor at the chancery. Things have been amazingly quiet this summer." He hesitated. "I'd been wondering if they might have stopped off somewhere on the way back from Tivoli, maybe on a personal errand. But I can't find anything here that might give us a clue."

"Another blank wall," said Ben.

"Yes, another blank wall." He turned his attention rather carefully to Maggie. "There are some personal papers, receipts and such, that you might want to look at more carefully than I have, Maggie. But I don't think you'll find anything."

Maggie picked up a sheet of fine vellum from the top of one stack. It was a thank-you letter from some friends of the French ambassador, who had visited Rome in May. She let it drift back to the desk. "Thank you, John. I'll go through these," she answered easily. The outburst might never have happened.

"And the president called. As you can imagine, he is extremely upset."

A shared glance of understanding passed between Maggie and Ben. How easily they fell back into the old patterns, she thought irrelevantly. Sternly she reproved herself.

They both were aware of Ian's close friendship with the president. She would bet that the man in the White House was calling people on the carpet right and left, demanding explanations from everyone from the lowliest clerk to the secretary of state himself. "I'm sorry I missed him."

"He said he would call back this evening to speak to you personally."

"Thank you," she said again.

"And now I must go." He straightened his tie and ran a palm over his already perfectly groomed hair. "I will probably see you tomorrow." He stopped on his way to the door as though a thought had just occurred to him. "There's one more thing, Maggie." Though he spoke to Maggie, he included Ben in his glance. His expression was a clear plea for understanding.

What now? thought Ben.

"A reception is planned for tomorrow night."

Maggie frowned, shoving her hands into the pockets of her white skirt. "I don't plan to do any socializing while I'm here, John."

"The reception is in honor of a U.S. trade delegation that has been touring the Common Market countries. It's being held here in the ballroom."

"Oh, God," moaned Maggie. The hands in her pockets made fists. Even without her background as a diplomat's daughter, she realized instantly the importance of such a delegation.

"Mr. Marston says that it will have to go on as scheduled. He wants things to appear as normal as possible. We'll come up with some kind of story to explain your father's absence, but it would be helpful—Marston wants you to act as hostess."

Maggie shook her head. "Absolutely not," said Ben, moving his hand to cup her shoulder.

Gandress held out a placating hand. "Mr. Altman, if these were ordinary times there would be no question of asking Maggie. My wife has acted as hostess for the embassy on many occasions.''

"Then let your wife do it again. Mine will not." Neither of them noticed the incorrect title, but Maggie did. It caused her a great deal of disquiet to think that the term *wife* came so easily to his lips in moments of stress.

"Marston believes Maggie's presence will help to dismiss any speculation about Ian's disappearance. He's adamant, I'm afraid."

"I'll talk to him. Only a monster would expect something like this."

"Ian would expect it," said Gandress quietly. "Wouldn't he, Maggie?"

Both men turned to look at Maggie.

Numbly Maggie nodded, urging her mind back to the situation at hand. Her father would expect her to carry on, doing whatever was necessary. "Yes, I'm afraid he would."

"Stiff upper lip and all that crap?" Ben said angrily.

"The diplomatic corps isn't all fancy balls and receptions, you know," snapped Gandress, with the first sarcasm he'd shown.

"I know." As he'd grown close to his father-in-law, Ben had begun to realize the extent of the pressure that Maggie had lived under from a very early age—pressure to perform with perfect decorum under all circumstances. When other American girls her age had been kicking up their heels at Fort Lauderdale, or worrying what to wear to the prom, Maggie had been acting as hostess for her father at diplomatic receptions. It wasn't fair.

And then she had married him, looking for stability in their relationship, a secure home life, free from that pressure. But the life of a news correspondent is anything but stable.

Ben found it easier, after many talks with Ian, to understand why Maggie had been so possessive during their marriage, why she was so alarmed when he went away, why she berated him when he returned. Ben had rebuked himself, too, wondering why he had failed to comprehend her reasons. And the answer was that he had, but by that time it was too late. She'd made it clear she wanted nothing to do with him.

Maggie walked with Gandress to the door. When she returned, Ben was lounging in her father's chair; he looked up from the handful of papers he was studying. His expression was disgusted.

She met his glare with a half smile, knowing his animosity wasn't directed toward her. "Well, at least he didn't say anything *really* trite like 'the ship of State must sail on.'"

"Thank God," said Ben sincerely. "Are you sure you're up to this, Maggie?"

"No, I'm not sure." She collapsed in a chair across the desk from him. "But I'll have to try, won't I? You want to hear something else really trite?"

He smiled sorrowfully, wishing he could spare her this ordeal. "Worse than Gandress?"

She dropped her gaze to the hands clenched in her lap. "I don't have anything to wear."

Ben's jaw dropped a the age-old complaint. Then he laughed softly.

Touched by the rich, warm sound of his laughter, she looked up and met his eyes with amusement in her own. Their gazes locked.

Ben leaned forward, holding out his hand.

She hesitated for only a moment before she put hers in it. He squeezed her fingers lightly. "That is trite, but at least it is a problem we can do something about. Now let's get to work on these papers."

When the president's call came through, Maggie took it, responding calmly to her father's friend's anxiety. For it was first as a friend that he called, then as president.

They talked for a few minutes and then he said, "Maggie, I want you to know that Marston's my best man. I trust him implicitly. You can, too."

"Thank you, sir. That's reassuring." She didn't tell him that there was a conflict between his best man and her ex-husband.

"Before we hang up, my dear, there's someone here who would like to speak to you."

"Maggie?"

She had been facing the desk, facing Ben, but at the sound of the voice, she turned away in surprise. "David?" What was David doing at the White House? Of course, he was on the Foreign Affairs Committee of the House.

"Darling, why didn't you call me?" he asked, his concern obvious even over the thousands of miles that separated them. "Do you want me to come? I can be there by tomorrow morning."

"No, David," she answered hastily. "I'm fine. I don't...that's not a good idea." Maggie cursed herself for the nervous tremor in her voice.

There was a pause on the line. He knew, without a doubt he knew. "I understand. Jamie's father is there, isn't he?"

She felt so guilty. David Gant was a wonderful man. Why couldn't she love him? "Yes," she said softly.

His voice lowered intimately. "Maggie, if you need me, you know all you have to do is call."

"Thank you, David. I do know that."

She said goodbye and hung up. Her fingers clung to the receiver for a minute. Finally she met Ben's enigmatic gaze full-on.

"Are you going to marry him?" he asked bluntly.

"No."

The terse answer pleased Ben. He didn't ask for more.

The butler found them there an hour later. "Would you like cocktails in here, Mrs. Altman? Dinner will be served shortly."

Maggie glanced through the French doors to the terrace beyond. Twilight had dimmed the outlines of the balcony and blurred the shape of the trees. She hadn't realized it was so late. "Oh, dear." She looked down at herself. "Dinner in the formal dining room?" she asked, knowing full well that unless orders were given to the contrary, that's exactly where it would be served. "I'm afraid I'm not dressed for it."

"Would you rather have your meal on trays in here?" he asked kindly.

She gave him a smile of grateful relief. "Thank you, James. I'm sorry to put you to the trouble."

Ben hid the curve of his lips behind his hand. It had always astounded him how everyone, from cab drivers to butlers, jumped to do Maggie's bidding the minute she flashed that warm, beautiful smile.

"It's no trouble, Mrs. Altman. I shall set up a small table under the window and leave it there for as long as you wish."

"That's very thoughtful. I think we'd be more comfortable here, under the circumstances."

"Very well, madam," said the butler. "And the cocktails?"

"I'll have a glass of Chablis. Ben?"

"Scotch and soda."

The butler disappeared only to return a few minutes later with their drinks. Holding his glass, Ben rose from his place behind the desk. "Let's take a break, Maggie," he suggested. He opened the doors leading onto the terrace. With the disappearance of the sun the air was cooler and washed by the earlier rain, fresher.

Maggie followed, welcoming the cleansing breeze that lifted the damp tendrils of hair from her neck. She leaned both elbows on the marble balustrade and looked over the formal garden beyond. The cool scent of lemon trees vied with the headier aroma of roses as she inhaled long and deep. "This is nice," she sighed.

"It is, isn't it?"

Something in Ben's voice brought her head around.

"Maggie." He set his glass down and faced her fully, leaning on one elbow. "I'd like to talk to you."

"You sound serious." She turned again to the shadowed vista before her. "Can't we just relax, Ben? I'm too tired to talk right now."

"Then you listen. I'll talk." He hefted himself up to sit on the wall and looked down at her bent head. "I've learned a few things over the years from Ian. The talk with our deputy ambassador brought some of them back."

"What things? Ben, please don't let's rehash the past. Not now. It's over."

"Will it ever be over? We have a son together. This afternoon showed us that we have other things together, as well."

"What are you trying to say?' she demanded. *If you say we should try again, I'll knock you off this wall, Ben Altman.*

"I was too blind to see that you had needs I didn't know about eight—nine years ago." He paused. "Your father expected a lot from you," he added quietly.

The implied criticism brought her head up. "Not any more than I was willing to give."

"I know that," he assured her. "He must have been devastated by the death of your mother."

"We both were," she whispered. But she remembered how willingly she'd taken on tasks that were beyond her maturity in order to ease her father's pain.

"Then you married me, and I began to expect even more of you than your father had. You were young, but damn it, you didn't look young. It was hard for me to remember. I expected you to be there waiting for me no matter where I went, how long I was gone, no matter how worried you were; I expected you to stay in the small part of my life I had labeled 'wife,' and not to ask for more."

Maggie didn't know how to answer. The things he was saying were true, but she had been even more guilty of destroying their marriage than Ben. Her love had made her afraid, then angry. She had cried, then pleaded; she'd threatened, and then she'd left.

"I suppose what I'm saying is that I'm sorry for everything."

"I'm sorry, too, Ben," she answered softly. "If I'd been older..."

He tilted her chin so that he could see her face in the dim light. "And if I'd been wiser. Maggie, do you think...?"

The sound of a door being opened in the room behind them broke off what he'd been about to say.

"I think our dinner has arrived," said Maggie.

Ben sighed and released her chin.

James entered the study carrying a small table. Behind him was a maid pushing a serving cart.

Ben sauntered through the doors with Maggie at his side. "We'll serve ourselves, James. Thanks."

"You're welcome, sir." He turned to Maggie. "Mrs. Altman, I want to assure you that the preparations for the reception tomorrow night have been taken care of. The flowers, the food, extra servants. You won't have to trouble yourself with details."

Maggie smiled her relief and her thanks. "That is a great comfort, James."

The butler left.

Ben lifted a silver lid and sniffed appreciatively. "We missed lunch."

Maggie wasn't surprised she hadn't noticed that. Just about at lunchtime they had been on Ben's big bed. "So we did," she said mildly. "Are you hungry?"

Ben met her gaze and knew that she was remembering the afternoon just as he was. The unvoiced thought of a moment ago was best left unsaid for now. It was not the right time; he'd seen that in her eyes. Maybe it would never be the right time. But strangely he felt better about them, much better. "Yes. Yes, I think I am. Fears blacker than the night can turn to hope, Maggie. It think we can help pull this off—you and I. We'll get back to work on those papers after we eat, and who knows, we may find something there."

"I'm hopeful, too," said Maggie, realizing with surprise that it was true. "Let's eat."

Gradually the meal disappeared, every crumb of the Italian garlic bread, topped with chopped tomatoes, every drop of the basil sauce that seasoned the braised chicken, every tiny vegetable, and every bite of creme caramel. At last Ben sat back and lit a cigarette.

He watched, amused, as Maggie delicately yawned over the last bit of custard on her spoon. There were dark circles beneath her eyes. It hurt Ben to see them. "I have a suggestion to make. I'd make it an order if I weren't afraid you'd throw me out."

She smiled. "What is your suggestion?" she asked pointedly.

He glanced at his watch. "It's almost nine, which means it's three a.m. in Washington. I suggest you go up to bed right now. It's been a long day."

"But, Ben, we have so much to do," she protested.

He leaned forward to take the spoon from her hand and stood, pulling her up with him. A hand at her waist, he guided her to the door. "Maggie, by my estimate you've been awake for at least forty-eight hours."

She thought for a minute and realized he was right.

"You're running on pure adrenaline, honey. You'll need your brain at full power tomorrow."

She paused on the threshold. "What about you?"

"I'll be up in a little while."

"Do you know which room is yours?"

"James showed me." He smiled and touched his knuckles to her cheek. "Are you sure you don't want someone in your bed?" he said softly, voicing the question he hadn't meant to ask. She still had the same disconcerting effect on him.

The suggestion brought her back to life. "I'm sure," she said firmly. She wasn't sure; she wasn't sure at all, but he mustn't know that.

"I thought you might be."

"Ben," she said, then hesitated.

He smiled again, encouraging her to say what she was feeling.

The touch of his hand on her cheek brought forth warm, sentimental feelings. "It would be easy to sleep together. Obviously we're still compatible that way. But it would be a great mistake. Don't you see?" *I might love you again,* she thought, but she didn't say it out loud.

"I do see," agreed Ben. This Maggie was so much more desirable to him, a handful of a woman. And, until he analyzed his feelings for her, it would be as risky as hell to get involved.

He walked with her to the foot of the staircase and watched until she disappeared. Reluctantly he retraced his steps. He needed to go through the papers Gandress had left. He needed to make a list of people to call tomorrow. He needed to get his thoughts in order.

He gave a bark of laughter, which sounded too loud in the silence, and sank into the chair behind the desk. His mind refused to be guided by the things he needed to do. Instead it was fixed on his physical needs and his emotional ones, focused obstinately on the number of different women that Maggie Altman was: the mother of his son, the woman he'd made love to this afternoon, the brittle woman, the vulnerable one, the woman who was so very much more ... More what? More mature, more beautiful—though he would have sworn no one could ever have been more beautiful—than the woman he'd married nine years ago. Linking his hands behind his head, he leaned back in the chair and tried to make the different images into a whole picture.

Upstairs, Maggie stood under the shower and tried to reconcile the sweet poignancy of this Ben with her bitter memories. Slowly she turned, facing forward, and closed her eyes under the hot spray, shutting out this Ben with determined efficiency, replacing him instead with the Ben of eight years ago. In an attempt to make herself immune to her ex-husband, she replayed the scene of their last meeting. It had been a small taverna around the corner from his office....

The Sermona was a favorite hangout for American network people, as well as print journalists, and she had left messages for him there before. Too many messages, too many tears and too much recrimination. This part was humiliating to remember, but she forced herself.

Maggie had just opened the door, thankful to see that the place was almost deserted. Hearing Ben's deep voice, she paused on the threshold, half hidden by a large potted palm.

He must have come in only seconds before. He eased his hip onto a stool. "A double Scotch, Vito. On the rocks."

"How ya doin', Ben?" someone said from the high-backed booth to Maggie's left. She recognized the voice of Ben's boss, Mac. "C'mon over," he said.

The bartender tipped the bottle over the glass of ice and handed it to Ben, who then crossed to join his colleague in the booth. Mac's back was toward Maggie. All she could see was the back of his head, but she had a clear view of her husband through the fronds of the palm.

"Oh, Mr. Altman, I almost forgot." Vito came out from behind the counter with her latest note in his hand. "Here's a message from your wife."

"Another one?" Ben took the folded paper from the man and stared at it for a long minute. Suddenly he made a sound deep in his throat, a sound like an angry animal. He crushed the unopened note in his fist and threw it violently toward the bar. "Blast it! Why can't she leave me alone?" he erupted.

Vito seemed taken aback by Ben's savage reaction, but he tried again. "She really sounded upset this time, Mr. Altman. Maybe you'd better read the note." A heavy man, he grunted slightly when he leaned over to rescue the paper that had fallen short of its target. He laid it on the table between the two newsmen.

"The diplomat's daughter *always* sounds upset when she doesn't get her way," Ben drawled sarcastically. He picked up the glass and downed the whiskey in three gulps. "Trash the damned thing and pour me another drink," he ordered.

"Ben, you shouldn't..."

Ben waved an arm, cutting off Mac's protest. "We've been legally separated for six weeks, Mac."

"I'm sorry. I didn't know," said his boss.

Ben folded his arms on the table in front of him. His head drooped. "She left me, because I wouldn't do what she wanted. Because I wouldn't change my life, my career, for her, she left me."

"You shouldn't be talking to me this way, Ben," Mac said quietly.

"I know. It's not the thing for a gentleman to do, is it? But she tried to interfere once too often, Mac." The violence in his voice was replaced by a soft, sad note of finality. "The one time I really needed her support, and she let me down. Hell, you know better than anyone."

Mac muttered something unintelligible.

Maggie bit down hard on her lip. She knew exactly what he was talking about.

Ben was good at his job; he was the best. Anytime there was trouble in this part of the world, they sent Ben

Altman. And sent him, and sent him. Until she couldn't bear the fear anymore. Their last fight had been because she had approached Mac on her husband's behalf, and without his knowledge or consent. She had begged Mac to transfer Ben to the States. When Ben found out, he was justifiably furious, so furious that he had immediately volunteered for the next assignment in the worst state-sponsored terrorist action in the area. And he'd been turned down. Finally he'd asked her to go to Mac, to retract her plea. She'd refused, putting the last nail in the coffin that held her dead marriage.

The man who got the story won a Pulitzer for it. She had fled to her father.

Behind the palm, she blinked at the humiliating tears that flowed too freely these days.

"This?" Ben picked up the paper and crumpled it in his fist again. "This is just another of her threats."

Maggie opened her mouth to protest but was interrupted by his angry fist slamming down on the table. "Damn it! I'd sell my soul to the devil to forget I ever knew her." The sincerity of his statement didn't escape either of the men, or Maggie, who now stood frozen at the entrance.

Mac tried one more time. "Why don't you talk to her instead?" he asked. "Sit down and have a reasonable conversation. Tell her how you feel."

Maggie wanted to scream at Mac to be quiet.

"Mac, have you ever tried to reason with a three-year-old?" Ben drawled tiredly. "Correction. A spoiled, coddled, pampered three-year-old? Trying to reason with my wife is the same thing. She knows very well how I feel." He took another swallow of his drink. "So, what have you got for me?"

Mac raised his glass; the bartender nodded. "As a matter of fact, there have been a few rumbles in Ankara. You want to go to Turkey and take a look around?"

She didn't move so much as a muscle, so how the man behind the bar knew she was there would forever remain a mystery. He looked up at her, and she saw in his eyes what she knew she would see, what she dreaded to see—pity. His expression showed her clearly, for the first time, the depths to which her self-respect had sunk. She was horror-stricken at the realization.

Something, perhaps the newsman's inexplicable sixth sense, alerted Ben, as well. He looked up at the bartender, then twisted slightly in the booth, following the man's gaze.

His eyes met Maggie's for a long, agonizing second. Silently they each asked the questions: How can it have come to this? How did the magic go sour? What happened to us? She thought she read regret and pain in his expression, but now it didn't matter; nothing mattered. She never knew how she did it, but she turned and walked calmly out the door. Ben didn't come after her.

Everything he had said about her was true. She had cried wolf once too often, and now, when she really needed him, he wasn't going to be there.

Chapter 5

Maggie was drifting, floating in the peaceful state somewhere between wakefulness and oblivion, when an odd noise began to intrude on her consciousness. She fought it briefly. Tired, she was so tired. There was thunder in the distance, she thought drowsily. Well, Washington certainly needed rain.

It wasn't thunder. Someone was knocking on the bedroom door. Squeezing her eyes shut, she rolled over onto her back. "Jamie?" she murmured.

Instead of answering, Ben entered the room, carrying two steaming mugs of coffee. He used his foot to close the door behind him and put the mugs on the bedside table. Sliding his hands into the back pockets of his jeans, he waited, looking down at Maggie with a small smile.

Watching Maggie come to life in the mornings had been one of his favorite pastimes when they were married. She began by squeezing her eyes tightly shut against the light; then she tested her torpid muscles, arching her back slightly, shifting her legs and flexing her feet under the covers. Finally she gave a big yawn, scraped her hair back from her face and opened those beautiful brown-velvet eyes. By the time she'd finished the long-remembered ritual, he was weak with longing.

During the endless hours of the night, Ben had promised himself that he would be casual with Maggie. They needed each other now, but when this was over, she'd return to Washington, and he—well, he hadn't made a decision yet about the job. But even if he went back to the States, there was still too much dividing them. He'd told himself he'd be a fool to get entangled with her again. Now seeing her like this, sleepy and warm and sexy as hell, his promise went out the window. He was entangled with her whether he liked it or not. And the end was going to hurt.

"Ben!" Maggie sat up with a jerk, suddenly and completely awake. Her eyes were glued to his, her heart pounding. It all came rushing back. "Something's happened."

"No, no." Ben shook his head and sat on the bed. He took her cold hands in his. "No news yet," he reassured her.

Maggie collapsed against the pillow. Her eyes fell shut, in relief or dread; she didn't know which. When she looked at him again, her gaze narrowed. "What's the matter, then? You look like death warmed over," she muttered huskily.

His hair was tousled, his jaw shadowed with stubble. His clothes looked as if he'd thrown them on. The tails of his wrinkled half-buttoned shirt hung loose over well-worn, well-fitting jeans. Dark hair clouded his chest, and he'd rolled up his sleeves to reveal strong forearms. Even resembling a refugee from Skid Row, he was a potent example of rugged masculinity. Too potent for the time and circumstances, she thought irritably.

She had hardly slept during the night. Because she was alone with her fears, they had grown to gigantic, horrifying proportions. The dark hours of the early morning had seemed endless.

"I brought you a cup of coffee, but I'm beginning to think I should have let you sleep." He handed her a mug.

Maggie muttered again, scooted up in the bed and arranged the pillow behind her, too aware that under the light sheet she was covered by only a sheer gown. She accepted the mug. "Thank you," she said formally. "Did you hear anything more about the car after I went to bed last night?"

"I checked with Alberto this morning. They are still going over it. They brought in a top-notch forensic man, but it may take longer than we expect. Marston warned us that waiting is another form of terrorism."

She watched him sullenly.

Ben hooked three fingers through the handle of the other mug and picked it up. Toasting her silently, he smiled, his green eyes glimmering over the rim. "I'd forgotten how grouchy you are in the morning," he said gently.

She glared at him. "I had an awful night, as I'm sure you did, too, so don't push me."

"Yeah," he said in a low voice, his gaze distracted by the smooth curve of her shoulders. "Ah, but I know the secret to putting a smile on that lovely face, don't I? I can remember what fun it used to be to cajole you out of your grumps."

"Ben—"

Ignoring the warning of her voice, he balanced his mug on his knee. He slid a hand beneath the heavy fall of hair at her nape and leaned forward to kiss the silky spot just behind and below her ear. His lips nibbled gently; his tongue snaked out to taste her warm skin. He closed his eyes and inhaled her delicate feminine fragrance.

Trying to keep the coffee from spilling, Maggie hunched her shoulder, denying him access, and shoved him away. "Damn it, Ben. Don't you have any feelings. Leave me alone."

Instead of retreating, he clasped her face in his big hand. "Look at me, Maggie."

His fingers were like warm bars on her cheeks, their heat setting off tiny explosions of desire throughout her body. Her lashes stubbornly shielded her expression from him. "I'd rather not."

"Look at me," he repeated.

As she raised her lashes, a tear fell on her cheek. She didn't know where it had come from.

Ben felt his throat close at the sight of the tear. He wiped it away with his thumb. "Honey," he said tenderly, "we're going to live through this thing. Ian will take care of Jamie and himself, too." His lips touched each eye and lingered on her forehead. "We have to live one minute at a time."

Ben's tenderness caused Maggie's heart to double its speed. If only she hadn't let down her guard yesterday. If only she had insisted he stay at least an arm's length away. But she hadn't. And now, instead of old, tired memories, she had fresh new ones that were infinitely harder to cope with. "I know," she said shakily.

"In the meantime, we have a lot to do." He smiled at her reaction. Her brown eyes had darkened to black pools of lazy desire. He had an overwhelming urge to strip off his clothes and crawl into the bed beside her. Instead he forced his voice to an easygoing lightness he didn't feel. "First, I'm going to fix you my special waffles—remember my waffles?" he asked.

Maggie nodded grudgingly. She remembered, all right, but she didn't want to. When they were married, Ben had always fixed waffles on Saturday mornings. "But it isn't Saturday."

"Ah-h-h. You do remember Saturdays," he whispered with a satisfied smile.

Her expression softened as she relented, letting the memory in. "How could I forget?" She had loved their Saturdays together; it had been a day to sleep late, to make love leisurely, to linger over breakfast—when he'd been in town.

"After breakfast we'll work on the papers again until it's time for the stores to open. Then we'll go buy you a dress to wear to the reception."

She closed her eyes, turning her face into his palm. "Oh, Ben," she said brokenly. "How can I think about buying a dress or playing hostess at some stupid reception when . . . when . . ."

"These are the things we do to get through the day, honey, to keep our sanity until we hear something." She was surprised to hear him voice the philosophy that had kept her sane so far. After taking both their mugs and setting them aside, he wrapped her close in his arms and lifted her, covers and all, onto his lap. He gathered up a handful of her blond hair and let it drift through his fingers.

His embrace was rock-hard and steady. Maggie relaxed against him, her own arms slipping around his middle. "I hope it's soon."

"God, so do I," he answered fervently into her hair.

Ben was reminding her that he was equally as shaken, equally as fearful as she. But Maggie was fighting guilt, too, because all she could think about at this moment was the masculine scent of his body, the muscles in the hard arms that held her, the strong heartbeat beneath her ear. She nodded, her cheek rubbing lightly against the hair on his chest. Her lips were only an inch away from his nipple.

God! Ben squeezed his eyes shut and made a fist in her hair. He wished she wouldn't rub against him like that; he wished she would do it some more. She would be disgusted if she knew where his thoughts had taken him.

After a minute Maggie pulled back to look at him, determination stamping her features. Ben would be disgusted if he knew what she was thinking. She had to put it out of her mind. Her smile was crooked but hearty enough to bring out her dimple. "When are you going to get started on those waffles?"

"Right now." He lifted her off his lap. "But you have to separate the eggs. I've never mastered that."

She turned an empathetic smile to him, but his smile was not there to meet it. His gaze had dropped to the deeply rounded neckline of her gown. His green eyes darkened to jade as they explored the shadowy hollow between her breasts. Her nipples responded instantly, as though it were his hands rather than his eyes that caressed her.

"Ben, don't." She was well past the age of blushing, so why did her skin feel so hot? Why did her breasts feel full and heavy, her nipples exquisitely sensitive? "I'd better get dressed," she said weakly.

Ben drew in a big breath and let it out, but he didn't get up. Instead he met her eyes with a rueful smile. "Yeah, I guess you'd better."

Resisting the too obvious urge to hide herself, she swung her legs out from under the covers on the far side of the bed and crossed the room on cat's feet. The closet door clicked audibly as the automatic light came on. Her terry robe hung inside the door. When it was belted and tied, and she felt more confident, she turned back.

Ben still sat on the bed. His back was turned to her. As she watched in disbelief, he lifted her pillow to his face and inhaled long and deep, as though he were inhaling the essence of her. The sensual gesture caused her breath to come faster. Her knees turned to water. Weakly she leaned against the door until the click indicated that the light was off.

At the sound Ben dropped the pillow and with a casual movement rose to his feet. He rubbed a hand over the stubble on his jaw. "I'm going to shave and shower. Marston will probably be pounding on your door any minute," he said calmly.

Maggie was careful to keep her expression noncommittal. If she hadn't seen it with her own eyes, she would never have known from his demeanor that the incident with the pillow had taken place. His offhand smile held nothing more than friendliness as he sauntered toward the door.

She finally found her voice. "I'll be right down."

After he had closed the door behind him, Maggie sank into a corner of the chaise lounge. She sat there until her knees stopped trembling.

The sexual magnetism between them was too strong. She greatly feared that the love she'd thought to be as dead as her youth was still there, hesitant and hidden.

She straightened. She intended to keep it that way—
hidden. A fully developed relationship with Ben was an
impossibility. The wounds inflicted by their divorce had
gone too deep. The pain would always be present as a
barrier to total commitment.

Commitment? Maggie wondered at her own sanity.
Ben might desire her; his actions yesterday might have
indicated more than a need for mutual comfort, but he
had given no hint that he sought to renew their relationship on a permanent basis. And she certainly didn't.

Annette Cabot was in the huge embassy kitchen when
Maggie entered. The lovely Swiss woman came to her
immediately, wrapping her in a warm hug. "Maggie, my
dear. I am so sorry."

Annette had always been rather reserved, and the
gesture surprised Maggie. But she was nonetheless
grateful. "Thank you, Annette. We're very hopeful."

"Of course, your father is a careful man, and smart.
I am sure everything will be cleared up soon. Now, can
I fix your breakfast before I leave to do my shopping?
Would you like an omelet?"

"No, Annette. You go ahead."

Annette rolled her eyes. "I received your message
about providing food for the people downstairs."

The chef had been out shopping yesterday, too, when
Maggie had looked for her. She had left word with
James Greenwood, and now she was afraid she'd offended Annette's pride by sending a message rather than
waiting to speak to her in person. "I hope it isn't too
much trouble. I'll be glad to help," she offered.

Swinging a shopping basket over her arm, Annette
said, "Of course it is not! All they seem to want is sandwiches and coffee. Now I am out of bread."

Maggie hid a smile. A sandwich, to Annette, was a sacrilege, an insult to her *cordon bleu* training. "I'm sure it's because they are so busy. A sandwich is quick and easy to eat."

"Poof! It is just as easy to eat a proper meal," said a huffy Annette as she left by the back door.

Maggie managed to locate a coffeepot of manageable size and set it to brewing. She separated eggs and left the whites in one bowl, the yolks in another. Then she waited.

When Ben joined her a few minutes later, she was leaning against the counter, sipping the hot brew, staring at a blank wall.

She looked cool and comfortable—and about eighteen again—in a pink cotton camp shirt and madras skirt. Her hair was tied back loosely with a pink scarf. But the mauve shadows beneath her eyes belonged to a heartsick woman. He was sorely tempted to go to her, to take her into his arms. Instead he swatted her bottom. "Have you done the eggs for me?"

The small boutique on the Via Veneto hadn't been there the last time she was in Rome. She looked at Ben suspiciously when he parked the car in front. "Been buying a few women's clothes, have you?" she teased.

He was suddenly still. Before he could speak, she hurried into the silence with an apology.

"I'm sorry. That was rather crude of me. It's none of my business."

"I've never bought clothes for any other woman, Maggie. I don't let myself get that involved," he asserted soberly.

"Oh, Ben," she sighed. "Please don't add to my guilt, not right now."

"Your guilt? I don't know what you're talking about."

She didn't think she could handle a heavy discussion, so she tried to respond with an idle remark. "I suppose I turned you off women pretty thoroughly, huh?" She reached for the door handle, but a large hand clamped down over hers, stopping her action.

His fingers spread around her jaw. "Maggie," he said roughly, leaning against her, unrelentingly demanding her attention.

Resigned, she lifted her eyes. She didn't see the accusation she'd expected in his. Instead he seemed genuinely puzzled.

"Surely you haven't been blaming yourself for our divorce for eight years?"

"It was my fault." She couldn't bear the disbelief in his eyes. "Come on, Ben; let's get this over with." Again she reached for the handle.

"Wait a minute!" Ben sank back into his seat, running a hand through his hair. He muttered an explicit word and turned to face her again. "Maggie, I'm only going to say this once. It takes two. I was just as much at fault as you were. If I'd had more patience, if I'd tried harder to understand, if I hadn't been so all-fired impressed with my own importance..."

She couldn't stand it any longer. She put her fingers over his lips. "No, Ben, don't say any more. I was selfish and spoiled, like a jealous child who had to have her way. I made you marry me."

"You used to say I was as stubborn as a jackass. Do you really think you could have made me do something I didn't want to do?"

"I went behind your back...."

Ben caught her hand in his grasp, holding it firmly. His short, hard kiss stopped the words spilling from her lips. The possessive brush of his mouth surprised him as much as it did her. He only knew that it hurt him to hear Maggie berate herself like that.

"You would never have done that if I hadn't pushed you to the wall." They sat there for a long moment staring at each other. The tension between them expanded to fill the car. Finally he could bear it no longer. He dropped her hand. "Shall we agree to stop blaming ourselves?" he suggested.

Maggie picked up her purse and, for the third time, reached for the handle of the door. "Yes," she said quietly. But she knew she would never stop.

"As a matter of fact, this shop is where I brought Jamie to buy your Christmas present last year."

Maggie had no doubt that Ben was sincere. The thought was unsettling. She forced her voice to show a brightness she didn't feel. "The ivory mohair stole? I loved it; it's as soft as a feather." She didn't add that she had assumed her father had helped Jamie pick out the beautiful stole.

The shop was doing a lively business. Two beautifully dressed clerks alternated at the register, and another, this one obviously French, offered to show them to a private room in the back.

Ben was directed to a chair, offered champagne, which he declined, and cappuccino, which he accepted. An ashtray was place at his elbow. Maggie watched all this with undisguised amusement. They probably ascribed to the marketing concept that a man would spend more than a woman would.

He met her laughing eyes and winked. "We're looking for a formal gown, something suitable for a diplomatic reception," he said.

"Ah, yes, *monsieur*. Your wife has marvelous coloring. Perhaps something in burgundy?"

Maggie opened her mouth to deny the woman's assumption with some heat, but Ben stopped her with another wink. He looked woefully at the Frenchwoman. "Alas, madam, she is not my wife. And I don't think burgundy is her best color. Do you have anything in white?"

"White is out this year, *monsieur*," she answered, not even repentant for her mistake. "I shall see what else I have."

Maggie swallowed, shot him an evil look and turned away to follow the woman to a curtained alcove. The time had come to assert herself. "Madam," she said to the woman when they were alone. "I simply want a dress in a hurry. It doesn't matter what color, as long as it is appropriate." While she was speaking, her clothes were taken and hung on padded hangers, handled as carefully as the finest silk instead of the practical cotton that they were.

"Certainly," the woman answered. There was about as much acquiescence in her manner as a bulldozer run amok, thought Maggie.

It had been many years since Maggie had shopped in an elegant boutique like this. Most of her things were grabbed off the rack nowadays, her shopping wedged in between finding shoes or a jacket for Jamie. Standing there in her underwear, and feeling rather like a fool, she was subjected to the woman's thorough scrutiny.

"Size thirty-six," proclaimed the woman, referring to the continental sizing number, and disappeared on a cloud of Parisian perfume. She was back in only a few minutes with an armload of dresses.

Maggie looked at them in horror. "Madam, I do not intend to spend all day trying on clothes."

She gave a Gallic shrug. "Of course not. You will try them on only for as long as it takes to find something suitable for you. Why don't you just let yourself be guided by your—um—friend."

Maggie's protests were lost in folds of luscious peau de soie.

Ben vetoed the dress without hesitation. Maggie agreed with him; it looked like a debutante's presentation costume. The next gown was fabulous, though, the colors, gold and silver, were interwoven as delicately as a cobweb, and the fabric clung to her every curve. As she parted the curtain, the woman whipped the scarf off Maggie's hair. It settled loosely across her shoulders.

Dazzled by the sight before him, Ben rose to his feet without even being aware of the movement. His mouth was as dry as the desert floor; his pulse skipped once, twice, then proceeded in double time. She looked like a Roman goddess.

He found himself experiencing the same overwhelming attraction he'd felt the first time he'd seen her. Like the first time, too, his emotions went far deeper, were more complete, than simple desire. Over the past couple of days he'd begun to wonder if there could be a chance for them to begin again. He wasn't yet sure that he could put the word "love" to his feelings, but whatever they were, his emotions were strong. "I can hardly tell where your hair leaves off and the dress begins," he murmured huskily. "It's perfect for you, Maggie."

Maggie smiled. "I like it, too." She appealed to the woman. "I hope you aren't going to tell me this is more than I can afford."

Ben frowned before the woman could answer. Maggie caught his expression out of the corner of her eye, and she lifted a brow. "Don't say it," she warned him. "Don't even think it."

"But, Maggie..."

She faced the woman again. "How much is this dress, madame?"

Maggie schooled her features to hide her disappointment when she heard the amount. "That's more than I can afford, I'm afraid. Let me try on the rose matte jersey."

The rose dress was just as pretty, she told herself. Besides, what difference did it make what she wore, as long as she was presentable? Other, more vital issues should take precedence in her thoughts. And she had already glanced at the price of the rose dress. It was stiff, but affordable. "I'll take this one."

"Don't you want to model it for *monsieur*?" asked the woman.

"I suppose so," she muttered. When she emerged, her chin was tilted, daring Ben to argue with her.

He came close to look down into her face. "You look beautiful in this dress, too, Maggie," he said softly, taking the wind out of her sails.

"Thank you." The words were more than the conventional response to a compliment. She was also thanking him for not being a threat to her hard-won independence.

"You're welcome."

The woman intervened. "While you're changing, I'll bring shoes to match the dress."

"I don't need shoes." She had a pair of high-heeled sandals in a neutral color that would do. She had no intention of spending any more money. While she was dressing in her cotton skirt and blouse, she tried to figure out which part of the budget she could trim to pay for the dress.

Maggie had been brought up with only a vague idea of the value of money. Her father was wealthy; Ben had made a good salary when they were married. But when she'd started living on her own, it was another matter entirely. She had realized that if she were to make a satisfying life for herself she would have to start thinking with a practical mind.

For the four years she'd been in school, she'd paid for her education and their expenses with an endowment from her grandmother, budgeting carefully so the money wouldn't run out before she finished. As soon as she'd found a job with the State Department, she and Jamie had begun to live on her salary alone. They managed quite well, considering that low-level civil employees didn't earn much.

One of her most cherished possessions was a framed copy of her first paycheck, the first money she'd ever earned for herself. It was a matter of pride with her that she'd managed on her own.

"Are you going to be in there much longer?" asked Ben from the other side of the curtain.

Maggie took her credit card out and opened the curtain to hand it to him. "Ask her to put it on this, please, Ben."

Ben hesitated for a minute, looking at the card in his hand, but resisted the impulse to pay for the dress without her consent. From things his young son had let slip, he had come to the conclusion that money was often tight. He also realized that this new, full-grown Maggie cherished her independence and would resent the offer. But he had a few questions.

He took the card to the front of the store and handed it to the Frenchwoman. At the same time he gave her one of his own cards. "Charge the lamé dress to me and have it sent to this address."

He would have liked to wipe the smirk off the woman's face.

Maggie whipped a brush out of her purse and pulled it through her hair. She retied the scarf and once again was plain old Maggie. Which wasn't so bad.

When they were back in the car, Ben turned to her, looking strangely unsure. "I'd like to ask you something. Please don't take offense."

She was instantly alert and wary. "What?"

"Why didn't you ever use the money I sent?"

A question about money was the last thing she had expected. She searched his features for a clue as to why he'd asked and was genuinely shocked by the hurt she found deep in his eyes. "If I'd really needed the money, I would have used it, Ben," she assured him gently.

The hurt was still there. She went on carefully, wanting to explain. It was very important to her that he understand this side of her. It was a side she was proud of, but it was also a side he didn't know. "It was vital to me at that time of my life to accomplish something totally on my own. I had a trust from Grandmother..."

"A very small one," he interrupted, toying with the keys in his hand.

"How do you know that?"

"From Ian. He was worried because you wouldn't accept money from him, either."

Maggie sighed and sat back in her seat. "Ben, please don't be unhappy about the money. Actually, though I didn't spend it, it was a great help just knowing it was there. I appreciated the security it gave me. But don't you see?" She turned her face to him. "I had to do it on my own," she finished softly. "I hope you can understand that."

"I do understand." The hurt was gone, she noted with relief. "I'm proud of you, Maggie. Very proud."

"Thanks. I'm proud, too. And Jamie has a sizable college account."

The mention of their son wiped the smile off his face. He jammed the key into the ignition. "I guess I'd better take a run home and pick up my tux. Do you want to come along?"

Maggie decided it wouldn't be wise to return to the scene of their lovemaking, not with her feelings so unstable. "No, I think I'll go through Daddy's papers once more. Maybe we missed something."

"I won't be gone long," he told her when he dropped her off at the mansion.

Maggie watched the car disappear through the gates. With the dress box under her arm, she turned to climb the steps.

James met her at the door and took the box from her. "Lola Orenda asked to see you, Mrs. Altman. I'll just put this in your room."

"Thank you, James. Is she in her office?"

"I think so, ma'am."

"*Signora*, please come in," Lola greeted her, indicating a chair. Maggie sat.

Lola hesitated. "I thought you might like to go over the arrangements for the reception tonight. Here is the menu." She slid a piece of paper across the desk. "And the guest list." Several papers, stapled together, were placed upon the first one. "The florist will be here in a few minutes."

Maggie interrupted, shaking her head, studying Lola. "I'll look into the ballroom on my way upstairs." She had an idea that the arrangements were an excuse. James had already assured her that the preparations were complete. Though her manner was brisk and business-like, the young woman's hand trembled. Obviously she had something else on her mind. "I'm sure everything is beautifully organized, Lola."

Lola glanced up nervously. "If you're sure."

"Was there more you wanted to say?" Maggie urged gently.

The young woman stared at her for a moment before bursting into tears. "I know I am a suspect because of my position, but, Mrs. Altman, I am innocent. That Mr. Marston—he is like a hunter in pursuit of his quarry. He will never let up." Her words were punctuated by sobs. She pulled a handkerchief from her pocket. "He fright-ens me, Mrs. Altman. He frightens me to death. I love little Jamie. And your father is such a wonderful man. I would never..."

Damn! thought Maggie as she rose to go to the girl. She put her arm about the slender shoulders. "Of course you wouldn't. Now, Lola, don't cry. I'm sure Mr. Mar-ston didn't mean to imply that you..."

"Yes, yes, he did. That man, he is a monster!"

At the moment Maggie was inclined to agree. Couldn't Marston see that this frightened girl was al-most a basket case? How could he suspect her of being a professional terrorist? Maggie sighed. She wasn't up to smoothing over Marston's rough treatment of peo-ple, and she would tell him so.

"Lola, why don't you go home for the day? You're distraught. A nice rest is what you need."

Lola sniffled into her handkerchief. "The florist..."

"If it's necessary, I'll see the florist."

Lola raised her beautiful tear-drenched eyes to Maggie's. "He told me not to leave."

Maggie had always hated women who could cry prettily; she looked like a hag when she cried. "I'll take care of Marston, too," she declared. As if she didn't have enough to cope with. She picked up a purse from the desk and thrust it at the weeping girl. "You're going home now. I'll see you tomorrow." She accompanied Lola to the front door and spoke to the guard on duty. "Miss Orenda is going home for the day. If Mr. Marston has any questions, refer him to me," she snapped impatiently daring the man to argue.

"Yes, ma'am," said the guard.

Ben fidgeted restlessly as he waited to escort Maggie downstairs. Marston and Gandress had made it clear that they thought it was important for Maggie to be present at this shindig, but they shouldn't have asked it of her. He wasn't sure she would be able to stand up under the pressure of the deception. They had decided to use the excuse that the ambassador had been called home for an unexpected foreign policy conference. Anyone with the least knowledge of diplomacy would see through the thin excuse.

They could only hope the members of the trade study group would be deficient in such knowledge. He didn't want Maggie faced with a lot of disquieting questions.

Her door opened; he turned, her name dying on his lips as he drank in the sight of the beautiful woman who had been his wife. She was magnificent. Tonight she had decided against the sophisticated chignon. Her hair was lifted with a comb on one side. The dress had been flattering in the shop this morning, its color lending roses to her cheeks; but tonight, with the addition of high heels to give grace to her movements and the soft fall of hair over one shoulder, it was even more becoming. The soft silk jersey dipped low from her shoulders, touched her breasts, fell free to brush her hips. The fabric moved when she moved, clinging so lightly that it appeared to float around her, and yet it magically defined unseen curves. The double strand of matinee-length pearls she wore had been his wedding gift to her. He swallowed when he saw them.

She smiled hesitantly. "Okay?" she asked.

The simple request for reassurance brought him out of his daze. He touched his black tie and then moved toward her. "More than okay, as I'm sure you know. I'm glad you still wear the pearls."

"I've always loved them." Ben had given the necklace to her the night before they were married. They had walked the banks of the Potomac in the moonlight; the cherry trees had been in heavy bloom, scattering their blossoms generously for the lovers to walk upon. She had been intoxicated by the scents of the night and the nearness of the only man she would ever love. She could still recall how cool the glowing pearls had felt against her overheated skin when Ben fastened them around her neck.

Ben remembered, too. He remembered making love to Maggie on their wedding night. She'd worn nothing but the necklace, which she'd refused to take off, until finally he'd convinced her that it was in his way.

So much love there, so much promise.

A high-pitched laugh from below brought them both back to the present.

Ben offered his arm. "Shall we go down?"

Maggie placed her fingers in the crook of his elbow. "If only we had a choice," she said, but she lifted her chin boldly.

As they reached the top of the stairs, she paused for a minute. "Why did you marry me, Ben?"

The question shook him deeply. He steeled himself against another thrust of regret. "Because I loved you," he answered after a minute.

"That simple?"

"Yes." He glanced at her out of the corner of his eye. "Why did you marry me?"

"Oh, I worshiped you, adored you and idolized you." She dropped her chin to her chest. "I'm not sure I even knew what a wonderful thing plain, simple love could be." She laughed, but the sound carried no humor. "I thought my prince had arrived to sweep me onto a big white horse and carry me away to live happily ever after."

"Never mind that the prince was very much the worse for wear."

"Never mind that Cinderella wasn't such a prize herself," she said, her voice heavy with self-blame. "I never should have—"

He cut her off. "Then we never would have had Jamie. And he is worth everything. So you see, something good did come from the fiasco."

He spoke in a joking tone, but the phrase caused a sharp pain in her chest. Their marriage had been like a flaming meteor, burning bright and passionate in the heavens for a brief time, only to fall to earth, cold and dark. She blinked to relieve her stinging eyes.

Ben noticed. He covered her hand with his. "Maggie, our marriage was destroyed by things you knew nothing about."

She stopped on the step above him, holding her breath. Her hand left his arm. "Like what?"

Intuitively Ben knew what she was thinking. "I was never unfaithful to you, Maggie."

She searched his expression. "I think I always knew that. But I didn't have the self-confidence to believe in you then. The women you worked with were so sophisticated. I envied them, and I guess I didn't see how you could possibly prefer me."

His chuckle was muted and slightly hoarse. "And I couldn't see how you could prefer me. Compared to what you were used to, I was a roughneck. I thought you were having second thoughts." He picked up her hand. Returning it to the crook of his elbow, he led her downstairs. "Enough of this conversation. Maybe when this is all over, we can sit down and have the talk we should have had eight years ago. But for now, duty calls."

"And we always answer," she said shakily. Ben Altman, uncertain? She didn't believe it. They paused in the door of the ballroom. Maggie put on her most charming smile and entered with Ben right behind her.

The prisms on the twin chandeliers glittered like dripping tears. Panels of blue brocade were framed by white wooden molding; gilt chairs with blue velvet seats were arranged formally but conveniently along two walls. The French doors leading onto the terrace were open to the sweet scents of the night.

There were at least two hundred people there. She probably didn't know more than one or two, but it didn't bother her to walk into a roomful of strangers despite the fact that she hadn't been in a situation like this for years.

The only thing that scared her was the possibility of a question or remark that would demolish her control.

"I'll stay close," said Ben. "Signal if you need me."

She glanced over her shoulder, and her smile wobbled a bit. "Thanks."

The fragility of her smile left Ben breathless. His hand tightened at her waist for a fleeting second, then he released her.

She did well for the first half hour. A small orchestra played at one end of the room, and some of the guests were dancing. Others gathered around the buffet table, while still others talked serious business in groups of two or three. Maggie knew better than to interrupt a discussion like that. She moved through the crowd, stopping occasionally to chat for a minute, or to explain her father's absence.

A tall, distinguished man asked her to dance. She accepted. But when he asked again, Ben got the signal. He cut in.

They danced for a moment like two marionettes before she gave up fighting his nearness and relaxed in his arms. "May I ask you another question, Ben?" she said after a moment.

Ben drew back to look at her, a smile curving his mouth. "Ask away."

"What did you mean when you said that our divorce was caused by things I knew nothing about?"

Ben's eyes took on a faraway look. Unconsciously he tightened his hold, bringing her closer to his body. "I meant war and killings, and famine and greed, and man's inhumanity to his fellow creatures. I've known them too intimately and for too many years. I wish you'd never had to. Those were—are—the things that make up my everyday world; my job is based on exploring them, trying to understand and put them into some kind of perspective for the public.'' The faraway look faded, and his eyes returned to hers.

''Eight years ago, your world was private schools and the hushed dignity of diplomatic life. Your life was as far removed from mine as heaven is from hell. And that was one strike against our marriage before we'd even begun.''

''Strike two was my immaturity, and strike three, the fact that I was too accustomed to having things my way.''

He brought their entwined hands to his chest. ''Hey, no more of that.''

She nodded decisively. ''No more. As you said, we have Jamie, and he's worth everything. At least . . .''

''Hush.'' Ben breathed the word against her temple. For a minute he held her close, moving to the rhythm of a soft ballad. ''Can you break away soon? It's ludicrous for you to be subjected to this.''

''I should stay for a while longer. But you can go if you'd like.''

''I'm not leaving you,'' he said firmly.

The last strains of the song were still fading when Ben suddenly raised his head to scan the ballroom. The muscles in his shoulder stiffened under Maggie's hand. She looked up at him, but he seemed to have forgotten she was there. She casually turned her head to glance over her shoulder at the formally clad men and elegantly gowned women, laughing, talking, dancing. Waiters moved among them with trays of champagne. The small orchestra began another song. Everything looked normal.

She couldn't spot anything that would have attracted Ben's sudden intense regard.

''What is it?'' she asked.

Ben shook his shoulders, freeing them of the tautness that had gripped him so unexpectedly. He answered Maggie's worried frown with an easy grin. "Nothing."

Chapter 6

Ben's instinct had picked up a slight disturbance in the festive atmosphere of the ballroom. Casually he scanned the room for the source. There. In the corner near the entrance. He smiled down at Maggie. "Nothing's wrong," he said. "I just realized that I'm hungry. I think I'll fix a plate. Can I bring you anything?"

Maggie eyed him speculatively. Finally she shook her head. "Liar." Her half smile was indulgent. The music ended, and she stepped out of his arms. "Come back and tell me what you find out, will you?"

He chuckled appreciatively. "You're too sharp. It's probably nothing. Be right back." Murmuring politely when it was necessary, he progressed easily through the crowd. Like the ripples from a disturbance in a pond, the commotion seemed to be spreading. Long before he reached his objective, he was aware of alarmed whispers. Catching the attention of one of the passing waiters, he lifted a glass of champagne from the man's tray and asked, "What's going on?"

"I am not sure, *signore*. One of the chauffeurs brought a newspaper...." The man moved on.

The blood turned to ice water in Ben's veins. No longer bothering with courtesy, he shouldered his way into the crowd. Someone thrust a paper at him. He read the headline with disbelief, stunned into immobility for a minute. When his heart resumed its beat, the sound was loud in his ears, shutting out the noise of the ballroom. He dropped the paper and turned, heading directly for Maggie.

Maggie's eyes met Ben's through a break in the crowd. From his somber expression she knew instantly that his instincts had been correct. Something was very wrong. He jerked his head toward the terrace. She nodded. Excusing herself from a group of Texans discussing current oil prices, she began to make her way to the French doors.

"What's happened?" she asked when he took her hands to draw her into a shadowy area on the terrace.

There was very little light, but as his eyes adjusted, Ben looked down at the elegant hands he held, hands bare of rings. Then he met Maggie's questioning gaze. "Someone has leaked the story. It's the headline in tomorrow morning's *Trib*."

It took Maggie a few seconds to comprehend what he was saying. The *Trib* referred to the *International Herald Tribune*. Printed in London, it was the most current English-language newspaper available in Europe. "Who?" she asked, horrified. Her hands tightened on his. "Who would do such a thing?"

One corner of Ben's mouth lifted. "Thanks for not immediately assuming it was me. Our friend from Washington certainly will."

Suddenly Maggie was assailed by doubt. Who else knew about the kidnapping? As she looked at Ben, she couldn't keep her expression free of the uncertainty she felt.

"I did not leak the story," Ben said firmly, emphasizing each word precisely. "There are other reporters in Rome with contacts in the embassy."

Maggie didn't respond. She looked away from his taut features. Her unspoken accusation had obviously been a blow, and she regretted that, but how could she be sure he hadn't told anyone? Trying to buy time, she disentangled her hands from his and turned half away.

"Do you really think I would do such a thing?" he demanded.

"Oh, Ben." Absently she fingered the pearls at her breast. "I don't know what I believe."

He put a leash on his temper. Nothing would be served by blowing up. "Look, Maggie, this situation will get a lot worse before it gets better. We're going to need each other for strength and support. You told Marston that lack of trust was never a problem with us. Did you mean that or not?"

When she'd said it, she'd meant it, thought Maggie. Now she wasn't sure. But she was sure of one thing; they did need to present a united front to Marston.

An increase in the noise level from inside drew their attention to the door. Their eyes met. Without further words they left the shadowy corner and hurried back inside.

Marston stood at the entrance to the ballroom, searching the crowd, his countenance as grim as a death's head. His gaze came to rest on the deputy ambassador, who immediately detached himself from the group he was talking to.

"Don't you think we need to see what's going on?" Ben asked mildly.

"Absolutely," said Maggie after only a moment's hesitation.

Nodding and smiling woodenly, Maggie skirted a group that had gathered to watch the dancers. Evidently the news hadn't reached this corner of the room. Ben was right behind her.

A very large man blocked their way. Maggie looked up to find him scowling down at her. California, her mind supplied automatically, California wine. She could remember that he wore burgundy cowboy boots with his tuxedo, but she couldn't for the life of her remember the man's name. *Anderson? Adams?*

"Little lady, what is this I hear about your father?"

Maggie stiffened at the appellation. She *hated* to be called little lady. "I'm not sure, Mr. Allen. I was on my way to find out. If you'll excuse me . . ."

He didn't move. "I don't like this at all, little lady. You told me he'd gone to Washington."

Maggie felt a movement at her side and put out a hand to restrain Ben. Her fingers fell on the bunched muscles in his arm. "Mr. Allen, I don't much like this myself. And I don't want to make a scene. Would you please get out of my way?" She was smiling, but no one who was listening to the icicles dripping from her words could doubt that the ambassador's daughter was very, very angry.

"Move your boots, cowboy," said Ben, the warning in his voice seconded by his glare.

The cowboy moved.

When they had gained the relative quiet of the hall, Maggie slipped her hand into Ben's, earning herself an enigmatic glance.

They found the two men in the study. Gandress blanched when they entered the room. Marston muttered a curse and rounded the desk, heading directly for Ben. "So, you couldn't keep your mouth shut, could you?" The telephone rang, stopping his progress. He glared at Ben as he put his hand on the instrument.

Ben glared back.

"Don't leave," Marston ordered, before he picked up the phone and barked his name.

Grateful for the distraction—it had looked for a minute as though the two men might go for each other's throat—Maggie asked, "What is that noise?" A low rumble, like thunder, was coming from outside.

Ben had already heard and identified the sound. "The paparazzi," he answered distractedly.

Marston's side of the conversation consisted of a series of one-word comments. He hung up and turned to them. "I suppose you know what's happened."

"Yes, I've seen the *Trib*," answered Ben, gritting his back teeth. "I had nothing to do with the leak."

"We only have one reporter involved in this situation, Altman," growled Marston. "If you didn't leak the story, who did?"

"I would imagine that any number of embassy employees could have done it. I don't know which one it was. All I know is that it wasn't me."

"I'm glad to hear you're so smart. You know, too, that I can have you thrown out of here, regardless of your ex-wife's wishes."

Ben bit off a smart comeback. He hated to have to defend himself or his job to anyone, much less Marston. Another time he would have told the jackass to stuff it, but he wanted... He called his angry thoughts to a halt. Wanted what? To be near Maggie? That was a hazard, too. "Are you telling me to leave?" he finally asked.

"I'm seriously considering it."

"Fine," snapped Ben. "I'll be out in five minutes."

"Will you two stop threatening each other?" Maggie broke in.

Marston spun toward her. "Do you hear that mob out there?" he challenged.

"It would be hard not to," she answered coolly.

Marston was furious. "They're all demanding an interview with the American ambassador. The telephone here has been ringing off the hook. I can't even get through to the chancery. Every network and news magazine in the entire world wants to know if the rumors are true. And do you know who started those rumors?"

"No, and neither do you," she said flatly. Crossing the room, she flipped on the television in the corner. "Conjecture won't help us at this point. Let's see what they're actually saying."

The news was not good. Speculation was rampant—everything from the ambassador having defected to the Soviet Union to his escaping an assassination plot by boarding a yacht on the Mediterranean. At the last theory, Maggie swiveled to meet Marston's gaze.

"We're checking that one out. Someone claims to have seen him in Cagliari, Sardinia."

"He was there for the festival of something-or-other in May," said Maggie.

"The Festival of Sant'Efisio," supplied Ben. "He went over to..."

The telephone rang again, interrupting the rest of his explanation. Maggie was closest. "Hello." She froze, the blood draining from her head, leaving her dizzy. Her eyes then took on the hard glitter of suspicion as they sought those of her ex-husband. "Yes, Mac, of course I remember you. Yes, he's right here." She extended the receiver to Ben.

Ben's heart descended to his toes. "Maggie..."

Her features had turned to stone. "The phone's for you, Ben," she said unnecessarily. "Your boss."

He accepted it but put his hand over the mouthpiece. "Maggie..." he tried again.

Ignoring him, she turned to Marston and Gandress. "Shall we leave Mr. Altman to have his conversation in private? We can use Lola's office."

"Maggie, damn it! Come back here."

She spun on him. "Just tell me one thing," she hissed angrily. "How did he get this number?"

"How the hell do I know? Maybe your father gave it to him."

"My father gave his private number to a network news V.P.?" she sneered. "Tell me another one, Ben." She whirled to march out of the room, followed by a triumphant Marston and a nervous Gandress.

Ben looked at the phone in his hand. He heaved a resigned sigh and put it to his ear. "Yeah, Mac."

Ben was relieved to find Maggie alone in Lola's deserted office. The next few minutes weren't going to be pleasant, and he'd just as soon not have an audience. She was sipping a cup of coffee. He wished he had one. Maybe the stimulant would help overcome his sense of wilting defeat. "Where's Marston?" he asked her quietly.

"In the basement."

He nodded. After unbuttoning his jacket, he slid his hands into his trouser pockets and hitched his hip onto a corner of Lola's desk.

"What did Mac want?" asked Maggie. Her anger had faded to sad resignation. She was proud of how calm she felt and sounded.

Ben crossed one ankle over the other and studied the toe of his black shoe. "He wants an interview," he said finally.

"Why did I ask?" Maggie said more to herself than to Ben. "What did you tell him?"

"I told him I'd discuss it with you," he said quietly.

Maggie put down her cup carefully.

Ben frowned, his dark brows meeting over his eyes. How could he put this so that she wouldn't despise him? He met her eyes, willing her to understand. "Before you say anything, please, just listen to me."

Maggie fixed him with a hard stare. Then she nodded. "I'm listening."

"I've told you, your father and I have become friends—more than that—good friends."

She nodded again. It was one of the reasons she rarely came to Rome, preferring instead to visit her father when he returned periodically to the States.

Ben levered himself from the edge of the desk. He took a few steps, then turned back and leaned forward, gripping the back of a chair. He dropped his chin to stare down at his hands. "Jamie was the reason, at first. Neither of us wanted his visits to be marred by tension between us. But I've always admired and respected Ian." His wry smile was directed inward. "Even at first, when he was furious with me for marrying his baby." He straightened and shoved his hands into his pockets. "Now I like to think the respect is mutual."

Maggie looked absently at the paper clip she'd picked up. "Your friendship means a lot to him. He always said you were a fair reporter." She raised her head to meet his eyes and went on in a lighter tone. "For Daddy that's the ultimate compliment. So tell me, how did Mac get the phone number?"

His eyes held hers. "Truthfully... I have no idea. Before you even arrived from Washington, Maggie, I had turned over responsibility for running the bureau to my assistant. I told both him and Mac that I wouldn't be available until this was all over. I swear I did not give this telephone number to anyone." He waited. "Do you believe me?"

She rose to refill her coffee cup from the pot on a side table. "I don't know," she answered at last.

Ben muttered something she couldn't understand. He raked his hand through his dark hair. "I realize how you once felt about my job, Maggie."

"It wasn't your job per se, Ben," she said wearily, tossing the paper clip aside. "It was what your job did to our relationship."

"Can we continue to condemn my job for everything?"

"Of course not." Crossing her arms under her breasts, Maggie paced to the window and back. "We've agreed not to rehash all our blunders."

"But not to forget them. Those who forget past mistakes are doomed to repeat them," he quoted quietly.

The remark brought her head up. Ben obviously wanted to make it clear that he had no intention of repeating his mistakes by becoming involved with his exwife. That suited her just fine.

"News of the kidnapping is public now, Maggie. Someone is going to do a follow-up. Isn't it better to give an official interview, have control of the information, than to let the speculation continue? I don't want the world to imagine even for a moment that your father might be a defector. Do you?"

"Of course not!"

"I won't do the story myself."

That surprised her. "You won't?"

Straightening, he released his grip on the chair. "Of course not. Jamie is my son, too. I'll be a subject of the interview right along with you."

Maggie's thoughts were in a turmoil. She wasn't sure. "We'd have to be very careful not to say anything that would anger the people who have them."

"Of course."

"I won't answer hypothetical questions, and I won't be badgered."

Ben smiled sadly. "I'll make him swear not to ask any. And I promise he won't badger you."

"Who?"

"My assistant, Mitch Harris, will do the interview."

She searched his expression. His gaze, as it met hers, didn't waver. Finally she shrugged. "All right."

"In the meantime, what about the reception?"

Maggie let out the breath she'd been holding. "Yes. I imagine the guests are already beginning to leave. I should be there, I suppose."

Ben moved to her side. "I'll go with you." He wanted to put his arm around her shoulders, but he didn't think she would appreciate it right now. Instead he offered his arm. After only a brief pause, she took it.

"That's a wrap."

Maggie was overwhelmingly relieved when Mitch

Harris gave the word. The interview had been necessarily brief, because of the lateness of the hour and the lack of information available, but heartbreakingly emotional. She hadn't anticipated the difficulty she would have discussing the two people she loved most in the world in a dispassionate way.

In response to questions about Dante, Maggie reiterated what she had told Marston. Dante was a loyal and devoted bodyguard. She felt her father and Jamie were safer since he was with them.

Mitch had been courteous, though Maggie was well aware of the seething impatience beneath the surface of his polite demeanor. But Ben kept his promise. Each time the man's impatience threatened to break free, a stern glance or a word from Ben brought it under control.

The hot lights were switched off, the tiny microphones removed from the neckline of her blouse. Men were busy rewinding cables and dismantling lights. Ben got to his feet to draw his associate aside for a quiet word. Maggie took the opportunity to escape.

She found James and asked him to bring a cup of tea to her room. She simply could not face Ben again, not tonight.

During the next day Maggie's courage was constantly tested. Judith had called immediately after the early-morning airing of the interview. Maggie had resisted the temptation to ask her to return to Rome. Instead she convinced the distraught woman to stay at home.

Rationally she could understand Marston's admonition that this waiting, this not knowing, was another form of terrorism. But emotionally she wasn't sure how much more she could take. She fought a constant battle with an overactive imagination determined to explore the grimmest possibilities.

Not having anything to do compounded her fears. If she'd been at home, she would have been cooking, cleaning, polishing—her panacea for attacks of worry, loneliness and desperation. She no longer had those attacks often, but when she did, they ended with a spotless apartment, a freezer filled to capacity.

Everything in the embassy residence ran quietly and perfectly.

She couldn't settle down long enough to read. Television was a constant reminder of her fears. Her father's papers had revealed nothing that she hadn't known or suspected. Ian was a generous man. He had his personal causes listed in a private diary. His correspondence was voluminous but predictable. He had helped Lola's brother find a job. A trust had been set up for Jamie. A college account for Dante's son wasn't drawing enough interest to suit him, so he'd transferred the funds to another bank. One of her cousins was applying to Annapolis; Ian had written a recommendation to the senator from Virginia.

Maggie's restlessness wasn't eased by Ben's attitude. The suspicion she'd shown about Mac's call had definitely come between them. They had avoided each other as much as possible since the interview, but there were times he watched her with a wariness that indicated he expected her to fall apart any minute.

She knew his own tension was mounting, as well. He'd spent the better part of the day on the telephone, ferreting out information, none of which had been useful, but he kept at it relentlessly, hoping that somehow he would come up with a glimmer of the truth, a tiny fragment that would be the beginning of a solution.

She had also searched for fragments, but the friends and co-workers she'd called at State either didn't know anything or wouldn't tell her. There was a bittersweet sadness in their attempts to voice their sympathy.

She understood the platitudes because she'd been on the other end. During times of emergency, which was most of the time, frantic relatives would call the Department of State daily with enquiries and bits of gossip. "Was it true that my husband was seen in Tel Aviv?" "Did my son really make a phone call to the Red Cross in Cairo?"

Oh, yes, she knew how difficult it was to calm and console someone when a loved one was missing. She knew the feeling well. After a long afternoon on the phone, she slammed the receiver down and filled the air with colorful curses.

Ben entered the room from the terrace in time to hear every distinct word. "Something wrong?" he asked with a one-sided smile.

She scraped her hair back, clenching her fists in its thickness until it hurt. "I'm frustrated as hell."

He reached for her hand. "Come on, let's take a ride," he said, pulling her to her feet. "I'll take the top off, and we'll blow the cobwebs out."

She opened her mouth to tell him she didn't need or want his pity. Then she closed it again. Thoughtfully she nodded. "I'm a mess." Her wrinkled shirt and slacks, the color of ripe peaches, had been crisp and fresh a few hours ago. Her hair was in one long braid down her back.

"You're fine," Ben said before she could find another excuse. He needed to get out for a while, too.

* * *

The view from Monte Mario, the highest of the legendary seven hills in Rome, was one of the most beautiful in the world. They were the only people around at the moment. Maggie waited in the graveled courtyard while Ben went inside the small café to order cappuccino for them both. When he returned, they wandered to the brow of the mountain, sipping the hot brew, which had a miraculous way of cooling one on the hottest day.

Where, Maggie wondered as she looked out over the view, where in all the buildings below her, where in the broad boulevards or twisting alleyways, in the parks or walled gardens, cellars or attics, where was their son? Or was he even in Rome?

They finished their coffee, and Ben took the cups back inside.

All of the city lay before her. Off to the right in the distance, the white marble columns of the Monument to the Kings glistened, bathed in the glory of waning afternoon sunlight. To her left and below, the Tiber cut through the city like a shining silver serpent. She felt grateful to the farseeing city fathers who had decreed that skyscrapers would never be a part of the skyline. The outline of the seven hills would never be blurred or obliterated by the hand of man.

Hearing the crunch of gravel that indicated Ben's return, she turned to look at him.

Ben was relieved to see that her features were calm, her lips curved in a serene smile.

"I'm glad you brought me here. It's so peaceful," she said softly. "The Eternal City has endured it all. Glory, cruelty, uncertainty. And yet it has survived."

The sunlight shone through her hair, framing her face with a golden aura. Magnetized by her, Ben took a step, and another. They were only inches apart. He put his hands on each side of her face. Slowly he lowered his head until he felt her breath on his lips. Softly, gently, he kissed her.

And suddenly he knew that he had never stopped, would never stop, loving this woman. The emotion that surged through him was powerful and compelling. He dropped his hands, but only to gather her into a loving embrace. "And we'll survive, too, all of us," he said huskily.

He wanted to tell her of his love, his regret for the missing years. He wanted to ask her to marry him again, to make a home with him for their son. He wanted to wake up with her every morning for the rest of his life, and he wanted to lie down beside her every night.

But she liked her life the way it was. She would have to make tremendous adjustments, and so would he. Would she be willing? It would be cruel to burden her with a decision like that now. She had enough to deal with. They both did.

Sighing, Maggie turned in the circle of Ben's arms. She rested her back against his broad chest. His arms tightened until they were a warm secure band across her midriff. "You know, Ben, for a long time after I left here, I thought it was a sign of weakness to lean on anyone. I'd leaned on you hard enough for two lifetimes, and I didn't intend ever to depend on another soul." She didn't add that she'd felt that way until the day she arrived in Rome, the day they'd made love, the day he'd said he needed her.

He tensed. "Is that why you've never remarried?"

"No. Well, yes. Maybe."

He laughed at her convoluted answer. The sound rumbling from his chest was tight and strained. Puzzled, she looked over her shoulder.

He grinned down at her, his green eyes sparkling with flecks of gold, but the tension in him wound a little tighter. "Is that what's known as the language of diplomacy?"

She smiled. "No, it's the language of confusion." Her gaze drifted back to the view. "David is a fine man. Jamie likes him. I don't know why I didn't agree to marry him."

After what he'd just discovered about himself, it hurt like hell to hear her talk about her feelings for another man. Striving for a release of the pressure building within him, he returned the conversation to the original topic. "We all have to lean occasionally, Maggie," he said against her temple. "It doesn't necessarily indicate weakness. It's important to interact with other human beings. To give and take."

"I think I understand that now." Restlessly she moved out of his arms. Reluctantly he let her go. She leaned one shoulder against the trunk of a juniper tree. "Sometimes I'm so lonely I can hardly bear it. And there's Jamie. There are a lot of reasons to remarry, but the fact is, I don't really want to."

Ben's tightly wound nerves could take no more. Grabbing Maggie's other shoulder, he flattened her against the tree. With his hands planted on each side of her face, he dipped his head and silenced her startled gasp with a kiss, a deep, thrusting kiss, a greedy, hungry kiss. One hand dropped to her waist, his thumb moving feverishly below the curve of her breast. His tongue plunged into her mouth, relishing every delicious drop of sweetness there. His knee parted her legs, his hips pinned her to the rough bark.

Maggie's heartbeat skipped once, then picked up speed; she felt her nerve endings come alive, under the movement of his thumb. She realized she was clinging to his shirt as though he were the only steady thing in a world spinning on its axis.

Breathing audibly, he lifted his head to glare at her. "Don't ever let me hear you talk like that again. You join a club for loneliness. You don't marry as a panacea. You marry because you love someone, desperately, deeply." His voice rose. "You marry someone because you can't exist in a world they aren't part of, damn it!"

Her head against the tree, Maggie stared at him, stunned by his ferocity. She forced her fingers to release their hold on the cotton shirt. Her eyes dropped to the wrinkled fabric. Absently she began to smooth it with her palms.

Ben groaned. Her hands moved on him as naturally as though they'd done the same thing every day for the past eight years. It felt so good, so right. "Oh, babe, don't . . . !"

Maggie's fingers stilled at the frustration in his voice. His black lashes hid his eyes almost completely. But a flush of desire had settled on his cheekbones, and his hand slid between the tree and her hips, holding her close to him. His body was hard and demanding against her.

An unmuffled motor split the heavy silence. The sound of car doors closing and laughter brought them slowly, relentlessly back to earth. "I'm sorry, Maggie," said Ben after a long sigh. "I shouldn't have done that."

She searched his eyes for the signs of regret she heard in his voice—and found them easily. "I guess we'd better go back."

* * *

The day after their trip to Monte Mario, Maggie decided she had to get out of the residence, at least for an hour, and alone. The mob of reporters had disappeared as soon as the interview aired—she'd heard from one of the guards that they were now haunting the chancery—so she shouldn't have any problem getting out unobserved. She told Marston where she was going, but no one else.

As she wandered aimlessly along the Via Rossini, she deliberately steered her thoughts away from Jamie and her father, and toward alternative courses of action. What more could they do?

In Washington David was pushing as hard as he dared for the State Department to do something, but without official public acknowledgment that the ambassador had, in fact, been kidnapped, there was little a lone congressman could do. And despite the furor of rumors, despite the interview and the multitude of police and intelligence agents who'd set up shop in the basement, official acknowledgment was being withheld pending proof of foul play. Even Marston was disgusted.

Maggie sighed as she turned a corner and paused, staring sightlessly at the array of merchandise in the display window of a small boutique. From that first day when he'd called, David had known—from the things she didn't say—that she wasn't going to marry him. But it hadn't slowed down his efforts on behalf of her father and son. She would always be grateful to him, she thought as she moved away from the window and into the mainstream of pedestrians. She was jostled, but felt no alarm.

On several occasions David had offered to come; but she'd been adamant. He'd accepted her decision with resignation, understanding without her having to put her feelings into words; that was another reason for her to be indebted to him.

Suddenly her arm was seized in a grip of steel. Her head snapped up. "Ben! You scared the daylights out of me."

"You need more than the daylights scared out of you. No one knew where you were. What the hell are you doing wandering the streets by yourself?" His eyes blazed with fury, but his face was also gray with the pallor of concern.

"I'm not a prisoner in the residence." She spoke more heatedly than she'd intended. "You were shut up in the study. Besides, Marston knew."

His gaze narrowed. "Did you count on his not telling me?"

"Don't be silly. Why should I try to hide from you?"

"Maybe you have some grandiose plan to be a heroine. Don't you know that anyone could pull up in a car and grab you?"

She couldn't resist the smile that twitched her lips. "Haven't you missed something?"

"What?"

"Just take a look behind you. My shadow is the one in the dark raincoat, about a dozen yards back."

Ben glanced over his shoulder. He relaxed, recognizing Maggie's shadow as one of the men who'd been hanging around the police van in front of the residence gates. "Sorry," he said with a fierce smile. "I didn't give Marston enough credit, it seems."

They walked on a few paces. "I had to get away for a while," Maggie explained. "I don't know why, but I was feeling stifled."

Instead of answering, Ben steered her down a side street. "As long as we're out, let's have lunch at the tennis club," he suggested. "I'm feeling stifled myself."

The tennis club was only a few blocks' walk, tucked into a corner of the grounds of Villa Ada. Many years ago, in another lifetime, they had played there together almost every day, the spirit of competition one of the few pleasures afforded them in the waning days of their marriage. From behind the hedges she could hear the muffled thwack of balls being hit, an occasional shout of triumph or groan of regret. Flowers still bordered the shallow steps leading into the clubhouse, laughter still rose from the tables in the courtyard. Such a sane world, thought Maggie.

A dark well-built man stood just inside the glass doors, beside a case of trophies, speaking earnestly to a young woman in tennis whites. The club still clung to the old standards. No color on the courts. He turned when the door opened, greeting Ben warmly before he turned to Maggie with a polite smile. The big man's smile suddenly broke into a wide grin when he recognized her. "Maggie, *mio amore!*" She was engulfed in a bear hug that threatened her ribs, but she returned it enthusiastically.

"Mario, how good it is to see you again," she said, meaning it. Mario di Conti was a friend as well as a tennis instructor. "You haven't changed at all."

"And you, little one. So beautiful, you are. That hasn't changed, either. But I knew so from the pictures."

"Pictures?" she asked, puzzled.

"Jamie's pictures. Didn't he tell you? I'm initiating another generation into the finer points of tennis. He definitely shows promise, that one. We have a lesson this afternoon. Is he with you?"

He didn't know? She couldn't imagine that anyone in the whole city, in the whole world, didn't know that the U.S. ambassador and his grandson had been kidnapped.

Maggie felt the blood drain from her face. Her fingers were grasped in a tight hold, and Ben spoke up, saving her from having to answer. "Mario, I'm sorry. Jamie and his grandfather are missing. It's been in the papers; I thought you would have heard."

Mario was devastated by his blunder. He wrung his hands. "I am so stupid. We finished a tournament this morning."

Mario's ignorance of the situation reminded Maggie that there was a world out there that didn't revolve around the acts of a terrorist. Such disregard weakened their position, and that pleased her very much. But, on the other hand, had the world grown insensible to such horror?

"When there is a tournament going on, I never read the papers," he went on. "Please forgive my callousness."

He continued to apologize all the way to the dining room. Maggie managed to assure him they weren't offended. She sat down in relief when they were shown to a table.

Ben stared across the table at his wife, trying to shake off the last remnants of fear he'd felt when he realized Maggie wasn't where she should be. "Your congressman called again right after you left. That's why I went looking for you."

"He isn't my congressman," she said pointedly.

The sharp retort pleased Ben. Maggie had said she wasn't going to marry the man, wasn't going to marry anyone, so why was he jealous? Because she could change her mind. There was still a possibility she would choose David Gant, and it scared the hell out of him. He considered telling her his feelings now, but his earlier reasons for not doing so still held. He didn't want to add to her confusion and worry.

Also, a niggling doubt in the back of his mind wouldn't let him. What if she agreed to his proposal because of their dependence on each other and later regretted it? No, he wanted her to be completely free to make the decision without pressure of any kind.

He'd go slowly, date her, send her flowers and candy—and a certain dress that made her look like someone from heaven. If she married him again, it would be because she loved him as deeply as he loved her. When this was all over, he would begin a campaign that would make Charlemagne look like a Boy Scout.

The green-jacketed waiter placed a bottle of chilled mineral water on the table. *"Potrei offrirle da bere?"* he asked.

"Drink, Maggie?"

"I'd rather have wine."

The waiter switched immediately to English. "The house wine is a nice medium-bodied white, sir."

"Fine," said Ben. He went on to order for them, consulting Maggie as to her preferences. The waiter disappeared, only to return in seconds with the chilled wine.

"Did you have any luck on the phone this morning?" Maggie asked after the wine had been poured.

Ben shook his head. "Nothing concrete. Pietro's boss will be back in town tonight. Maybe he'll be able to find out something for us."

"I hope so. This waiting is unbearable." She put her elbows on the edge of the table and rubbed her upper arms. "I think I'm so strong, until suddenly I realize the horror of it all. Then I want to crawl in a hole somewhere."

Ben stretched out his hand, palm up. Without hesitation Maggie placed her hand in it. His fingers closed around hers tightly like a warm glove. "You are strong," he said softly, his eyes sending a message she wasn't ready to read. "You may be the strongest woman I've ever known. To go through a pregnancy totally alone, to finish school, to care for Jamie by yourself. Only a very brave, very strong woman could have done all those things."

It was the first time either of them had ever referred to the circumstances surrounding the pregnancy. Maggie found herself unable to resist the warmth in his eyes or his hand. She dropped her gaze. "I wasn't brave at all. I was scared to death."

"That's why you're brave. Anyone can cope when things are going well."

The waiter returned with their appetizers, saving her from having to answer.

"I was there on the day Jamie was born," Ben said when the man had left.

Maggie had been toying with her antipasto. At the announcement she dropped her fork. "You're kidding."

Ben chuckled. The sound startled Maggie. "You aren't kidding? You were there?"

He told her then, of the meeting with her father, the days in Washington spent haunting the hospital, even the lengths he'd gone to in order to avoid her cousins. "You've done a damned good job with Jamie. He's a wonderful kid. Most women in your predicament would have been bitter as hell and would have tried their damnedest to keep their ex-husbands away."

Maggie blinked at the sudden change of subject and the slight huskiness in his voice. She didn't know how to respond to such a stunning revelation. He had actually been at the hospital, and she hadn't been aware of it. She wondered how she would have reacted if she had known. "I love Jamie. I don't think I would be showing that love very effectively if I kept him from knowing his father. Besides, his visits with you are good for him," she replied. "I couldn't deny him that."

"Yeah, we have fun together, but you have the hard part. You're responsible for his day-to-day development, the rules and regulations, the homework." He shrugged with a self-deprecating grin. "The one time he was sick while he was here in Rome... Do you remember?"

Maggie nodded, a smile playing about her lips.

"Your father and I went to pieces. We called in doctors, world-renowned specialists, to tell us that he had a cold virus. We both felt that you had entrusted him to us, and we'd let you down by allowing him to get sick."

"It wasn't your fault that he had a cold, for heaven's sake," she protested.

"I know that now, but I didn't then. God, I was scared." He shifted in the seat. "From the very first, you've been generous, letting him visit, not criticizing me to him...." His voice trailed off.

Maggie wondered why he was paying her compliments with a scowl on his face. Did he resent having to pay them? "We're both lucky," she said quietly, thinking of their son, the only remaining link between them.

Lucky, hell! thought Ben. He felt lonely, not lucky. He looked across the table at his wife. Her silvery blond hair was lifted off her neck in a noble, if prim, chignon. Suddenly he felt an overwhelming urge to plunge his fingers into her hair, raking the pins out of it until it tumbled free over her shoulders, down her back to her waist. He wondered... No! He jerked his attention away from Maggie and speared a piece of tortellini. She'd made it clear that she wasn't interested in anything physical, and until he could declare himself, he'd better keep his mind off sex. But it was hard; it was damned hard.

The waiter had just placed their entrees before them when the man in the dark overcoat appeared at the entrance to the dining room. Ben saw him first, talking to the maître d', who gestured toward their table. The man looked grim and disturbed.

Oh, God... Jamie. Ben felt the blood drain out of his face. A ringing in his ears drowned out all other sound in the restaurant. Slowly he laid down his fork and waited, feeling more helpless than he had ever felt in his life.

He didn't realize that he had risen to his feet until Maggie touched his forearm. "Ben?" She looked over her shoulder and froze, the fingers on his arm turning to talons.

The man approached the table. When he saw their faces, he must have known immediately what they suspected. He put out a hand, palm up. "It's not what you're thinking."

Ben's lungs were burning. He let out the breath that was dammed up inside. "What is it, then?" he grated.

"I've been notified by radio that contact has been made. They want you back at the residence."

Maggie placed her napkin on the table and stood. The emotion that swamped her was one of relief, which was ridiculous. She still didn't know what was happening to her son. But the waiting was over.

"I called for a car. It should be outside now."

Maggie slipped the strap of her purse over her shoulder. Her other hand sought Ben's. Their fingers linked tightly, they walked beside the man in the dark overcoat, out into the sunshine.

Chapter 7

Marston was waiting at the front door of the mansion. One look at the man who never had a hair out of place told them that the news was significant; the waiting was over. He had discarded his jacket, revealing a leather shoulder holster. His tie was askew as though he had jerked at it in frustration. Wordlessly he spun on his heel and led the way down the hall to the study. Ben closed the door after them and held Maggie's hand in a tight grip.

"What's happened, Mr. Marston?" Maggie asked, attempting to keep the trembling out of her voice.

He took a long breath and looked at Ben, then Maggie. "It's worse than we feared."

"Don't gloss it over, Marston," said Ben. "Give it to us straight."

"As we suspected, the IRA has nothing to do with it."

Marston removed his glasses, changed his mind and put them back on. "A local radio station got a note in the mail this morning from the TAC—Tactical Action Commandos.''

Ben felt the kick in his gut as though it had been delivered by a heavy boot.

Maggie looked confused. "I've never heard of them."

Marston avoided her eyes. "You tell her," he said to Ben, surprising them both.

Ben's voice was even as he explained, but his stomach churned with fear and dread. "They're a new group, claiming to support the poor and downtrodden victims of political tyranny generated by the United States. But they also have another distinction that makes them extremely dangerous," he told her in a dull monotone. "They are trying to organize as a representative body, the force that will unite all the terrorists in Europe and the Middle East."

Maggie listened in horror as Ben recited the facts as if by rote.

"They're so new we haven't been able to infiltrate the group," added Marston.

"What are their demands?" Ben asked him.

"They want the release of three prisoners being held in Italian jails in return for the release of the ambassador and Jamie."

"Can I guess which three?" Ben asked very quietly after a long silence.

Marston nodded.

"Not the men who were responsible for the World-Star air crash last year?" asked Maggie, remembering a briefing she'd been in on a week ago. "Their trial starts next week, doesn't it?"

Neither man answered; neither had to. Their expressions answered for them.

Maggie sagged slightly, and Ben's arm came around her shoulders. She straightened immediately. "I'm all right," she said huskily. But she was lying.

The policy of the United States was not to deal. She knew that. She agreed with it. In principle. If you gave in to terrorist demands, they would up the ante next time. And there would always be a next time if you gave in.

But, dear God, when it was your baby... your father...

Ben couldn't say anything for a long minute. "What do we do next?" he asked finally in a choked voice.

Marston shoved his hands into his pockets. "We still wait. The note is being analyzed, though I doubt there will be a lead there. The stationery was common bond; and I'm sure these people are smart enough not to leave fingerprints. The note said they would call the embassy tonight at six, but that place is a madhouse. I've arranged with the chancery to reroute the call to our switchboard in the basement. We'll tape, of course. I'll let one of you answer the phone in the study, but be careful what you say."

Ben listened to the agent's plans, but his concern was for Maggie. Her features were pinched and white. The slender shoulders under his arm were too straight, too stiff. "Maggie, why don't you go upstairs and lie down. I'll call you if we hear anything."

"No. Please quit trying to protect me from this, Ben." She turned to the other man. "Mr. Marston, may we go down to the basement?"

They paused at the bottom of the stairs; the scene before them was one of quiet, constructive order. In response to a question from a uniformed policeman, Marston left them standing there; Ben moved to join his friend Alberto in front of the map. Maggie followed, but it took only a few minutes for her to realize that she was useless here. Worse, she was making these people uncomfortable. She gave up and headed for the steps.

Ben hesitated for only a moment before following her. He found her on the sofa in the library, her knees drawn up, her arms folded around them, and her head bent. "Oh, God, please help us," she prayed. "Please, please."

The sight of her huddled there stabbed Ben like a white-hot sword. He fought for control over the blackest thoughts a man can have. Frustrated beyond belief, he wanted to roar against the evil that allowed human beings to do this to each other, scream aloud against the injustices and the hand of fate that had brought them to this moment.

But he did none of these things. Silently he went to a cupboard set into the paneled wall and drew out a woolen afghan. "Come on, Maggie. Lie down here on the sofa. You haven't slept well in days. You're running on pure nerves."

Lifting her head, she sighed heavily and speared her fingers into the heavy knot at the back of her head. The action of her fingers dislodged several pins. "They're as good as dead. Italy will never agree to release those men." Her tone was lifeless.

"No!" shouted Ben. With a visible effort he lowered his voice. "No," he repeated, but a muscle in his jaw jumped; his nostrils flared; his fists clenched. "I refuse to believe that. I refuse to think it or even listen to you say it. Do you hear me?"

She saw the violence in him, and understood it. But there was no violence in herself. She couldn't dredge up the anger that would give her strength, only hopelessness and a vision of the long bleak tunnel she had to travel through. "If only I could *do* something." She surged to her feet. "All those people downstairs—they're busy! If only I could be busy, too."

A conversation surfaced in Ben's mind. A few days ago he and his son had had a mild altercation on the subject of chores. *"Ah, do I have to? Mom works me to death, Dad. She's always got to be busy."* Was it only a few days ago that Jamie had complained about making his bed? He felt as though it had been years. He'd give his own life to hear Jamie complain again.

He dropped the afghan and helped dispose of the rest of the pins in Maggie's hair. His fingers remained to massage the nape of her neck, her shoulders, until he felt some of the tension ease. "We will do something. As soon as the call comes in, but you won't be much use if you drop from exhaustion. Maybe they'll let us speak to Jamie. Would you want him to know you're afraid?"

"No." Maggie shook her head to free the tangles. "That's better. Thanks."

He picked up the afghan he'd dropped. "Come on. Lie down."

"What are you going to do?"

He indicated the bar. "I'll fix myself a drink and confiscate Ian's favorite chair for an hour. Don't worry. I won't leave you." His last remark was in response to a look of panic in her eyes.

Ben had read Maggie's thoughts perfectly, her fear of waking in confusion, unaware of developments. But, Lord, she was tired. And he was offering to keep the vigil. "Thanks. I believe I will lie down."

She slipped off her shoes and stretched out on the couch. "You know, Ben, Marston's not so bad," she murmured as her heavy lids closed. "He's just never had any children, so it's hard for him to understand our fears."

Feeling a compulsion to be near her, not to leave even for a second, Ben watched her while she slept. Eventually he dozed, too.

He recognized the black abyss. He'd stood before it when he first realized Jamie was missing. Now it was deeper, wider and blacker. The walls shifted, as if they were about to crumble. Slowly he became aware that he was not alone at the edge.

Maggie stood beside him, a younger Maggie with a baby in her arms. He was delighted. They could go back, live through all the years they'd missed. But he must be careful; he mustn't startle her. If she moved she might fall, and the baby...

She smiled at him, a soft, lovely smile of recognition. She lifted the baby's tiny hand, waving it "hello," and took a step toward him... God! No!

Ben sat up abruptly in the chair. Sweat poured off him; his heart threatened to burst from his chest. His hands gripped the arms of the chair so tightly his muscles screamed for release.

When he saw Maggie curled up on the sofa, he collapsed in the chair again like a limp rag. His head lolled from side to side as he tried to throw off the aftereffects of the nightmare. A picture of Ian with the president of Italy was on the bookshelf in his line of vision. He stopped the motion of his head and stared at the face of his friend. "Don't disappoint me again, Ben," he seemed to say.

Ian had always been careful not to lay the blame for the dissolution of their marriage on Ben. But Ben knew that Maggie was the most important thing in the ambassador's life. He never talked much about his wife, but the few things he did say convinced Ben that he had absolutely adored Maggie's mother. She had died when Maggie was only twelve. He hadn't even considered leaving his child with relatives. She had grown up in her father's house—wherever that house might be.

A soft knock on the door interrupted his reverie. Lola stood there with a tray in her hands. "Mr. Marston ordered this for you," she whispered. "He said to tell you that the call should come through any time now."

Ben took the tray from her and set it on a table. "Thanks, Lola."

"*Prego*. Also, this note came while you were out." She handed him an envelope. "Is she asleep?"

He took the envelope, which was loosely sealed, and turned it over in his hand. His name was printed on the front. He felt strangely reluctant to open it in Lola's presence. Nodding toward the figure huddled in a corner of the couch, he answered her question. "She's been asleep for quite a while."

"I'm sorry you must wake her."

"Yeah," he said, his features grim. "It would be easier on her if she could just sleep through the whole thing."

Lola lingered at the door, speaking softly. "She would not like that, I think."

"You read her well. She most certainly would not like it." He gave up and opened the note. As he scanned the contents, he felt a surge of hope. "When did you say this came, Lola?"

"I'm not exactly sure. I found the envelope on my desk after lunch. It may have come over with the mail from the chancery. Is it important?"

He moved his stiff shoulders in what he hoped was an indifferent shrug, but his mind was racing. "Probably not. Just business." He was only vaguely conscious of the door closing behind Lola. The message in his hand was from Pietro, saying that his boss had returned and might have some information. He wanted to talk to Ben. Would Ben call so they could set up a time and place?

Would he? Ben felt the energy return to his body. Things were beginning to break. He reached for the telephone.

Ah, hell. He couldn't call from here. Every phone in this place was bugged. And he couldn't leave until the call from the kidnappers came in. Frustration sent him pacing, but excitement began to build within him, as well. He paused. Should he share this with the people downstairs? No, he'd wait and see. It might not amount to anything.

He crossed to the couch and knelt on one knee beside the sleeping form of his wife. She lay on her side, her fingers linked and tucked under her cheek. A fat blond curl masked one eye. Gently he lifted it. It wound itself around his finger, the individual strands clinging to his skin.

What would they say, these people who had his son? What would they say? *Maggie, oh, my darling, hold tight to me. The call is coming in, and I'm scared. I'm so scared.* He brushed her hair away from her face. "Maggie, honey, wake up," he said gently.

Her eyes opened immediately, the brown irises warm with an emotion Ben couldn't decipher. His heartbeat accelerated; his pulse echoed loudly in his ears. Their gazes clung for a breathless moment. It was Ben who broke off the silent communication. He stood abruptly, plunging his fists into his pockets. "Lola brought us a tray. It's almost time."

Maggie swung her feet to the floor. She hunched her shoulders and slid her hands under her thighs to hide their trembling from Ben. "I'm not hungry," she said, her voice husky with sleep. *I'd either choke or throw up,* she added to herself.

He brought the tray to the sofa and set it between them on the middle cushion. "Neither am I, but we both should eat something. I don't want you to pass out on me." He reached for a sandwich and a cold bottle of beer.

Maggie's resistance withered under the meaningful look he gave her. She simply didn't have the strength to argue with his reasoning. "Okay."

The taste of the sandwich was lost on her. She chewed, but her eyes kept straying to the telephone on the desk, willing it to ring. The instrument remained maddeningly silent. She changed her tactics, deliberately ignoring the black bastard, as though she didn't give a damn whether it rang or not. It didn't.

Ben finished his food and drained the last swallow of beer. He laid his head against the back of the sofa and took a cigarette from the pack on the table beside him. "I have to go out after the call comes in."

She dropped her half-eaten sandwich on the tray and reached for a napkin. "Go out? Where?"

He avoided her eyes as he cupped the flame of his lighter. "I need to make a phone call that I can't take care of from here."

Maggie's gaze sharpened. What kind of phone call? she wondered. He'd been using the telephones to stay in touch with half the people in Rome, and suddenly he had to go out? "Fine. I'll go with you."

"Not this time. I won't be gone long."

"Ben Altman, you may as well get it through your head right now that I'm in this all the way! I'm not staying here with my hands folded while you go off somewhere following a lead." She swept the air between them with a hand. "Just think of me as one of the boys."

"But you're not one of the boys, damn it. And you're not—" The telephone rang. They both leaped for it. Ben got there first.

"Dad?"

Ben's arm caught Maggie close; he angled the receiver so she could hear. "Jamie? Oh, Jamie..." He had to swallow hard. "Are you all right, son?"

"We're okay, Dad. I'm not allowed to say much." His voice sounded surprisingly strong on the first sentence but quavered slightly on the second.

"Jamie, darling, it's Mom."

"Mom, you're there, too?" The quaver was more pronounced now. "I'm scared, Mom."

"I'm here, darling. We're doing everything we can to get you back." Maggie squeezed her eyes shut. "Just do whatever the people tell you to do, Jamie. Don't argue with them, sweetheart."

"Granpa already told me that."

"How's Granpa?"

"Granpa is fine at the moment," said another, harsher voice. Maggie couldn't distinguish the accent—was it Slavic? "But neither of them will be fine for long unless our demands are met. Listen to me and don't interrupt. We will communicate only with the radio station from now on. We will call them at midnight, and again at four p.m. tomorrow for progress reports. If we are not satisfied by midnight tomorrow that our comrades are going to be released, we will kill either the ambassador or his grandson. That gives you over twenty-four hours to arrange for the release of our freedom fighters. I suggest that you not waste any time.'' The connection was broken.

Ben hung up and headed for the door. Maggie didn't have to ask where he was going. She followed him out to the hall and down to the basement.

Marston looked up from where he was leaning over the communications center. Wordlessly he shook his head.

''We couldn't trace the call, Ben,'' said Alberto. ''They had it timed to the second. We will try to analyze the voice recording, however. It may give us something.''

All the stiffness seemed to go out of Ben. He closed his eyes and massaged his temples with his thumb and forefingers. Then he straightened. ''Where do we go from here?''

Marston answered. ''We're sending a team of trained negotiators to the radio station. If we can keep them talking longer when they call back tonight . . .''

Ben and his police friend exchanged glances. Not much chance of that: as Alberto had said, these people knew what they were doing.

Ben drew Maggie with him to the steps. She hadn't opened her mouth throughout the exchange, and he knew that she was stretched to her limits, as he was. He had never found the simple act of climbing stairs such an effort. ''Jamie sounded okay,'' he observed quietly when they'd reached the top.

A shudder shook the slender body under his arm. ''Yes, he did,'' she choked out. ''Scared, though.''

He put his other arm around her, too, and held her tight against him. "Cry if you have to, baby. Cry and get it all out."

"I can't," she whispered. "I wish I could cry, but I can't."

"I can't either," he admitted. "God knows, I'm crying inside."

Maggie lifted her head to look deeply into his eyes. "Please, let me go with you, Ben. I can fight my fear for Jamie and Dad, but I can't fight you at every turn, too: I don't have the strength for that. Please don't shut me out."

He studied her upturned face, weighing and examining the alternatives. Putting Maggie in the slightest bit of danger was unthinkable. He loved her too much. But what if their positions were reversed? What if she tried to shut him out, if he were the one who had to plead? He reached a decision that he prayed he wouldn't regret, but it was the only decision open to him. "Okay, Maggie. We're in this together. Whatever comes up, we'll handle it together. But we've got to hurry. I want to get hold of this man while he's willing to talk to me."

Maggie sagged in relief. "Thank you. I promise I won't slow you down. If I'd had to stay here alone, I would have been a lunatic by the time you got back."

"Let's go."

"I'll get my purse." She ducked under his arm and headed down the hall toward the library.

"Get my jacket, too, will you?"

She nodded. The purse was on the floor beside the sofa, and the jacket hung across the back of the desk chair. As she reached for it, the phone at her elbow rang again. Her heart did a somersault. "Hello?"

"Mac, Maggie. Ben there?"

Maggie had recognized Mac's voice immediately. "I'll get him," she said shortly, and dropped the receiver on the desk with a thump that she hoped rattled his eardrums. "The telephone's for you," she told Ben when she joined him. "It's Mac again."

Ben muttered a curse under his breath as he disappeared into the study. Maggie lingered at the door, unabashedly eavesdropping.

"Yeah, Mac," said Ben shortly. He was silent, listening; then he spoke. "I told you I've put Mitch in charge of the bureau until this is over."

Aware of the agitation building in his voice, Maggie wished she could hear both sides of the conversation.

Ben's next word was bitten off sharply. "No." He listened further. "Damn it, I said no! Screw you and your damned job—this is my son!"

Maggie heard him slam down the phone; a moment later he joined her. "Let's go," he said angrily.

She watched him for a sign, some outward guarantee that the scene she'd just heard was not simply for her benefit. "What was that all about?"

Ben jerked open the front door. A blast of heat came into the air-conditioned hall, hitting them in the face. "What?"

"Don't be evasive with me, Ben Altman. You know very well what. I heard you tell Mac where he could, uh, what he could do with his job. Did you mean it?"

"I meant it. He wanted another interview. I am more interested in getting my son back than reporting on it."

Anger lent him extra vigor. By the time they reached the driveway, she was practically running to keep up with his long-legged stride. "Ben. Slow down, please."

"What? Oh, sorry," he said absently. But he slowed.

For the first time Maggie was totally convinced that Ben's energies were directed toward one thing and one thing only—the return of his son. He'd even put his job in jeopardy to do it. She felt a surge of gratitude that they were in this together. "Let's go find a phone," she said, matching her stride to his.

They passed through the gate unchallenged. The man in the raincoat took his place behind them.

The nearest phone kiosk was less than two blocks away. "I need to talk without his overhearing," Ben told her, indicating the bodyguard. "My contact may be shady, but he isn't a convicted criminal, and he wouldn't want the authorities listening in on our conversation. Can you draw him out of earshot?"

"Sure," she answered, but she had no idea how she would accomplish it.

"We're almost there." As they neared the booth, Ben snapped his fingers as though remembering something. "Now," he said softly. Maggie stopped and casually retraced her steps, pretending interest in a bookstore. Ben patted his pockets and looked around as though just spying the telephone kiosk. The pantomime must have been effective, for the man stayed with Maggie as Ben stepped into the kiosk and lifted the receiver.

A few minutes later Ben rejoined her, a smile on his face for the benefit of their tail.

Chapter 8

It's set. He's agreed to meet with me," said Ben. "He isn't sure if the information will be helpful, but he's been asking around." He chuckled. "He was almost indignant. I think he believes terrorist groups give crime a bad name."

"When is the meeting?" asked Maggie.

"Tonight. He has a dinner appointment at the Hotel De La Ville. He'll meet me afterward."

"Us," Maggie corrected. "He'll meet us."

"Look, honey, I know I said you could come along. But this meeting is only to gather information. Nothing will happen tonight."

"Good, then there's no danger, and no reason for me not to go with you."

Ben growled, but he didn't argue further. Maggie would be safe enough. The area around the Spanish Steps was the international gathering place in Rome and, as such, was never completely deserted. Tourists and shoppers roamed the nearby streets, wandering in and out of boutiques with such famous names as Gucci and Valentino; business deals were closed over coffee at one of Rome's oldest cafés; the Hotel De La Ville was only one of three hotels nearby with their ever-present taxis. The Steps themselves were a perfect place for a meeting—clandestine, casual or romantic.

"There remains one small problem. Your escort," Ben said. "The man I'm meeting can smell a cop from a mile away. I can come and go, but I sure can't hide you in the trunk of my car. And I can't see him letting you out of his sight."

Maggie remembered how secure she'd felt this afternoon with the man nearby. Now his vigilance was a hitch in their plans. Suddenly her brow cleared, and she chuckled under her breath. "Don't worry about him. I know a secret way out of the grounds."

Ben looked down at her, astonished. "You do? And just how, may I ask?"

Her expression lightened. "Jamie told me about it after his visit last year. He was playing archaeologist, pretending to excavate the latest ruin, when he found a door in the side wall that's grown over with ivy. Probably originally a servants' entrance. It was locked, but there was a rusty key still in the lock. He hid the key, but I think I can find it."

Ben looked worried. "If he got out, others could get in."

"I scolded him. Made him promise he'd never do it again. He said the lock was really rusty; it took him an hour to make it work. He never did get the door open. We may not be able to, either."

Ben chuckled drily. "He's a persistent little devil when he gets started on something, isn't he?"

The amusement in his eyes softened the lines in his brow that seemed to have grown deeper with each passing day. Maggie swallowed the lump in her throat. "He's intelligent, too," she said lightly. "He gets that from me, of course."

Their laughter was strained but sincere. And she was surprised at how much better she felt for it. Ben, too, must have felt better. He hugged her close. "The door may be sealed, and I'm not so sure we'll get away with it, but we'll give it a try."

"You can leave in your car, drive around the block and pick me up at the corner. It'll be a piece of cake."

Looking down at her, Ben sobered. "Don't take this lightly, Maggie."

Instantly she was as serious as he. "I'm not taking it lightly at all."

They separated after dinner to rest. It was almost nine when they met in her room.

Ben had changed into jeans, a knit polo shirt and deck shoes. He had to hide a smile when he entered Maggie's room. Her getup was straight out of a Hitchcock movie.

The black jeans she wore hugged her derriere the way any good spy would hug the night. The black oversize sweater would have her sweltering the minute she stepped out of the air-conditioned mansion. Her blond hair was hidden completely by a scarf tied intricately to resemble a turban.

"Aren't you hot in that thing?" he asked, indicating the sweater. "Where did you get it?"

"I'm roasting," she snapped. "And I found it in Daddy's closet. I don't want anyone to see me climbing through a hole in the wall."

Ben felt his smile spread to a rueful grin. This was the Maggie he remembered lovingly, the Maggie who plunged headlong into a situation, giving it her all. He was pleased to find there was some of the old Maggie's enthusiasm under the calm exterior of the mature woman. "Honey, if Marston sees you in that getup, you'll never make it to the wall. You couldn't broadcast your intentions any clearer if you hired a hall. Don't you have a cool blouse that isn't black?"

Maggie eyed her ex-husband. He was dressed conventionally, but he was going to drive out the gate. He didn't have to sneak through the bushes. She looked down at herself, all the way down to her white running shoes. "With these white shoes it would be hard to be invisible, anyway," she admitted. "I guess I might as well be comfortable." She tugged the turban off. One thick braid fell down her back. Opening the closet, she took a blue cotton shirt from a hanger and disappeared into the bathroom to change.

The terrace off the study was deserted. Ben had thought it would be. When the entire estate was surrounded by a nine-foot wall, when security guards patrolled the gates, and dozens of intelligence agents were temporarily housed on the ground floor, why should anyone keep an eye on the gardens?

He watched Maggie disappear into the shrubbery in the direction of the gate. Finding it earlier hadn't been easy. He smiled as he pictured his young son crawling through the undergrowth on a quest for the lost city of Embassaria. He could imagine Jamie's eyes, green in color like Ben's own but warm like his mother's, lighting up when he spied the hidden gate. Ben swallowed hard and shut his eyes against the burning there. Jamie.

He shook his head hard to rid his mind of the image. Thinking of the danger to Jamie would distort his reason; it would only be counterproductive. He must concentrate on the task ahead. If they were lucky, the importer would provide a lead to follow, but if not, there would be other directions, other paths. He couldn't dwell on his fears of what he might find at the end of this search; he had to concentrate all his energies and abilities on the search itself.

Sliding his hands into his pockets, he sauntered around the corner of the house. He nodded briefly to the man at the front entrance, pulled out his keys and unlocked the car.

The Hotel De La Ville sat in the shadow of Trinità dei Monti, the cathedral that looked down upon Piazza di Spagna and the Spanish Steps. The Steps themselves separated into three flights as they climbed the hill; some were broad, some narrow, some divided, the contrast effectively exaggerating their height.

Ben decided to park in a small piazza half a block from the foot of the landmark. He paused uneasily, his hand still on the key. A heavy bank of clouds hit the moon and even the man-made lighting seemed to have dimmed. The area was almost deserted.

"I want you to take the keys to the car, Maggie." He disengaged them from the ignition and handed them to her.

She automatically held out her hand. "Why?" she asked when he'd dropped them into her palm.

"If something goes wrong, I want you to get the hell out of here, as quickly as you can."

Maggie wisely didn't reply that she wasn't about to leave the square by herself, but she did put the keys into her pocket.

When they were on the street, Ben drew her into the curve of his arm, sauntering slowly as though they had all the time in the world. But adrenaline was surging through him.

His eyes were busy, and what he saw reassured him to a degree. Despite the threat of rain, there were a few people on the street. A little girl played next to the fountain at the foot of the broad steps while her parents watched fondly. A well-dressed con artist talked earnestly to a couple of tourists who were trying valiantly to deal with dripping ice cream cones. A group of teenage girls giggled and flirted with a group of teenage boys. Everything looked fairly normal. His eyes went back to the child at the fountain. The little girl reminded him...

At first Maggie resisted the restriction of Ben's arm, impatient to reach their destination. Then she realized his intentions. They were to look like any other couple out for a stroll.

"Maggie, have you—" She looked up at him, and he stopped. "Ah, hell, I don't know how to say this."

"Say what?" she asked, mystified by his hesitance.

"Do you know whether you're...? Are you pregnant?"

She bit her cheek inside to keep from laughing out loud. It really wasn't funny, but there was a certain satisfaction in seeing Ben Altman discombobulated. She nestled closer and slid her arm around his waist. "I don't know yet, but I'll be sure to let you know."

Ben gave her a look that spoke volumes as they circled the fountain, his strong white teeth the brightest thing in the dark night. They started up the steps. At the first level he nuzzled her ear, whispering, "You're a dangerous woman, Maggie."

"Dangerous? Why do you say that?"

"Because you could distract a man from his duty with no trouble at all," he answered absently. A distant rumble of thunder had drawn his gaze to the sky. The breeze picked up.

"So could you," she shot back.

Ben didn't answer. She wasn't even sure her words registered. He was scanning the area again. The family at the fountain had disappeared. The laughter of the teenagers faded as they wandered away. The con artist was fighting a losing battle as the tourists edged toward a waiting taxi.

Ben and Maggie reached the midpoint of the gigantic staircase and sat down on a warm marble step to wait. Sitting close together, they were partially hidden by the shifting shadows of the huge potted azaleas that decorated the steps in the summertime.

Maggie looked around. Seldom was the area as completely deserted as now, and it was disconcerting. True, there was the threat of rain in the air, but usually someone could be seen, a policeman, at the very least.

"Sh-h-h." A loud footstep sounded in the night. Ben's attention was focused on a man dressed in a black suit and chauffeur's cap who had appeared beside the fountain below them. Maggie hadn't even heard the limousine drive up, but there it was, parked at the curb across the street.

The man looked around nervously, turning first one way and then the other, as though he were searching for something or someone.

Ben frowned. "That's his chauffeur." He rose, showing himself, but put a restraining hand on Maggie's shoulder. "Stay there." Casually he sauntered down a step or two, until his head was on a level with hers. His broad shoulders partially hid her.

The man hesitated for a minute, then quickly climbed the steps, moving smoothly for one of such bulk. Maggie suddenly felt that something was not right. The man looked like a thug—even his posture was threatening. There was a rather obvious bulge under his coat.

"Signore Altman?" he inquired.

"Yes, I'm Ben Altman."

He gave a rather contemptuous bow. "My employer was to meet you here. Have you seen him?"

"No, we just arrived. He hasn't come down yet." With his head he indicated the top of the steps, where the lights of the hotel could be seen.

The wind picked up a strand of Maggie's hair and swept it in her face. She lifted her hand to brush it aside. The gesture caught the man's attention. She froze, and he looked back at Ben.

"*Signore*, he is not there. He dismissed me during dinner and told me to return at ten o'clock. The doorman at the hotel told me he had left at about nine-thirty, alone. I am greatly disturbed, *signore*. My employer never goes anywhere alone."

I'll just bet he doesn't, thought Maggie. She sat very quietly, but she didn't like this at all. The man's manner was hostile, his tone, belligerent. He seemed to be blaming Ben for his employer's negligence in not keeping him apprised of his whereabouts.

Ben stood rock-still, his hands thrust casually into the pockets of his jeans. He eyed the man steadily. "Perhaps the doorman was mistaken. As I said, we only got here a few minutes ago."

The big man stared at Ben. Finally he shrugged his bulky shoulders. "Perhaps," he said. "I shall return to the hotel to see." He hurried down the steps to the limousine.

"What do you think that was about?" asked Maggie when Ben was sitting beside her again.

He glanced at his watch, then at her. "I don't know, but I don't like it. The man was right; his boss never goes anywhere without a couple of bodyguards. Maybe we should get out of here."

"No, Ben. Let's wait a little longer. There may be a perfectly simple explanation for his being late."

"Okay. Fifteen minutes, if the rain holds off. Then we're leaving."

The shiver that tripped across her back couldn't be blamed on the wind. Maggie hunched her shoulders, gripping the edge of the marble on either side of her hips. One of them came away wet and sticky. "Yuk, someone's ice cream," she said. "Do you have a handkerchief?"

Preoccupied with his uneasiness, Ben took one from his back pocket and handed it to her. Maggie was about to comment on their isolation when suddenly she froze. She shifted to the left, into the cone of light from the lamppost above her and stared in horror at the square of white linen she'd used to wipe her fingers. "Ben..." she choked out.

Lightning split the sky, and at the same moment Maggie heard a loud clap of thunder. Ben leaped to his feet and spun around, looking toward the top of the steps.

Maggie forgot the horror of what was on her fingers as another loud report rang out. But this one seemed to have come from above, from the Egyptian obelisk in front of the church. "What on earth...?" Oh, God! Shots! She started to jump up, but Ben slammed her back down, putting himself between her and the source of the sound. The report was followed by another, simultaneous with the sound of a soft impact. Ben reeled against her.

He'd been hit! Frantically Maggie lurched to her feet, grabbing him around the waist from behind, slowing his impetus enough to keep him from pitching headlong down the steps. With a surprising strength, she dragged him back into the shadowed protection of one of the planters. He was unbelievably heavy.

Her eyes darted madly from the top of the steps to the bottom, seeking help, seeking rescue, but there was not a soul to be seen. She opened her mouth to scream, but voices from above cut off the sound before it could leave her throat. Someone was coming down the steps. "Ben, we've got to get out of here. Someone's coming," she said softly. When he didn't answer, she looked down. A black stain blossomed on the side of his shirt above his belt line. "Ben," she whispered wildly. "Are you all right? Ben, speak to me, damn it!"

Ben groaned.

Maggie sagged in relief. But her relief was short-lived. She heard a shout from above and the sound of heavy feet. She turned him, looping his arm across her shoulders and stood up.

Ben straightened with effort, grateful for the support of her slender body. His side felt as though someone had branded him with a hot iron. He'd been dazed by the shock, but his reeling senses were beginning to clear, to settle into some kind of order. "I'm all right now."

"Sure you are," she muttered.

"This way," he hissed. "We've got to get off these steps."

This was no time to question his judgment. Maggie was too relieved that he seemed to be in charge again. They angled laterally across the wide expanse of stairs, staying in the shadows of the planters as much as possible, until they reached the low wall that bordered the steps.

The next thing she knew Ben had picked her up bodily in one arm and swung her over the wall. Her feet dangled in the air...it was at least a ten-foot drop. "Ben, don't..."

But he did. "Run," he commanded.

Maggie landed on all fours, uninjured but stunned and disoriented by the teeth-rattling fall. The narrow space between the wall of the adjoining building and the foundation of the steps was pitch-black. Ben let out a moan when he hit the ground beside her.

"Are you all right?"

"Damn it, I told you to run," he grated.

"Which way?" she growled back. "I can't see a thing."

"Hurry," he whispered, grabbing her hand.

Afterward she had no idea which direction they took. It seemed that one alley led into another, a dark labyrinth. Once Ben sagged against a bolted gate to catch his breath. He put a hand to his side; it came away wet and sticky. He looked at his hand, then at their surroundings dazedly, as though he didn't know what they were doing.

Hearing the relentless footsteps that still dogged them, Maggie took the initiative. "This way," she directed. They were off and running again.

Ben's pace began to slow; he staggered once. Maggie could hear his breath coming in harsh gasps. He was pushing himself to the point of collapse. Surely they were safe now. She stopped, pulling her hand out of his grasp, and listened. Only the wind raced through the alleyways behind them.

"I can't go any farther," she said, satisfied that they were no longer being followed. "And neither can you. Let's rest for a minute."

Ben turned to look at her. Her image swam and tilted slightly as he put out a hand to a wall for support. Even in the dim light that filtered down from the street he could see the determination in her eyes. He relented, but they were too exposed here. "There," he gasped, unsteadily retracing his steps to a deeply shadowed gap between two buildings, not wide enough for a car.

There was nothing here for cover, no refuse, no niche. The only thing breaking the straight shadow of the wall was an old wooden kitchen chair, propped at an angle beside a door. If someone shone a light into the gap they would be outlined perfectly. But she was right. He could barely manage to put one foot in front of the other. His head floated somewhere above his body. The shot . . . he must be losing blood.

The next thing Ben knew, he was lying on the cobblestones in the stinking alley with his head and shoulders cradled in Maggie's arms.

She rocked him, made soothing noises and left tiny kisses against his temple. The urge to relax, to accept her tenderness, was a brief one. A sense of inexplicable urgency took over, though for a minute he couldn't remember why it was so urgent that he get up. There was something he should be doing, something . . . "Maggie," he whispered.

"Oh, thank God." Maggie's voice caught on a sob of relief. For a heart-stopping minute, when he'd collapsed at her feet, for a horrible eternity, she'd thought he was dead. And she'd wanted to die, too.

Recollection swept over Ben in a dizzying wave. They had to get out of here. He pulled himself free of her arms and sat up resolutely. "How long was I out?"

"Just a few minutes." She hesitated. "You've been shot," she said, as though he didn't know.

Ben smiled tenderly and touched her cheek. "It isn't bad, honey." He looked down at his shirt. He was covered with blood, but the bullet had gone through his side, the fleshy part just above his waist. "I don't think it got a rib."

"Or something else? Like a heart or lung or..."

"Maggie," Ben said sternly, hearing the note of hysteria in her voice. "I'm very proud of you, babe. Don't fall apart on me now that the danger is over."

Maggie slumped, tilting her head back to rest it against the wall behind her. "I won't. But is it really over?"

"It is for now." Ben took in a long, painful breath and let it out. "We've got to get back to the residence. Marston has to know about this."

"Ben, I think I should go for help. You're in no condition to..."

"No!" he interrupted harshly. "You're not going anywhere by yourself."

Maggie made a sound of disgust. "I should have left before you came around enough to argue. Do you have any idea where we are?"

"I think we're near the Piazza del Popolo, but I don't know how near."

The Plaza for the People was one of the busiest inter-sections in Rome. There would be traffic, taxis. Feeling her energy return, she got to her feet. "I'll get us a cab."

Ben caught her ankle in an iron grip. "Help me up," he ordered.

"Ben, I know the city. Let me go alone."

"We're staying together. I'll lean on you."

Maggie muttered under her breath as she helped him to his feet, something that sounded like "damned macho mentality." Ben grinned to himself, agreeing with her judgment. Where Maggie was concerned, his macho mentality did lie awfully close to the surface. He had a feeling he'd never get over the urge to protect her, whether she needed protecting or not.

The gathering storm broke with a vengeance as they made their way to the Piazza del Popolo. By the time they found a taxi, they were both drenched to the skin. The driver obviously thought Ben was drunk; then he saw the blood. He would have driven away, leaving the crazy Americans to their crazy games, except that they were already in his cab.

"What is it about you and rain?" asked Maggie when she had given the man directions. She shook the water from her hands and arms and pulled her soaked shirt away from her body. "Every time we're together, I seem to end up wet." She was chattering to cover up her ner-vousness. If she allowed herself to dwell on what they had been through, or worse, what might have hap-pened, she would start blubbering like a baby.

Ben subsided against the cushion. "Surely you re-member Italian summers. Hot as hell, but if you don't like the weather, wait . . . five . . . minutes."

Alarmed, Maggie stared at him. His voice was slurred, his eyes closed. She had to keep him awake. "Damn you,

Ben Altman, if you pass out on me again, I'll leave you where you fall," she threatened.

He grinned drunkenly, his head rolling to the side. "When we were married, you wouldn't have told me off. Oh, babe, have you changed."

"Have I? How?" If she could keep him talking . . .

"You're . . . better."

"You're delirious. Come on, Ben. We're here."

The taxi parked beside Ben's car. "Wait here, will you, until we make sure it will start?" she asked the driver over the pelting tumult of rain on the roof of the cab.

The man looked suspicious but nodded his agreement. Maggie helped Ben into the passenger seat and circled to get in on the driver's side. She dug into her pocket, hampered by the wet denim, and finally pulled out the keys.

Roused by the effort of changing cars, Ben watched her competent hands maneuver the wheel in a U-turn. He reached out to grab her braid.

"What are you doing?" She moved her head, trying to free her hair from his grasp, but he held on.

"Lord, I dread the third degree we're going to get when Marston hears that you drove through those gates in my car."

Maggie glanced across at his profile. His jaw was tense, his skin pale, and there was a drawn look about his brow, as though he were trying to keep from frowning. He needed a doctor, not an interrogation. "He won't harass you," declared Maggie firmly.

Ben swiveled his head around in surprise. It seemed she was feeling a bit protective, too.

The man with the walkie-talkie did a double take before he opened the high wrought-iron gate to admit the small car. Maggie smiled at him. In the rearview mirror she watched him lift the instrument to his lips. He looked like he was shouting.

Marston met them in the driveway. "How the hell did you get out of this compound?" he demanded of Maggie. "And you!" He whirled on Ben. "I'll have you up on kidnapping charges."

Ben winced as Maggie helped him out of the car. "Fine, Marston. Would you just let me get cleaned up first?"

The agent spied the blood. "Good God, what happened to you?" He replaced Maggie's support with his own. "Get a doctor," he said to the man who stood at the open door.

"Get Chief Alberto up here first," Ben protested. "This is something you both should hear."

"And we will," vowed Marston. "If we have to take the thumb screws to you, we'll hear every word, you idiotic bastard. And you!" he roared at Maggie. "How the hell did you get out? In the trunk?"

Maggie thought it prudent not to reply. Let him think that. She might need her escape route again. She noticed something else. Marston might be shouting threats, but his complexion was almost as white as Ben's. He was as concerned as he was angry.

"The doctor's on his way," said the security man as Marston lowered Ben to the couch.

"Good."

Ben spoke to the man. "Is Alberto downstairs?"

"I think so, sir. Most of them stayed the night."

"Would you ask him to come up here, please?"

The man looked at Marston, who nodded.

Maggie knelt on the floor in front of Ben. Her blond hair was bedraggled and coming loose from the braid, her clothes filthy and smeared with his blood. She had never looked so beautiful to him.

"Let's get rid of this shirt," she said, reaching for the hem.

"No," said both of the men simultaneously. Maggie withdrew her hands instantly.

"The bleeding might start again, honey," Ben explained softly. "Leave it until the doctor gets here."

"But . . . okay." Maggie dropped her hands in her lap and looked up at him helplessly. She wanted to be doing something for him.

Ben understood the need in her eyes. He put out a hand to stroke her cheek and smiled. "You're one helluva woman, Maggie Altman. Maybe you could ask James for coffee, and go upstairs and get me a clean shirt."

She scrambled to her feet. "I'll be right back."

"Don't hurry. Take a hot shower and change your own clothes," put in Marston. When she paused on the threshold, he added, "I'll take care of him."

Maggie studied him, then nodded. "Thank you."

Upstairs a few minutes later, she propped her forehead on the shower wall. Gratefully she let the tears flow and mingle with the hot water. What was it Ben had said when they were on Monte Mario? *You marry someone because you can't exist in a world they aren't part of . . .* If he had been killed, would she have been able to survive without him?

The answer was clear.

Yes, she would survive—she had Jamie—but she would be only half alive. The love she felt for Ben had been relegated to the back of her consciousness, but instead of withering there, it had grown, secretly, encouraged by her own burgeoning maturity and fed by the love they shared for Jamie. Now, in the fertile atmosphere of their interdependency, it had blossomed, fed each time he touched her, each time their eyes met in silent communication. And now it had reached full-blown maturity. She didn't know whether anything would come of this revelation, but it warmed her.

She was still apprehensive about his safety, but she no longer fell apart when he was in danger. She had confidence in him. In a flash of insight she realized that faith in him was the one vital thing that had been missing in their marriage. From the very first time when he had been ordered out on assignment, she had lacked faith.

The sound of her own sniffles brought Maggie back to the realization that there was much to be done before the nightmare would be over. The time remaining before TAC's deadline was ebbing away. She picked up a bar of soap and began to scrub herself briskly.

Suddenly she inhaled through her clenched teeth, her naked body as motionless as a statue. Ben's was not the only blood on her hands! She had completely forgotten the horrible discovery she'd made just before the shots rang out.

Quickly she turned off the tap and, reaching for a towel, stepped out of the shower. Five minutes later she was dressed in clean jeans and a soft shirt. She skipped every other step as she hurried downstairs, a bundle of clothes for Ben in her arms.

She burst into the study. The doctor, at least she presumed he was a doctor, gave a last pat to the white bandage across Ben's lower chest. "There, I think you will heal very well. The wound is superficial."

Relieved at the doctor's pronouncement, she waited for him to finish. He took a syringe and a small bottle out of his bag.

"No, doctor," said Ben, struggling to rise. "No sed-atives."

The doctor didn't blink but kept filling the syringe. "How about an antibiotic? Does that meet with your approval?"

Ben had the grace to look chagrined. "Yes, sir."

"Even in the American embassy," he said, eyeing the two other men in the room, "I am supposed to report treating a gunshot wound."

Alberto folded his arms across his chest. "You know who I am?"

The doctor smiled pleasantly. "Of course. You are Alberto, the *principale* of the police."

"Then consider it reported."

"Certainly. I am grateful not to have to fill out all of your forms." He turned back to his bag to withdraw a white envelope, which he handed to Ben. "These are the painkillers. You may take them or not, as you wish. But I would recommend some rest."

"Thank you, doctor," said Ben, accepting the packet.

Maggie could barely wait to pass on her news. As soon as the door closed behind the little man, she spun around to the group. "There was some more blood, on the steps. I thought at first it was ice cream, but it wasn't." Her eyes sought Ben's. "Don't you remember? It's on the handkerchief you gave me."

Ben's furrowed brow cleared. "Right before the shooting started." He explained to the others. "We were meeting a man I know. He didn't show up." He turned back to Maggie. "Where's the handkerchief?"

"On the Spanish Steps," she said ruefully.

"I don't know that a bloodstained handkerchief will have any value, but, Alberto, can you have a man take a look there? See if he can find it? Damn the rain. It's probably soaked clean by now.''

''Forensics can do some remarkable things. It is worth a try.'' Alberto crossed to the telephone.

Ben took his clothes from Maggie and entered the small bath off the room. He returned in only a few minutes, his clean jeans and crisp blue shirt contrasting sharply with the fatigue in his eyes. He was toweling his hair dry.

Marston made them repeat the story of the shooting over and over until Maggie thought she would drop from exhaustion. Ben avoided the mention of any names, annoying the agent even further each time the account was retold.

The telling was interrupted only to tune in the radio station at midnight. They all clustered around a small portable set of her father's. The kidnappers repeated, word for word, their demands. When one of Marston's negotiators attempted to ask a question, the connection was broken.

At last the men left them alone with a suggestion that they get some rest. ''There isn't anything you can do tonight,'' Alberto said kindly. He was beginning to show the effects of their vigil too, Maggie noticed. His normally pinkish complexion had a gray pallor.

''Come on, Ben. Alberto's right. Let's go upstairs,'' said Maggie tiredly.

''To sleep?'' He gave a harsh laugh.

''You can stretch out on the bed for a couple of hours and rest. Ben, a gunshot wound is a dangerous thing. You've lost a lot of blood.''

Arm in arm, they mounted the stairs. When they reached her door, she turned to him. ''Would you like to stay with me?'' Maggie didn't know where the words had come from. She had never intended to make such an offer.

His dark brow lifted in that sexy way. He tucked a strand of hair behind her ear and let his knuckles linger at the side of her neck. "I don't think that's a very good idea, Maggie," he said gently.

She fit her spine firmly against the door and stared at the floor. "I wasn't talking about making love, Ben, but..."

"I didn't think you were," he said with a hint of irony.

She raised her gaze to his. "I need someone to hold me," she whispered, her eyes searching his anxiously, bravely. He would never know what it cost her to ask.

"Someone?" said Ben quietly.

"You."

The muscle in his jaw didn't exactly jump, it was more like a slow contraction. "I can't, Maggie."

Maggie shielded her eyes with her lashes. Oh, God, she couldn't believe she had pleaded with him. Memories of the last days of their marriage surfaced to haunt her as she turned her head away. Memories of herself, begging—*"I need you, Ben."* Demanding—*"Can't you ever stay home?"* Accusing—*"You don't love me anymore."* When she'd finally left, she was running from those memories as much as from Ben. And in the bleak days following their separation, she had vowed never to beg again. It was degrading; it was humiliating.

The admonition he'd voiced two days ago rang in her ears: *"Those who forget past mistakes are doomed to repeat them."*

"I understand," she said softly. "Good night, Ben."

Chapter 9

Ben closed the door of the guest room behind him and leaned against it thankfully. She'd stood there, so brave and steady, so desirable as she'd asked him to hold her. And he'd wanted to. How he had wanted to. Now that he'd admitted his love for her, to himself at least, it seemed to swell, to expand with every passing minute. There was no way in hell he could have been in a darkened bedroom with Maggie and not have made love to her.

And Maggie didn't need that. She'd been through enough for one night. When he'd heard those shots ring out... God, he'd never felt such fear. He'd been in physical danger many times, but his own mortality seldom occurred to him at those times. Tonight, however, he'd been screamingly aware of the danger to himself and Maggie.

Tonight Maggie needed comfort, peace. He loved her, and he wanted her—even half-conscious and in pain, he wanted her. He wanted her, not as the enchanting girl she had been, but as the glorious woman she'd become.

His laugh was harsh in the darkness. He flipped the light switch and pushed himself away from the door, reaching for the buttons of his shirt as he went. An unexpected pain shot through his chest as he lifted his arm. If she thought he could lie beside her in bed and not be aroused, she was still very naive.

Working carefully with one hand, he finally got the shirt off. The snap of his jeans was easy, the zipper more difficult, since Maggie had forgotten to provide underwear. The memory of her sweet face turned to him, the soft utterance—''you''—set his heart to pounding and left him with an intense hunger that was a definite hindrance to getting his jeans unzipped. He had almost pulled her into his arms then. He had almost told her he loved her, wanted to be her husband again. But he hadn't.

The search for Jamie and Ian was the most important thing right now, the only thing any of them should be concentrating on. When he declared his love, he wanted time to defend his proposal against any objections she might raise.

Damning himself heartily, he finally stepped out of the jeans and headed for the shower, which presented another problem. The doctor had done a neat job; the bandage was on to stay, but what would happen when the water soaked through it?

He shrugged and turned on the shower. He would have to put physical comfort aside. Forget his wound; forget his desire. Jamie and Ian needed him.

When he had dried himself and dressed, including underwear this time, he opened his bedroom door quietly and headed for the basement. Feeling better for the shower, he turned back the cuffs of his shirt as he ran lightly down the stairs. His adrenaline was pumping.

He found Marston there. The man looked like hell, thought Ben. A scowl seemed to have become a permanent part of his expression. Ben sensed that this had become a personal crusade for the agent. Marston seemed almost as deeply troubled as he and Maggie; it was no longer just a job. Time was ticking away. They had less than twenty-four hours left.

"What the hell are you doing down here?" Marston demanded belligerently when he saw Ben. "The doctor told you to get some rest."

Ben didn't take offense, but he sagged visibly. Suddenly he was spent, consumed by his worry, his fear. He didn't want to bait the man anymore. And he didn't want to be baited. "Look, Marston. Just give me something to do. Anything."

Marston looked at him through narrowed eyes for a long time. At last, satisfied by something he saw in the younger man's eyes, he nodded abruptly. "Take the phone upstairs. See if you can get any information about what happened tonight. Chances are the ambush had nothing to do with our problem: if your contact operates in a gray area of the law, he probably has a few enemies who would be curious and angry about his meeting with a well-known reporter. But just on the off-chance that there is a connection, see what you can find out."

"Are you taping all the telephones?" Ben asked mildly.

"Hell, yes!"

"Then I'll use a phone outside." Ben turned to go.

"You damned fool!" erupted Marston. "Someone tried to kill you and your wife—ex-wife."

Ben dragged a hand through his hair. "If I thought my contact was involved in the kidnapping of my son, don't you know I'd say to hell with him? But I don't. In fact, I have a suspicion that I may have gotten him involved myself." He remembered the bloodstained handkerchief. "If anything has happened to him, it may be on my conscience," he added soberly.

"They didn't find the handkerchief," said Marston, correctly reading Ben's thoughts. He sighed heavily. "Okay, I'll turn off the machine on the phone in the study."

It was a major concession. Ben wasn't quite sure he believed the other man. "Why would you do that?" he asked, unable to hide his suspicion.

"Because, hero," Marston sneered, "we need the information—and hell, look at you. You couldn't walk a block in your condition."

Ben hated to admit the truth of the observation, but by the time he made it back upstairs, he was weak. His hand was shaking as he reached for the telephone.

"I can't talk to you!" The unsteadiness in Pietro's voice was unquestionably caused by panic.

"Shut up and listen," Ben said, his own voice hard. "I want to know what happened tonight."

"I swear to you, I don't know. My employer has disappeared. No one knows where he is, and that makes everyone nervous."

"Don't try to make me believe you won't find out. I know you and the others who work for him will move heaven and earth to find your boss, Pietro. You'd better let me in on it when you do. I want to know if there is a connection. If you don't call by—" he glanced at his watch "—noon, I'm coming to your house."

"No, *madre de Dios*, please do not involve my family. *Signore*, I will get the information for you, but maybe not by noon." He paused. "If I do not call, I swear to you I will get in touch somehow."

"I don't want to involve your family, Pietro. But my family, my little boy..." He couldn't go on. His jaw hardened in resolve. He hated to threaten Pietro, but he would do whatever was necessary. "Noon, Pietro," he repeated harshly. "You have this number." He hung up before the frightened man could argue further. Time was running out. He'd been on the damned phone half the night, and a more frustrating and unproductive night had never been spent.

Maggie found him there shortly after five. "Have you had any sleep?" she asked as she stood over him.

"Have you?" he returned, evading her question.

"No. But I do feel better for the rest. Is there anything I can do?"

"I've done everything I can think of. The police are still trying to trace the calls to the radio station. Undercover agents are combing the less savory streets of the city. I can't even get through to most of my regular contacts. They all seem to be terrified. I finally tracked down Pietro, who swears he knows nothing. I put the fear of God into him in the hope he'll find out something for us. He's going to call back at noon tomorrow—today." He raked his rumpled hair for the umpteenth time and squeezed his eyes shut. With a teeth-rattling blow, he brought his fist down on the desk. "It's so damned frustrating!"

Maggie was deeply affected by the grief and defeat that ravaged his face. She wanted him to do all he could to find their son and her father, but Ben had plainly reached his limit. He had to have some rest.

"Oh, Ben," she murmured. She went to him then. Rounding the desk, she held out her arms. She could do it because she was offering comfort this time, not asking for it.

Surprised, Ben swiveled the chair to face her. She stepped between his legs and wrapped her arms around his shoulders, bringing him against her. Reaching for her, he closed his eyes against the exquisite pleasure of being held like this. She smelled fresh and clean, like Maggie. Her breasts were soft and firm under his cheek. Her heartbeat sounded steady in his ear.

Maggie laid her head on his. "I don't expect you to sleep, but you're not going to be any good to anyone if you don't relax for a while. If you'll go upstairs, I'll fix you a hot milk punch and bring it up."

Ben kept his arms around her hips but looked up. Lord, she was so pretty. Her figure blurred. He blinked hard and relented. "Okay."

He was stretched out on the bed a short time later when she brought the punch. He'd kicked off his shoes, and his shirt was unbuttoned. A smile twisted his lips as she set the small tray on the bedside table. "I haven't had a milk punch in years," he said. "Not since..." His sentence trailed off.

Maggie finished the thought. Not since she used to make them for him when he would come in from covering a story, dead tired but unable to relax because he was so keyed up. "Come on. Drink it," she said briskly.

He propped himself up on one elbow and reached for the napkin-wrapped glass. "Um-m-m. That's good," he said as he drained the contents. He licked the milky mustache off his upper lip.

With a sharp pang Maggie remembered the times she'd performed that little chore for him ... and what it had led to. She had to get out of here, she thought as she stretched out a hand for the glass.

Instead of giving it to her, Ben set it on the table and wrapped his long fingers around her wrist. The pressure he used was more persistent than demanding. Slowly, slowly he drew her closer, until her knees touched the side of the mattress. He looked at her as though he wanted to reach into her soul. What she saw in his eyes was so much more than hunger, more than desire. If she responded to that look, she would be lost.

"Ben, don't," she protested, but she rested her knees on the edge of the mattress. She leaned forward, her fingers brushing the white gauze on his chest. "Your bandage is wet."

"Cold shower," he murmured as he covered her hand with his and held it to his chest. "Miserable things, but necessary occasionally."

Maggie felt his answer deep inside her. Her fingers combed through the wiry hair that covered his skin. "Why—?" She had to clear her throat before she could continue. "Why was it necessary?"

His voice lowered an octave, became a husky rasp that sent a shiver through her. "You wanted me to hold you. I couldn't do that, Maggie. But I can make love to you."

Maggie closed her eyes. He hadn't been rejecting her. "I thought you didn't want me."

He tugged even more persistently this time, and she sat on the bed beside his hip. His eyes had darkened to a compelling, glittering jade. "In another life, maybe, just maybe, I won't want you. Never in this one." His fingers combed her hair and caught there.

"Ben, you're injured." But she was relieved when he heeded the message in her eyes rather than the message of her words.

A half smile, so sexy that it stole her breath, curved his lips. "Then be gentle with me," he teased. That induced a husky laugh.

The corners of the room were shadowy, leaving them together in a pool of light from the small bedside lamp. The illuminated space was like a small island in which they were briefly isolated from pain, separate from the world of fear. Maggie had no will to deny either of them the healing power of love.

He lifted her hand from his chest and put a soft kiss in the palm. "I hurt the most here." Holding her gaze, he placed both their hands over his hard arousal and pressed. The growl that issued from his throat was quiet but harsh. "Oh, Maggie, I'm aching."

Maggie's eyelids were heavy; her lips parted on a breath of air. Even through the heavy denim, she was aware of his desire; it became the source of her own pulse, shimmering through her entire body.

His hand left hers, and he reached up to stroke her arm lightly, to undo the buttons of her blouse so smoothly she didn't know it was open until his gaze dropped to her breasts. He frowned at the bra, but his brow cleared when he discovered the front hook. His eyes widened in appreciation. "Your breasts are fuller," he murmured as he tested the weight of one in his hand. "Beautiful. Did you nurse Jamie?"

"Yes," gasped Maggie. "Oh, Ben..."

"I wish I'd been there." He grinned devilishly. "Your breasts always were sensitive. I love to watch them." His fingers traced her hardening nipples.

She was the one who was disoriented now, dizzied by the touch of his big hand as it roamed freely over her. She arched slightly, thrusting her nipple into his palm, begging unconsciously for a firmer touch. He answered her need, squeezing her tender flesh.

His hand abandoned her breasts, reaching suddenly for her nape, pulling her down until their lips were only a heartbeat apart, their eyes locked. "Kiss me," he commanded hoarsely. "Kiss me the way you want to be kissed."

Willingly, fiercely, Maggie covered his lips, her tongue sliding over his in a sensual caress. She shook with the force of her desire. Their mouths came together, broke apart, slanted on each other again.

Ben took gentle bites of her, murmuring passionate words against her lips. When she opened his jeans to caress him, he thought he would explode. It took all his strength to remove her hand. "I want to love you slowly, babe. If you keep doing that, it'll all be over in seconds."

He still reclined on one elbow, with Maggie bending to him. At his words, she whimpered softly in her throat, and Ben provided the last small tug to bring her down beside him.

Now he was leaning over her, his smile hungry and tender. He smoothed the hair from her temples, from her shoulders, until the gleaming mass lay across the pillow. Her eyes were glistening darker than night, shielded partly by the thickness of her lashes; her lips were red and swollen from their kisses. His tongue sought the corner of her mouth, traced her upper lip to the other corner, dipped inside. "Nothing in the world tastes as good as your mouth does," he breathed. "Unless it's your breasts." His tongue followed a delicate vein from her throat to her nipple. The hand that wasn't tangled in her hair slid between her denim-clad thighs to rub lightly there. "Or your..."

Maggie clasped his head between her hands and brought his mouth back up to hers. He refused to abandon his quest, however. Hastily he unsnapped and unzipped her jeans. "Ah, babe, you're so sweet," he whispered.

Her hips writhed beneath his touch. "Yes, Ben, yes. Please."

He pushed the jeans off her hips. She toed off one sneaker, then the other. They hit the floor, to be followed by the jeans, then her shirt and bra.

Ben disposed of his own clothes even more quickly. "Let me," he said huskily when she began to slide her panties over her hips. He knelt, straddling her thighs. His eyes took in every inch of her body as he slowly drew the bit of silk down her legs. His hands retraced their path, cradling her hips, lifting her to meet his hungry mouth. His tongue dipped into her femininity.

Maggie reached for her sanity, but held on only briefly under his tender assault. "Ben, no, please," she cried, her head rolling on the pillow, her nails digging into his shoulders. "I want you inside me."

"I will be, darling. I promise," he said against her skin. His teeth nipped. His tongue soothed. "But tonight . . . I want you every way there is."

Maggie felt the tension within her build, grow, soar, until it burst in a star-bright release. She bit down hard on her lip to stop the scream of completion that welled up in her throat. Her body shook with the spasms coursing through her.

And then he filled her . . . to the limits of her soul. He filled her and moved. Slowly at first, with deep rhythmic thrusts, he moved. Gradually the tempo increased until he was driving into her with deep, penetrating surges. Maggie cried out from the sheer excitement of the onslaught. His mouth captured her cries. What she had thought was fulfillment was only a prelude to the crescendo that shook them simultaneously, leaving them gasping, their damp bodies suddenly limp.

Ben had just enough remaining energy to pull the sheet over them.

She must have slept, but it seemed only moments before she felt his hand stroking the planes of her face. She opened her eyes to smile tenderly at him. "Did I sleep long?"

"Not very long," he answered. "I watched you." He was smiling, and there was a soft amused expression in his eyes.

She smiled, too, unsteadily. "That must have been greatly entertaining."

He chuckled. "I love to look at you like this. When you're around other people, you present such a proper picture. But when I look at you, I remember the way you go wild in my arms." He reached to cup her breast firmly in his palm. "Go wild for me again."

Later they both slept, but Maggie was awake when Ben carefully eased his arm from underneath her shoulders and got out of bed. She felt, rather than heard, his soundless grunt of pain. He pulled on his clothes in the near-darkness and leaned over to kiss her with lips that were warm and hungry.

She steeled herself not to respond to the kiss, to keep her breathing to a regular tempo. If she let him know she was awake, he would turn on the light. She was too vulnerable after spending the past hour in his arms. He would be sure to see all the stored-up love in her eyes.

He sighed against her temple and strode to the door.

* * *

Ben watched as Maggie raised the cup to her lips to sip her second cup of coffee. They were in the kitchen, which was deserted at the moment, lingering over the remnants of breakfast. James had been horrified when they'd insisted on eating there, but Annette had seemed pleased.

Maggie had on the same skirt and pink blouse she'd worn the day he took her shopping, and looked just as young. But her features were pinched and white. Her long fingers trembled as they grasped the cup. She avoided meeting his eyes.

Ben pushed his plate away, crossed his arms on the table in front of him and looked at her. "Okay, let's have it."

"I don't know what you're talking about." *Smart, Maggie,* she said to herself. *When in doubt, resort to clichés.*

He put a warm hand over hers. "Maggie, we made love. Is there anything wrong with that?"

She looked down at his hand, and his arm, dusted with dark hair. He'd pushed up the sleeves of the white cotton turtleneck that was tucked snugly into his jeans. "There is when Jamie...when Daddy..." Her throat closed on the end of the sentence.

His fingers tightened. "Look at me," he demanded. When she complied, he went on in a gentler tone. "Do you feel guilty about making love with me?"

Inexplicably her temper flared. "Why don't you quit calling it that?" she challenged. "We had sex."

Before he dropped his eyes, she saw the sudden shock in them. But when they looked at her again, he had his emotions under tight rein. Nothing in his expression revealed that her careless words had hurt, and she wondered if she'd imagined it.

Maggie's own torment was more obvious. She was unable to hide it. She placed both fists on the table, squeezing until her nails dug into the flesh of her palms. Her features twisted with the turmoil going on inside her. "Yes, I do feel guilty. But I feel guilty about sleeping, too. And eating and breathing and walking and . . ."

Ben felt a hard knot form in his stomach as he watched her growing distress. His chair scraped across the floor. He reached out to pluck her from her chair and onto his lap. His arms were a tight band around her shaking body. He buried his face in the curve of her neck. "So do I, love. Oh, God, so do I."

Clasped tightly in his arms, she was soothed. Her shaking gradually stopped. She stroked his hair, her fingers gently tangling its dark thickness. "Ben, I'm sorry. That was a rotten thing to say. I don't seem to have any control over myself."

Ben slid his hand into her hair, pulling her head fiercely against his chest. "I know you didn't mean it, babe."

Lola's high heels sounded on the hardwood floor, announcing her presence. Maggie slid off Ben's lap and back onto her chair before the secretary, dressed in a smart gray suit, entered the room. "Has there been any news?" she asked as she poured herself a cup of coffee from the urn.

News. Yes, Ben had been shot. They'd been chased through the back alleys of Rome. Someone else's blood had been on her hand . . . When she opened her mouth to answer, Ben glared at her. "No, nothing since the call," she said.

"I'm so sorry," said the younger woman. She approached the table but didn't sit down. "I was hoping—well, just hoping.'' She reached down to squeeze Maggie's hand.

"Thanks, Lola," said Maggie, returning the squeeze. Ben had become very still beside her. She could almost feel the rigidity in his body.

"I've been requisitioned downstairs. See you later." Lola left on a cloud of perfume.

"You've thought of something," Maggie said as soon the other woman had gone.

"It probably doesn't mean anything," he said guardedly.

She sighed. "Not Lola again?"

"Why not? She's really got you snowed, hasn't she. All those tears, that sad puppy look. The woman's trying to ingratiate herself with you."

"Nonsense, she's . . . anxious! And young."

Ben sighed. "Maggie, have you ever seen some of the pictures that come out of the terrorist training camps? I guarantee that age doesn't have a thing to do with fanaticism." Filled with a surge of energy, Ben got to his feet and began to pace. "Lola is your father's appointment secretary. She is the one person who always knows his whereabouts." He spun on his heels and faced her again, his hands sliding into the pockets of his jeans. "She also gave me the message to call my contact yesterday, and we were almost killed."

"She didn't know where we were meeting him. You didn't even know yourself until we made the call." Maggie simply couldn't believe his speculations.

"We discussed the thing to death, Maggie. You and I talked about it while we were eating dinner. Besides, the envelope wasn't sealed securely," Ben said, disgusted at himself for his carelessness. He should have known better. He'd been worried about Marston discovering their plans, but he hadn't been overly circumspect about anyone else who might have been listening.

Maggie crossed her arms over her chest. "I still don't believe she's that good an actress." She lowered her voice. "She reminds me of myself."

Slowly he withdrew his hands from his pockets. "Of you?" he asked disbelievingly. "What do you mean? She's nothing like you."

She avoided looking at him. "Not like me as I am, but as I used to be."

"That's crazy."

"Crazy? Is it? The tears, the agitation, the moodiness. I think she's just like me," she said stubbornly.

Ben came down on one knee beside her. Taking her hand, he tried to hide his amusement. "Honey, you were never that much of a weeping willow, believe me."

Maggie let her eyes return to him then. She smiled a small smile and touched his face. "I think you either have the worst memory in the world, or you're only remembering the good times."

"And which do you remember, the good or the bad?" he asked quietly.

She didn't even have to consider. "I'm afraid I'm as guilty as you are, wanting to recall the good times. But I make myself think about the bad ones, too. As you said, history repeats itself if you forget it."

His eyes were steady on hers as he rose. "Not anymore," he said decisively. "We're two different people. And from here on in we begin fresh. Okay?"

To hide the gleam of expectation that she knew was in her eyes, Maggie picked up her cup again. "Okay."

"Now, back to Lola...."

"Ben, I think you're wrong. She's been so *concerned*. She's scared to death of Marston. She's fond of Jamie, and she worships Daddy."

"Our time is short, Maggie. Tonight at midnight." Ben paced a few more steps, stopping behind Maggie's chair. "There's a way to find out," he said quietly, but his excitement was beginning to build.

She twisted around to ask, "How?"

"I can follow her when she leaves work. I can see where she goes, if she contacts anyone."

"I don't like it," Maggie said flatly. "You've already been shot, Ben. You'd be taking a chance."

"But if you're right, if she is innocent, there's nothing to fear, is there?" he inquired smoothly as he headed toward the door.

Maggie put down the cup and got to her feet. "That's what you said yesterday."

He scowled over his shoulder at her. "I'm going downstairs."

She hurried after him. "All right, we'll both follow her."

"Not this time." He entered the stairwell leading to the basement. "It's for your own good."

"Oh, Ben, that's the oldest one in the books," she said disgustedly. "If you think I'll accept that for a reason, you'd better think again."

"Because I said so?" he offered, smiling to himself.

Maggie was right on his heels. "That reason's even worse. You're not going alone. I'll go after you," she threatened.

Ben stopped, and Maggie plowed into his back. She grabbed for something to regain her balance at the same time that he turned to catch her around the waist. The action put their eyes on a level, and their mouths. He pulled her against him and gave her a hard kiss; then he grinned. "No, you won't. I'm going to tell Marston how you got out last night."

It took Maggie a minute to remember what they were squabbling about. Then she rested her forehead against his. "Oh, Ben, don't do that," she begged softly.

Suddenly the light of excitement glittered in his eyes. She was familiar enough with the look to know what he was thinking. He grasped her shoulders. "I have a feeling about this, Maggie," he said earnestly. "My intuition tells me that something's about to happen."

Maggie knew enough to trust Ben's instincts. Eight years ago she'd hated them, resented them but never doubted that they were genuine. Those elusive, intangible feelings made him one of the best reporters in the world. He'd once told her that they'd never failed him. "Okay."

His brows lifted in surprise. "Okay?" He'd expected more of an argument.

She shook her head indulgently. "I'm not totally unreasonable, Ben. Besides, I trust your intuition."

"And you'll stay here?"

"If you'll take Marston with you."

His brows lowered again, but in contemplation instead of the irritation she'd expected. "I might just do that," he said.

Pietro didn't call at noon. Ben went to his home, as he'd threatened. He'd never been there before, but he knew the location of the apartment where the young man lived with his wife and two children. It was empty, not one stick of furniture in the whole place.

He wandered through the rooms, his footsteps ringing hollowly. He dreaded having to return to the mansion to report another dead end to Maggie.

In a dusty corner of one room, apparently over-
looked by the occupants in their haste, Ben found a worn
stuffed bear. He picked it up. Jamie had had one very
much like this. He almost choked on the thought.

He fought his tears, fought them furiously, afraid that
if they began today they would never stop. Finally, as he
stood there motionlessly, staring down at the brown
bear, they overflowed, wetting his cheeks.

Maggie didn't react the way he'd expected her to at the
news that Pietro had disappeared. She simply nodded as
though she'd known.

The TAC leader called again at four, his strange harsh
accent coming over the radio wires like the voice of Sa-
tan.

Maggie and Ben stood arm in arm in front of the map
in the basement, listening with the others to the broadcast. "Tonight at midnight one of them dies."

The Italian negotiator replied calmly, trying to reason with the man, trying to keep him on the line long
enough for the call to be traced. But, just as before, the
connection was broken.

A man with headphones signaled to Alberto. "We
have it narrowed down to this twenty-one-square-block
area," the chief explained to Maggie and Ben a few
minutes later, pointing to a spot on the map. "We have
every available man in the area, searching. Roadblocks
have been set up. If they would only call one more
time..."

At seven o'clock Maggie stood in the front hall. Lola
was about to leave. No one in the residence was keeping
regular office hours. The young woman checked her
purse to make sure she had change for carfare and set off
down the drive, waving goodbye.

Maggie returned the wave.

As soon as she saw Lola disappear through the gates, she signaled to Ben and Marston, who had been waiting in the study. Marston passed her without a word. A grim-faced Ben would have done the same, but Maggie caught his hand. "Please be careful."

His mouth tilted slightly. "I will, princess." He pulled her against him, brushed her lips with his. "And you stay put." He made a decision, perhaps a rash one, but as necessary to him as breathing right now. "I love you, Margaret Anne. I love you very much."

Maggie's head flew up. She opened her mouth to speak, but no words came out.

Ben smiled sadly at her attempt. "A shock, huh? Don't worry about it, honey. We'll talk later. But if you say it's just sex, I'll throttle you." His mouth came down in another kiss, this one very different from the first. This one was hard and possessive and left Maggie feeling warm to her toes. Then he was running down the steps after Marston.

Only after Ben had driven away in the sleek black Ferrari was she able to comprehend the significance of what he'd said. He loved her...again...or still. A small smile curved her lips, and she got her voice back. "You picked a hell of a time to tell me, Ben Altman," she said out loud.

She wandered back down to the basement. Nothing was happening there. The study was too empty, likewise the bedroom. There was no place to go where her thoughts didn't follow, so she simply wandered from room to room, waiting, wondering what was happening...for an hour, two hours. It was as though death had already entered the mansion.

By nine-thirty her nerves were tight and screaming; when the telephone rang in the study, she cried aloud. "Get hold of yourself," she commanded as she reached for the receiver.

"*Signora*, this is Dante."

"Dante!" she cried in disbelief. "Oh, God, Dante! Where are you?"

"*Signora*, I am very frightened. I've managed to escape from the kidnappers, but I'm afraid to come back to the residence. They will be looking for me. I am going to hide in the country."

The man sounded as though he was about to fall apart. Maggie strove for control. She had to calm him down, to reassure him. "Dante, of course you're frightened. How did you manage to get away?" When he didn't answer she went on, "It doesn't matter. But, Dante, you've got to help us. Where are they holding my father and Jamie?"

"I—I'm not sure, *signora*. I don't trust this telephone. A person who works at the residence is involved. They could listen. I could maybe show you, but . . ." There was a gasp and a muffled exclamation from the other end of the line.

Maggie's palm was suddenly wet. The receiver slipped slightly. She tightened her grip. "Dante? Are you still there?"

"Someone is approaching. I must go. Do you remember the young one's favorite site?"

Maggie didn't even have to think twice. Jamie's favorite place in all of Rome was the largest of the ancient monuments, the Colosseum. "Yes, I . . ."

"Come there now. Alone."

The phone was dead in her hand before she could say another word. She stared at it as her mind raced over the conversation. Dante didn't trust the line. He'd said that someone in the embassy *was* involved. Could Ben have been right? Was it Lola? She'd promised Ben she would stay put, but if there was a chance of saving her father and Jamie, could she live with herself if she didn't take it?

She had been too suspicious another time and ended up feeling like a paranoid idiot when the nice man in the three-piece suit had returned her red scarf. This was Dante, for heaven's sake. Her father's bodyguard.

Maggie thought about changing out of her cotton skirt and blouse to more practical jeans but dismissed the idea. She didn't hesitate another second. She had to go to Dante immediately, to learn what he knew. She'd call Ben when she had the information.

Her purse was on the desk. She grabbed some money for a taxi and left it there. At the door of the study she paused. Should she tell someone she was leaving? The only one she trusted at this point was Ben.

She recrossed to the desk and scribbled a note on the pad, then let herself out the terrace door.

Chapter 10

Ben observed his growing impatience reflected in Marston's scowling countenance. They had followed Lola to the area near Monte Mario known as Medaglie d'Oro. She had entered a neighborhood café, and when the maître d' had shown her to a table near the door, she'd shaken her head, indicating a preference for one near the back.

Marston had grinned at Ben knowingly. "I think this is it." Surely this was a rendezvous of some kind. All they had to do was wait for her contact to arrive. They had felt more and more foolish as she proceeded to eat a leisurely and solitary dinner. At nine-thirty she had risen, paid her bill and left, passing within a few feet of where they stood. She merged easily into the crowd.

They followed for another two blocks, until the streets narrowed, and the crowd began to thin out. They had to drop back to avoid being spotted.

"She's almost home," muttered Marston disgustedly.

Suddenly, from out of the shadows, a figure approached her, a man. Lola appeared to be alarmed. She sidestepped, but the man grasped her arm. It was too dark for Ben to identify the stranger, but the man didn't seem to threaten Lola or want her to accompany him. He simply held her elbow and talked, his determination indicated by his posture. Ben and Marston were running toward the two people.

The man released Lola and strode away to melt once again into the shadows. As he turned to glance over his shoulder, Ben got a glimpse of his face. "Pietro!" he shouted. What the hell was going on here?

"I'll get him; you take the girl!" cried Marston, signaling to a car that had been following them. Three men jumped out and set off at a dead run after Pietro and Marston.

The people on the street around them eyed the man warily. In a few more strides Ben caught up with Lola. "Okay, *signorina*, suppose you tell me what you and our mutual friend had to discuss."

"He's not my friend, Mr. Altman. I swear. I don't even know the man's name."

The fear in her eyes seemed real enough, but Ben wasn't in the mood to take her at her word. "Spill it, Lola," he snarled.

Tears fell prettily on her cheeks. He ignored them. She groped for a handkerchief. "He—he said to give you a message."

"A message?"

She nodded. "He said to tell you that his employer died from his wounds. He wants revenge for his employer's death."

So it *had been* the importer's blood on the steps. "That isn't all he said, is it?" Pietro wouldn't have taken a chance like this to tell him he wanted revenge. "Did he say why he didn't call me?"

Lola sniffed into the handkerchief and nodded. "He says he was trying to get information, and you should check out Eibo's in the warehouse district."

"Ah, hell!" The district was dark and cluttered and dangerous. Half the unsavory things that went on in Rome went on in the warehouse district. He stopped. And the twenty-one-block area that the call had been traced to included the warehouse district.

"You have a few hours. His people will go in and bomb the entire district if they have to. And Dante—Dante's involved."

Dante! The "too clean" man. Marston had said no one was that clean. Ben damned himself for not pushing for more information on Dante. "What else did he say?"

"Nothing. I swear!" She gripped his shirt in alarm. "Oh, yes, one last thing. He said to tell you he'd moved from his house."

That was no news.

Marston loped around the corner, breathing like a marathon runner. "We lost him," he wheezed. "The bastard had a motorcycle around the corner."

"I don't think it matters," Ben answered thoughtfully. He fixed Marston with a heavy look. "That was my contact, with a message."

"Really?" said Marston.

Ben's first impulse was to drive straight to the warehouse district and tear the place apart, brick by brick, until he found his son. He put a tight leash on his urge. This would take careful planning and a lot of help from all the agencies involved. The situation was getting uglier and more dangerous by the minute. And their time was running out.

His jaw was stone as he turned to the young woman. "Lola, would you do me a favor? Would you go back to the embassy...?"

"I am arrested?" she asked fearfully, looking up into his intransigent features as though he would be the one to arrest her.

"No, no," he reassured her. "We—I just have a feeling that Maggie might need someone with her tonight."

Lola's eyes softened. "Of course, I will be glad to go. I would not want her to be alone."

Maggie had been wrong about Dante, but right all along about Lola. She was a frightened young woman. When he had time, he would feel badly for having misjudged her. When he had time. "Thanks." He squeezed her elbow.

Marston was uncharacteristically silent on the walk back to the car. But when they had put Lola into the back seat of the other agents' car, he caught Ben's arm and steered him aside. "When do you plan to let me in on the story, hero?"

At the sarcasm in the epithet, something in Ben snapped. His anger erupted violently. He jerked his arm free to whirl on the man. "When we get to the residence!" he snarled. "You need help, don't you? Or do you think you can do this on your own? You son of a bitch, do you want the responsibility for the lives of both the ambassador *and* my son? The U.S. government might not have your hide, but I sure as hell will!" He circled the hood of the Ferrari and got in; the car was started and in gear before Marston recovered from his shock. He grabbed for the door handle and heaved himself in as the tires spun, spitting gravel and dust.

Both cars roared through the gates and came to a screeching halt in the drive. "I'll meet you in the basement in two minutes," Ben bit out to Marston as they entered the residence. "Follow me, Lola." He took the stairs two at a time, calling for Maggie.

Her room was empty.

So was his.

Lola was halfway up the stairs when he started down. "She must be in the study," he said as he passed her.

But she wasn't. Ben felt the cold hand of dread clench his heart. The kitchen. He sprinted down the hall.

No one. God! What had happened? She couldn't have gotten out without being seen. His mind denied the fact that she certainly could. He refused to believe it.

He burst through the door leading downstairs. "She's gone!" he shouted.

More than fifty men turned as one to see the ghost-white face of the distraught reporter, agony etched on his features.

"Gone?" said someone.

"Yes, damn it! Gone!" His voice was slurred with emotion. He spun around again and then came to a dead halt; he raked a hand through his hair. He didn't know where to go. The thought brought tears to his eyes. *Where shall I go? Where shall I look?* he cried silently, like a lost child. *Maggie. Maggie. Damn it, how could you do this to me?*

"Pull yourself together," said Marston from behind him.

He spun on the agent, ready to do damage, but Marston went on in the matter-of-fact voice that was just what Ben needed to regain his control. "She's a smart lady. She wouldn't just disappear."

"Then where the hell is she?" he demanded, but in a more reasonable tone.

"Maybe she left a note."

Ben looked at him as though he would have liked to wring his neck for being first with the idea. He headed for the study where they had spent so many hours together.

And there it was. Right next to her purse. He grabbed the white sheet off the desk, looked first for her signature, scrawled hastily at the bottom, then at the body of the note.

But his eyes refused to comprehend what he was reading. He shut his eyes, shook his head. Then tried again.

His son, his friend and now his wife. His arm fell lifelessly to his side. The paper fluttered toward the floor, to be retrieved by Marston before it settled.

Ben—Dante has managed to escape! I'm meeting him to find out where they are holding Jamie and Dad. I'll call you—Maggie.

"Dear God," Marston breathed. He wasted no more time on self-recrimination than the second it took to utter the words. "Come on, Altman."

Ben looked at the man blankly.

Marston's face grew hard. His fist shot out to grab Ben by the shirtfront. He shook him. "Snap out of it, man! We've got work to do." He left the room, not waiting to see if Ben would follow.

Suddenly energy surged back into Ben's body. He'd get them back, he swore. He'd get them all back. And then he would never let them go again.

The debris of centuries-old stones crunched under Maggie's feet. The night whispered in her ears with the voices of those long dead, drowning out even the sound of the sparse traffic on the boulevard that curved around the huge edifice as though to contain its barbarity with what man called progress. But Maggie walked away from the boulevard, away from the lights, away from the trappings of civilization into the darkness.

The taxi had let her out at the foot of the drive leading to the hillside remains of a temple overlooking the Colosseum. Nervously she glanced up at the columns, trying to keep her mind on trivial ideas instead of the fears that threatened her control. She wondered if Jamie had ever been here.

The gigantic monument with its ghostly memories of the past was overwhelming in the daylight, but at night it loomed twice as big, twice as threatening. Her feet lagged. She took a short breath and let it out. Deliberately she increased her pace. Silly to be afraid. Dante had been with her father ever since he'd been assigned to Rome. He was trustworthy.

However... Ben's contact had said someone attached to the embassy was involved.

No. The embassy did not necessarily mean the residence; the chancery had hundreds of employees. She herself didn't know the man well, but she was sure Dante was loyal. When his wife had died, leaving him with a young son, her father had been the first one at his home, offering condolences, arranging and paying for the funeral, taking the mundane burdens off the chauffeur's shoulders, which were already burdened heavily enough with grief. That was—what?—nine years ago? It had happened shortly after her father had been assigned to Rome. She and Ben had still been together, and Jamie hadn't even been thought of.

"Dante took me to the Appian Way, Mom. Granpa was busy, and Dad was out on a story, so Dante took me to get ice cream at the Piazza Navona...to St. Peter's...to the movies." Dante wouldn't hurt Jamie.

She reached the outer perimeter of the arena. Her footsteps now whispered like hollow sighs on the stone. The arches cast deep shadows, with short patches of light between. She hurried from one patch to the next, circling, ever circling away from the traffic, away from the presence of other human beings. She kept walking slowly, so that Dante could see that she was alone. So that she could get his precious information before he left town.

The area seemed so completely deserted. Had he changed his mind? Had he decided to run anyway? Had he thought it was too dangerous to meet her, after all? Had he been followed? Was he even now...? She swallowed and stopped for a breath, closing her eyes. When she opened them again, she searched the ground at her feet through a blur of tears, half expecting to see Dante's bloody body.

When her vision began to clear, her eyes were shocked by a pair of dark, highly polished shoes. *How strange, that shine,* she thought incongruously. *It's so dusty around here.*

Her gaze climbed to the man's face. "Dante!" she cried gladly. She ran forward to hug him, her relief overwhelming, but he remained stiff in the circle of her arms. *I've embarrassed the poor man,* she thought fleetingly. "Dante, I'm so happy that you are safe." Her hands, still on his arms, squeezed lightly; she forced herself to smile and take a step back. "Where are Jamie and my father?"

"Signora..." His expression was ... expressionless.

"They're dead."

Maggie didn't realize she'd spoken the terrifying fear aloud until Dante answered. "No, *signora*, they are not dead, not yet."

She shook her head in confusion. "I don't understand. How did you get away? Couldn't you have gotten Daddy and Jamie out, too?"

"It was not as difficult for me," he said guardedly. He stood perfectly still. Only his eyes spoke: of remorse, of regret and pain. And of culpability.

Her body denied what she read in his gaze. She took a step back, away from the unspeakable thing, back until she was brought up against a wall. She sagged against the stone behind her.

Dante looked the picture of guilt. Or was she misreading his expression? She dragged her fingers through her hair. "I don't understand," she said again.

"Signora, I did not know the young boy would be with us. Believe me, I did not know."

She stood erect, stepping once more into the pool of light. "Dante." Her whisper was disbelieving. "You aren't a part of this? Are you?"

But she'd lost Dante's attention. The light poured in over her shoulder to illuminate his shocked face. She watched him stiffen, watched his skin turn the color of the marble behind him as he stared beyond her. She should turn her head, she should look into the face of her enemy, but she couldn't. Her gaze fell to her own shadow at her feet.

Two other shadows moved silently out of the night to stand guard over her.

"I didn't mean this, *signora*," said Dante.

"No, he did not," spoke a voice in heavily accented English. "He tried to double-cross us, and now he is in the same position as any other hostage."

Dante's chin came up. "We should have left the child," he said, his voice full of conviction. "I never agreed to taking him."

"You are a sentimentalist," spat the other man. "We have no room for such emotion in our cause. You will be killed along with the Yankee pigs."

Maggie raised her head to examine her captors. They could have been taken from a poster describing what the typical terrorist should look like. They wore camouflage fatigues and laced boots, with caps pulled low on the brow, their feet were slightly apart, their jaws unyielding. Her eyes traveled slowly from one man to the other. Each held a small but lethal-looking machine gun.

Fear settled in Maggie's knees, touching off a trembling that threatened her ability to stand. She clamped her lips between her teeth, biting back a bark of hysterical laughter. She couldn't fall apart now.

She tilted her chin and looked back at Dante. His countenance said it all. He was responsible. He might regret it now because he'd been caught, but he was responsible.

Suddenly she remembered what she should have remembered days ago. Dante's wife had not died of natural causes; she'd been killed—an innocent bystander killed by the Italian police in a raid on the headquarters of a group of terrorists. The hostage they had rescued was an American military officer.

The hatred must have been brewing in him for all these years, hatred and a desire for revenge.

"You lured me here deliberately, didn't you?" she accused.

"No," he said sadly. "I didn't know they were following me. I wanted—I thought I could help you to get Jamie away from them. I never meant for the boy to be a victim."

She believed him. But a sour taste rose in her throat. "Just my father."

"A life for a life," Dante proclaimed. She wanted to fly at him in her rage; she wanted to scratch his eyes out. But she didn't. She simply glared at him. It seemed to make him uncomfortable, and that pleased the devil out of her.

"As you say, *signora*." The man to her left spoke again. He had a black patch over one eye. "Just the criminal representative of an evil power." He shrugged. "Too bad. But now we have a bonus in you. Maybe now the officials will listen to our demands. I am sure our compatriots will agree that there is something rather romantic in having three generations of prisoners. Shall we go?"

"Go?"

"Yes, *signora*. Now. After Dante." The wrong end of the machine gun nudged her painfully in the back. She thought about running, but the man behind her was showing signs of nervousness. She would be dead before she could take a dozen steps.

"Is Lola Orenda a part of this?" she asked suddenly.

Dante looked back over his shoulder, genuinely surprised. "Lola? The secretary? No. One of the downstairs maids is a member of TAC. She was the one who let us know about your meeting with the importer."

Maggie groaned. If Lola had been involved, Ben might might have learned something from her. But she wasn't, and he wouldn't. Maggie's feelings of isolation and desolation had never seemed so intense.

"Silence!" said "Eye Patch."

Chapter 11

They weren't even going to let her see them.

Maggie had pleaded for permission to see her father and son. She had used threats, which the terrorists had laughed off, and tears, which only annoyed them.

"Tie her up," said the man who was in charge, the man whose voice was so familiar from the radio broadcasts, the one with the slightly Slavic accent. "And gag her."

Oh, dear God, no. So much for the State Department's indoctrination. Rationally she knew she should cause as little trouble as possible, but emotionally her responses had been as predicable as those of any unwary victim.

The man with the patch over one eye approached. She looked at the rope he held in one hand and the filthy rag he had in the other. If he put that nasty piece of cloth in her mouth, she would suffocate without a doubt.

She whirled on the leader. "Please, I won't say a word. Please, don't gag me."

"If I hear a squeak out of you . . ."

"You won't, I promise."

He nodded. "Tie her up and get her out of here."

Eye Patch looked disappointed. He trussed her hands and ankles, then half lifted, half dragged her to a door in the back wall. She had only a quick glimpse of a storeroom of some sort before he shoved her toward a corner and slammed the door, plunging her prison into total darkness. Her forward motion and bound ankles sent her sprawling. Her cheek scraped the rough floor, and her head made contact with the wall, dazing her. For several minutes she allowed herself to rest where she had fallen.

She would not be defeated, not as long as there was breath in her body. Tears came and she let them flow. She was alive, and so were Jamie and her father. As long as there was life there was hope. Gradually she calmed; her senses settled. She had to think.

Levering herself to a sitting position, she rested her back against the wall and listened. A heated argument was going on outside the door.

The rapid Italian exchange sent her heart diving to her toes. They were arguing over which of the captives to murder first.

While she listened, she began to work frantically on the ropes that bound her. She recognized two voices. Eye Patch, who apparently was second in command, could be heard above the general babble.

"I am tired of the runaround we are getting from those fools who call themselves negotiators. The time has come to show the Yankees that ours are not empty threats."

The second voice was that of the leader. "We gave them until midnight."

"What difference can an hour and a half make? I say we do it now."

"We wait," said the leader. He seemed the more compassionate of the two, but how long could he hold out against the mutiny that Maggie sensed was forming?

Maggie heard a woman's voice—the downstairs maid Dante had mentioned? "Are they men of their word, Anval?" The woman's tone dripped sarcasm. "Do you think they are even now acceding to our demands? Maybe our friends are walking out of prison, free men, at this very moment."

The Leader—Anval?—answered decisively. "We will wait."

There were several muttered responses; Maggie couldn't understand the words when they all spoke at once, but the volume seemed to grow to a dangerous level.

Then she heard Dante's name and guessed that they must have turned their attention to their former compatriot. There was the sound of a slap followed by several thuds. They were beating him. Oh, God!

"That will teach you to betray us," someone said.

Maggie slumped against the wall. She could only pray that Ben would somehow find them.

Meanwhile she continued to struggle against her bonds. The ropes cut into her wrists and ankles, but she welcomed the pain. It helped to keep her abysmal fear at bay.

Suddenly the door to the storeroom was thrust open. The light stung her eyes, and she blinked at the man who stood over her. It was the leader, Anval.

"We have brought you some company." He laughed unpleasantly. "I don't know how much companionship he will provide, however." Two men dragged Dante's limp body into the room and dumped him unceremoniously on the floor. The three of them left.

"Dante?" said Maggie.

There was no answer. Was he dead? A shudder ripped through her body. She strained to hear the sound of his breathing, but beyond the door, chairs were scraping across the floor, as though in preparation for action of some kind.

She closed her eyes and went to work on her bonds again.

The police van came to a halt a block away from the Eibo warehouse. Marston, Ben and Chief Alberto huddled together in the small space in the back that wasn't given over to communications equipment.

"We had men in the area. Two of them are already in place on the rooftop of the adjoining building. They're watching the loading dock," said Alberto as he spun the dials on a short-wave radio. A crackle of static followed. Finally he gave the dial a twist that brought in a man's voice, loud and clear.

"Give me a report," commanded Alberto, speaking in English for the benefit of the international team.

"There are lights on the ground floor, shadows moving behind the loading door. Half of the top floor seems to be taken up by offices. There is movement in one of the rooms upstairs, but it's difficult to distinguish figures. We need a high powered telescope and a sound pistol," the man replied, asking for the latest equipment. Ben had seen a demonstration of the gun-shaped device that could pick up a whisper at a thousand feet.

"Everything we'll need is on its way. Along with the commando team. Any other movement?"

"You mean the woman? No. But they might have returned with her before we arrived. I would guess that the prisoners are upstairs, with maybe a guard or two. They'd want them out of the way."

Alberto half stood to look through the small rear window of the van. "Here are our experts now. Your telescope's on the way." He replaced the microphone and opened the back door. All three of them climbed out.

Ben thought he would explode with impatience as the professionals discussed the situation to death. He realized the necessity of fine-tuning the rescue plan, but he was almost frantic at the lack of action. He lit one cigarette from the butt of another.

The telescope had been in place for fifteen minutes, and the man on the rooftop had reported that a man and a child were alone in the second-floor room. Where the hell was Maggie? Why wouldn't they put her in with the others if they'd brought her back here?

Ben ground his cigarette out beneath the heel of his shoe. "Alberto."

The chief of police glanced over his shoulder. Something in Ben's eyes must have alerted his friend to his state of mind, because he moved immediately to Ben's side.

Marston noticed the exchange and joined them. "What's up?" he asked.

"I am going in . . . quietly and alone, but I'm going."

"No, Ben," said Alberto.

"Alberto, let me ask you something. Why are you hesitating? Why didn't you send your men in fifteen minutes ago?"

"There are some logistical problems to be worked out," said Alberto.

"You're hesitating because when your men storm the warehouse, someone is going to be killed. One person, going in alone, might be able to get the hostages out before that happens."

Marston interrupted. "Listen to me, you fool. You're not going to screw up this operation by playing hero."

"I'm not playing," said Ben in a voice of steel. "The three most important people in the world to me are in that warehouse. If there's a chance in a million I can get one of them out safely, I'm going to take it."

Alberto looked thoughtful. "One man might be able to accomplish what a team of men could not," he said to Marston.

"Then I'll go," said the agent. "It's my job."

"And it's my family," declared Ben. "Butt out."

"Alberto has jurisdiction here," Marston reminded him.

Both men turned to the chief of police. He studied Ben for a long minute, then turned to do the same to Marston.

"You know me, Alberto," said Ben. "I've been in tight scrapes before. God, man, I'm begging! Don't send your men in there until I have a chance to try!"

"Ben, I wish I could give you permission to try. I cannot." But his eyes glittered with something else: consent.

Ben felt relief, overwhelming relief, flow through him. His lips twisted in a parody of a smile, and he nodded almost imperceptibly to let Alberto know that his message had been received.

Marston was silent, but there was no doubt he knew exactly what was going on and that he would do everything in his power to prevent it. Ben prepared himself to fight him, if necessary.

Alberto turned to a man behind him, a man obviously outfitted for commando action, and included Ben in his order. "Come and study the plans we've obtained of the building."

A man stuck his head out of the back of the van. "Signore Marston, the president is standing by to talk to you."

Marston stepped inside the van. Seconds later, taking advantage of the agent's absence, Ben disappeared down the alley toward his objective.

When Marston emerged from the van, he found the chief alone. "Why the hell did you let him go, Alberto? He's going to get himself killed."

Alberto spared him only a glance. "Because Ben was right: only one man was needed."

"But to send a civilian . . ."

"He was going, anyway. It would have taken more men than you or I have to prevent him. If my loved ones were in that warehouse, I would have felt the same."

Damned Italian macho mentality, thought Marston. But in a way, he understood.

Alberto turned back. The American agent would never understand, he reminded himself sadly. He tried one more time to make it clear. "I would have had to arrest Ben Altman to keep him out of that building."

That wouldn't have been a bad idea. The agent stalked away. But he stalked in the same direction Ben had taken.

Ben found the small window on the landing of the stairs. Alberto had agreed that the window offered the most auspicious entry to the warehouse. For one thing, the stairway was unlit, and Ben needed the cover of darkness. For another, it was around the corner from the loading-dock door, where, at random intervals, the police had spotted an armed man stepping out to look over the street.

The latch was rusty from disuse and wouldn't open soundlessly. If there happened to be another guard on the stairs, his attempt at rescue would be over before it had begun. He turned the knob slowly and carefully holding his breath at the grating of metal against metal. Sweat was pouring off him by the time he had it open.

Levering himself up, he threw a leg over the sill. He sat for a moment, listening to the audible sounds of an argument going on in a room below.

"The woman is the least important."

"I say we kill the old man first. Americans are sentimental about women and children."

"Whatever we are going to do, let us do it now! I, for one, am tired of waiting."

The muscle in Ben's jaw jerked, then clenched. The sound of the argument masked any noise he might have made as he ran lightly up the steps. Judging from the comments and responses he'd heard, there were eight to ten people in the area below who were ready for action. So was he.

He flattened himself against the wall of the staircase and peered carefully around the corner. In front of him was a hallway that stretched the width of the warehouse. The wall to the left was punctuated with doors. To his right the wall was solid, with what looked like a matching stairwell at the opposite end, maybe sixty feet away. All this he observed in the blink of an eyelash, because he also saw the burly figure of a guard grinding a cigarette beneath his heel.

If the man hadn't been watching the floor, he would have spied Ben immediately. The guard resumed his pacing, steadily approaching the spot where Ben waited. Every booted tread was like a death knell for Ben's chances. He looked down the stairwell. It was perfectly straight, no turns, no place to hide.

Ben scowled, his mind racing, coming up with ideas, then discarding them. The only weapon Ben had was surprise. And his greatest fear was noise. All it would take was one shout from the man, and the whole crew would be up here. He'd have to go for the throat. He crouched as the heavy steps drew nearer.

Surprise proved to be enough. Ben sprang forward the instant he saw the toe of a boot. The heel of his hand connected with the man's windpipe.

The force of the blow crumpled the man's knees, sent his head back, his eyes bulging, but it didn't render him unconscious. He grunted and staggered, trying to regain his balance. Struggling to free the gun in his holster, he opened his mouth to draw in a noisy breath. He was going to call out.

Ben cursed silently and swung a hard right to his jaw.

The man sagged, toppling forward. Ben caught the burly guard before he could hit the floor and eased him down as quietly as he could. He paused for a moment to listen to the muffled conversation below. They still seemed to be arguing, but there was no sudden outcry.

He went through the man's pockets and came up with a key. If the information he had was correct, Ian and Jamie were behind the fourth door on his left. He inserted the key, pushed open the door and stepped inside.

"Stay quiet," he murmured even as he opened his arms to his son.

Jamie raced forward to clamp his father's waist as though he'd never let go, and Ben's arms enclosed him in a binding embrace. He shut his eyes thankfully and bent his head to press his lips against his son's head. "Jamie," he whispered. He raised his eyes to Ian and held out one arm to bring the older man into their embrace.

Jamie muffled a sob against Ben's chest.

"Ben, I don't know how the hell you got here, but I'm glad to see you," whispered Ian. His weary features split into a grin.

Ben reminded himself that the reunion would have to wait. He had to get them both out through the window, silently. Then he had to find Maggie before the commandos charged the building and all hell broke loose.

"Jamie, listen to me," he whispered. "We've got to get you out of here. I want you to follow me without making a sound. Can you do that, son?" Though he addressed his words to his son, he watched Ian's face. The older man nodded.

Ben noted the bruises. Ian's eye was swollen shut and blue-black. There was a yellowing spot on his jaw.

Ben inhaled sharply and tilted his son's face up. Jamie's features were without blemish, but there was a bruise on his arm. The sight of those marks hardened his resolve. He'd get Ian and Jamie out, go for Maggie, then *kill* the sons of bitches!

"You're going out through a window, Jamie. There'll be a short drop. As soon as you hit the ground, run toward the alley to your right. Granpa will be right behind you, but don't wait, just run. One block down is a police van. It has no markings, but it is blue. Can you do all that?"

Jamie swallowed and nodded. "Yessir," he whispered.

Ben cupped his son's head to his chest. "Good boy. Remember, absolute silence. Let's go."

Ian took one step, and Ben stopped him. Jamie had on sneakers—he was okay—but Ian's leather-soled shoes had to go. He pointed to them.

Ian understood immediately. He slipped out of the shoes.

Jamie's eyes grew wide and round at the sight of the unconscious guard. Ben checked the man's condition and noted with grim satisfaction that he had left a few bruises himself.

He had taken a chance leaving the window open. If any of the terrorists had noticed it, they would have known their hideout had been breached. But now he was grateful not to have to endure the squeak of rusty metal again. The conversation downstairs had grown quiet, a soft buzz that wouldn't mask any unexpected sounds.

Ben lifted his son in his arms, hugged him tight for a split second, and lowered him feet first through the opening. He held him in a controlled slide until only their hands grasped; then he dropped him. But he didn't hear Jamie's feet hit the pavement.

He stuck his head through the window. A large dark figure held his son. His heart lodged in his throat until Marston lifted his head, gave him the thumbs up sign and a grin.

Ben sighed his relief, nodded and turned to Ian. He gripped the older man's arm. "There's an agent down there waiting for you," he breathed.

The ambassador fixed him with an uncompromising stare. "You said 'Granpa will be right behind you.' Where do you intend to be?"

"Ian, please go."

"Not until you tell me what you're planning to do. Maybe I can help. I have a few scores to settle, too, you know."

Ian Bentley was in excellent physical condition. For a minute Ben was almost tempted to accept his offer. But Ian had been through an ordeal that would tax a man half his age. Besides, if the worst happened, Jamie would need his grandfather.

"They are holding Maggie downstairs," he said.

"God! How did—forget it, it doesn't matter how." Ian searched Ben's eyes. He understood without being told what the consequences of the next few minutes could be. He grasped his son-in-law's arm in a brief salute and turned and put a leg over the windowsill.

Ben smiled wryly. One thing about a diplomat: you didn't have to repeat yourself, he thought. Ian's footsteps were quieter than Marston's, but he heard them both fade to nothing. He headed for the top of the stairs.

He had already decided that the opposite stairwell was farther from where the group downstairs was gathered. If he went down this way, he would step right into their midst.

Maggie's head throbbed, and her wrists were raw from the abrasion of the ropes, but she was nearly free. She clenched her teeth and gave her right hand one more vicious jerk.

She tossed aside the rope that had bound her wrists and set to work on her ankles. Her fingers were numb and clumsy, but finally she managed to release the last of the knots. She crouched for a minute to regain her balance and moved stealthily to the door.

Now what? How was she going to get out of here and
find her father and son? The kidnappers were right outside the door. There was no back entrance to the storage room, no window. She folded her arms across her
bent knees and rested her head on them, wishing she had
one of Ben's cigarettes. *Think, Maggie! Think!*

Ben reached the foot of the stairs. Large boxes provided a screen from the group. They had begun to argue
again, with even more heat than before.

"One of them goes. Now!" said an angry voice that
brooked no opposition. Ben wondered; he didn't recognize the voice as belonging to the man he'd dubbed
bossman. He heard the unmistakable click of a safety
being removed from a pistol. "I am the leader now, and
I say we kill the . . ."

Ben held his breath, bracing himself for a move. The
ambassador? The child? The woman?

At Maggie's touch, Dante groaned and moved. He
was alive but still unconscious. She stood erect, determination hardening her features. She couldn't, she
wouldn't cower in this room for another minute.

Eye Patch spoke on the other side of the door. "I am
the leader now, and I say we kill the . . ."

Maggie put her hand on the knob, opened the door
and stepped out.

Ben heard the commotion by the loading ramp at the
same time that he saw Maggie step calmly out of a door
to his right. Good God, she was walking right into the
line of fire!

Suddenly all hell broke loose. Wood splintered, metal clanged, gunfire erupted. *"Polizia!"* shouted a voice. "Throw down your guns."

A body hurled itself out of nowhere, sending Maggie back into the storeroom, while bullets flew and ricocheted around her.

"Jamie!" she screamed and couldn't even hear her own voice over the tumult. "Daddy!" A light exploded next to her head. She fought the weight that held her down, but her struggles only provoked a shifting of the body above her. She used her knee, her nails, her teeth, frantically struggling against her captor. Her burning wrists were caught in an inflexible grasp and pinned. She cried out at the anguish, both physical and emotional, of being helplessly imprisoned.

Then Maggie fainted for the first time in her life.

Chapter 12

When Maggie regained consciousness, she knew immediately that she was in heaven. She was being held close in Ben's arms, Jamie was on his knees in front of her swabbing at her face with a wet cloth, and her father was crouching behind her son, silent tears wetting each side of his broadly grinning mouth.

"We made it?" she asked. "We really made it?"

Throwing aside the cloth, Jamie lunged forward into her arms, and Ben's embrace tightened around them both. "We made it, my darling," he said in a choked voice.

Maggie's head bent over Jamie's. "All of us," she finally sighed, reaching for Ian's hand and bringing him into the circle.

"A bit battered but whole," said Ian. "Whole, thank God."

Maggie combed her fingers into Jamie's hair, lifting his head. She was too moved to speak for a minute. She drew him close, putting her lips to his forehead, closing her eyes in a prayer of thanks.

Jamie wiggled a bit, and she released him with a smile. The bruise on Jamie's arms, and her father's swollen, battered face suddenly registered. "Jamie, Daddy, you're hurt!"

"Not anything serious enough to worry about, my dear," her father replied. "As a matter of fact, we're already beginning to heal. But you, on the other hand..."

Maggie put a hand to her own cheek. It came away streaked with blood. Her wrists were stinging, too. "I'm fine," she said, grinning. Bruises, scratches were nothing. "I've never felt so wonderful in my life!"

Ben's arms were shaking with the intensity of his joy. The relief was overwhelming.

Marston came over to the group and hunkered down, his rugged face gleaming with relief. "Mrs. Altman. Mrs. Altman." He shook his head in mock reproach. "You don't follow orders any better than your husband does."

Maggie interrupted, grinning. "Mr. Marston, don't you think we know each other well enough by now to be on a first-name basis? I'm Maggie."

His hard eyes were suspiciously moist. "And I'm Clay. You're a hell of a woman, Maggie." He paused, unable to say more for a minute; then he spoke again, his voice husky. "If you weren't—" his eyes flicked to Ben, whose arms tightened around her "—taken, I'd be awfully tempted to propose to you."

She rubbed her cheek against Ben's hard arm. "If I weren't taken, I'd be awfully tempted to give it some thought."

"I'll say goodbye here. When you get back to the States, give me a call. I'm in the book."

That was enough, thought Ben. "We're both coming back. *We* will give you a call."

Ian's eyes took on a glitter, but he didn't say anything.

"Dad! Really?" said Jamie. "You're moving back to the States? For good?"

"For good," Ben assured his son.

Maggie had a dozen questions about that statement, but she put them aside to be answered later. She held out her hand. It was immediately grasped in Marston's hard one. "How can I ever thank you enough, Clay, for getting us out of here alive?"

Marston's jaw dropped almost comically. He dropped her hand. "You mean you don't know...?"

"Know what?" she asked.

The man who had come up beside him relieved him of the need to answer. "Mrs. Altman, I am Doctor Manuzio." He spoke softly. "We have an ambulance waiting to take all of you to the hospital."

Everyone protested at once.

Ian rose, holding up his hand. "If I may have a word with you, doctor." He drew the man aside. Jamie went, too, protesting heatedly.

Ben watched, a small smile on his face. His eyes returned to Maggie's. "Sometimes it helps to have a diplomat handy."

Her amused gaze clung to his, gradually sobering. "Yes, it does. I don't think I could stand to be separated from any one of you right now."

"I love you, Maggie." Ben's voice was hoarse. He seemed to be holding his breath as he waited for her to answer.

"Yes, I believe you mentioned something about that," she teased unsteadily.

"Maggie, damn it, tell me . . ."

"Are you feeling better, Mom? Do you want to try to stand up?" asked Jamie, returning to her side.

Maggie took her son's proffered hand, but she held on to Ben's, too, and felt him relax slightly. "As a matter of fact, I feel quite rested. I've never fainted before. It's amazing."

Jamie looked dubious as she struggled to her feet. Her head spun for a second, then her senses stabilized. He held on to her even when she straightened. "You should take it easy, Mom. You're going to have a black eye."

"That man knocked me down. . . ." She shuddered.

Ben chuckled, drawing her questioning gaze. "The man who fell on you was me, my love. And if I'd known you could put up a fight like that one, I wouldn't have worried so much about you." He leaned closer to whisper for her ears only. "If you've permanently damaged the goods, it's your own fault."

Maggie recalled her last act of defiance and the satisfactory grunt of pain it had produced. "Ben! That was you? And I—with my knee! Oh, Lord, I'm sorry."

He grinned. "Sorry is what you very well may be."

Ian interrupted before she could reassure herself that she hadn't really done any permanent damage. "Well, he's going to follow us to the residence and examine us there. I think I've convinced him that we'll benefit more from hot baths and food than from X rays and blood tests."

"Needles, yuk!" said Jamie. "They're gross!"

The three adults gaped at him. Five days in the hands of terrorist kidnappers, and he declared that needles were gross. Suddenly they were all laughing helplessly.

Arm in arm, the stronger supporting the weaker—
though none of them could have told which was which—
they headed for the loading dock and the police van that
would take them back to the residence.

Jamie was asleep almost as soon as his head touched
the pillow. Hand in hand, Maggie and Ben stood
watching him for a long time, reluctant to leave him.
Finally they made their way back downstairs to the
study.

The men and women from the basement straggled up
in ones and twos to say goodbye. Some would return
tomorrow for more in-depth questioning of Jamie and
the ambassador. They would bring in their psycholo-
gists, their psychiatrists, their political analysts and
specialists, hoping, trying to understand what provokes
an attack of terrorism. But for tonight the weary group
was simply relieved and happy.

Maggie and Ian thanked each one of them personally
while Ben watched with admiration, occasionally add-
ing his own thanks.

But it was the ambassador and his daughter who were
center stage. Their behavior reflected on their country,
and they weren't about to scrimp on their thanks. They
offered coffee and sandwiches, which were for the most
part declined, and talked to each person as though they
had all night to spend personally with him or her.

They were exhausted and injured, and no one would
have criticized them if they'd gone straight to bed. But
it was more important to show their gratitude to the
people who had worked diligently to free them. Ben was
so proud of them both, and impatient to see them get
some rest.

Ian had been correct when he'd said that he and Jamie were beginning to heal. Their bruises hadn't required medical treatment.

Their inside bruises were another matter. Time alone would tell about those. And if Jamie had nightmares, Ben would be there with Maggie to hold him, to comfort them both. From now on they were going to be a family. Now all he had to do was convince Maggie of that fact. The sooner he got started, the better.

He tried to catch her eye, but her attention was fixed on Alberto, who was the last to leave. His whole being rebelled at the sight of the white patch on her cheek. Maggie, beautiful, loving Maggie, his Maggie, injured at the hands of a monster. Ben's own hands began to shake at the thought, and he looked down at his scraped knuckles. He squeezed his hands into fists. *Why didn't I kill the bastard?*

Resting his head on the back of the sofa, he closed his eyes, forcing his thoughts away from the picture of Maggie, limp and bleeding in his arms as he'd carried her out of the storage room. *Because it would have made me no better than they are,* he thought, answering his own question. He smiled to himself. But there had been a certain satisfaction in leaving his own marks on that guard.

"He seems to be having pleasant dreams," said Maggie. "What do you think he's dreaming about?"

Ben opened his eyes to see Ian and Maggie standing before him with their arms around each other. His smile spread, then faded under the force of emotion. The love he was feeling flowed from his heart until it filled every part of his body. He couldn't speak.

Ian cleared his throat, then gave his daughter a final hug. "I'm going to bed. Good night, you two."

Maggie was caught in the spell of Ben's gaze. "Good night, Daddy," she said huskily. Then she remembered. Her eyes sent Ben an apology. "Daddy, wait a minute. What about Dante?"

Her father sighed. "I don't know, honey. He is mentally unbalanced, would have to be to go along with kidnapping. But he did stand up to the others when it came to Jamie. And he was obviously surprised by the death threat. I really think he expected that the men in prison would be freed and we would be returned unharmed."

"A disillusioned idealist," put in Ben.

Ian nodded thoughtfully. "He'd become a very quiet man after his wife was killed. I should have realized how deep his grief was, and how far he'd go for revenge. I don't blame him completely. I'm going to talk to the authorities to see if I can arrange for psychiatric treatment."

"And his little boy?" whispered Maggie. Even though Dante had been responsible for putting her own child and her father in grave danger, she couldn't help thinking of his son.

"I'll make arrangements," said Ian. Maggie's heart warmed at her father's words. She put her arms around his neck and kissed him. "I love you very much," she whispered.

He returned her hug, lifting her off her feet. "And I love you. Good night, you two."

"Come here," Ben ordered softly when Ian had left. He snaked out a hand to pull her down on his lap. "I haven't held you for an hour at least."

Maggie curled into his warm embrace, her head tucked under his chin. He lifted her feet to the sofa and disposed of her shoes.

"This feels good," he murmured contentedly.

"Wonderful," said Maggie, wiggling her toes.

"I'd like to keep you right here forever." He placed his lips on her temple. "Here against my heart," he said softly against her skin. "Safe."

Maggie was silent. Her hand rested lightly on his chest.

He let his head drop back to the cushion. "Tonight, when you were in danger, I think I understood for the first time what you must have felt eight years ago."

Maggie smoothed the fabric under her hand, feeling the strong beat of his heart. "And I understood why you must do what you feel is right. I discovered I'm a bit of a fighter, too."

He chuckled. "More than a bit. I'm living proof."

She raised her head. "Did I really hurt you, darling? I know I kicked pretty hard."

"Like a mule," he teased. "We'll have to test the equipment later. To make sure it still works."

"Um-m-m," she murmured, putting her face against his neck. "Jamie seems all right," she said tentatively.

"He'll probably have nightmares. There could be other repercussions. We won't know all the effects for a while. It might be a good idea for him to talk it out with someone."

She sat up and slid off his lap to face him. "A psychiatrist, you mean? You think he'll need one?"

He nodded thoughtfully. "Or a counselor of some kind. We should take care of finding someone as soon as we get back to Washington."

"We?" she said softly.

"I love you, Maggie. I think we should be a family again."

She nodded, but slowly. "Then we'll both be there for Jamie."

"And for each other." He hesitated. "I meant to woo you slowly. With flowers and candy—I even bought that lamé dress for you. But I can't wait that long. Will you marry me?"

"Yes, of course," she said, surprised that he'd have to ask.

"What do you mean, 'of course'? You haven't even said you love me." He pulled her close again, inhaling the scent of her hair. "But as a matter of fact, I'd rather that you show me. Let's go to bed."

"I love you, Ben. I'll always love you. And I want nothing more than to go to bed with you. But..."

He was stung by the "but," then he relaxed. "But what?" he asked tenderly. She'd said she loved him. She'd said she'd marry him. It couldn't be too serious.

Maggie played with a button on his shirt, avoiding his gaze. "Do you remember the first day I was in Rome, out at your place?"

"How could I forget?" he answered huskily, his lips roaming over her face.

"I didn't get pregnant."

Ben pulled back to stare at her. "You mean...?"

She nodded. "I'm sorry," she said with a small smile.

Ben collapsed against her, shaking with helpless laughter. When he could speak again, he shook his head and got to his feet. "I guess we could both use some sleep," he said, reaching down to scoop her up in his arms.

Maggie put her arms around his neck. "But you could hold me," she suggested. "If it wouldn't be to painful."

"Don't worry," he gritted. "I don't intend for you ever to sleep alone again, no matter what."

"A few weeks ago my family and I lived through the horrifying nightmare of an act of terrorism. We were lucky. And I say that without taking one iota of credit away from the men and women who participated in the rescue. At any moment during the ordeal, the people who held my son and his grandfather, and later my wife, could have killed any or all of them. It could have been done in cold blood, in anger, or on a whim.

"How is it that some people can live out their lives under the most appalling conditions, go through the horrors of Job and survive with their humanity intact? And others, what turns them into terrorists? It is a question for which I have no answers. The memory of my fear is too fresh; I am too involved to be objective. But society must find an answer, and find one soon, or we shall all return to the level of animals. The hunter and the hunted. No one in the world will feel safe.

"This is Benjamin Altman, ABS News, Washington."

Maggie reached forward and turned the television off. She nestled under the outstretched arm of her husband.

"Well?" asked Ben. "What do you think of my swan song?"

"I think Mac will be sorry to lose you," she said quietly.

He tilted her chin to look steadily into her warm brown eyes. "Something's troubling you. What is it, honey?"

"I just hope you don't regret leaving your job with the network. You didn't have to do it because of me, you know. I could have handled it. I really could."

"I know you could, my love. I'll never doubt your ability to handle anything again."

His smile was filled with trust and faith. Maggie leaned forward to touch her lips to his. "Thanks."

Ben responded to the sweet caress of his lips with a low growl. He tumbled her back on the sofa and covered her body with his. "But as I told you, Margaret Anne Altman Altman..."

She laughed at the crazy name Ben had insisted on calling her.

He propped himself on his elbows and played idly with a strand of her hair. "I really wanted to make the switch. It was half decided before we remarried. The *Post* is enthusiastic about what I've done so far, and they're sure the column can be successfully syndicated." He dipped his head to kiss the little hollow at the base of her neck. "I want to spend more time with you and Jamie. I've missed so much of his childhood. And I can write at home...if and when we ever find a home."

The apartment was cramped with the addition of another person, especially such a big one. They had begun house-hunting right after their short honeymoon.

"So we won't have to arrange day-care for Jamie while you're at work," he went on.

Happiness bubbled up in Maggie. Happiness that had bubbled so frequently over the past few weeks that she felt as if her mouth were permanently fixed in a grin. She laughed again and threw her arms around his neck. "Ben Altman, house husband! I'm not so sure what your fans would say, but I love it! Now *you* can plague Jamie about his homework. You can discipline him; you can wash the mud off him when he comes in from playing in the rain."

"Maggie..."

She was covering his face with kisses. "You can do the laundry and the shopping. You can plan all the meals and cook. Except breakfast. I'll do breakfast."

"Maggie..." His hand slid under her sweater to cup her breast.

"And you... what is it, Ben?"

"I threw your birth control pills away."

"You did wha-at?"

"I thought that might get your attention." He grinned unrepentantly and covered her lips in a long, slow kiss. "Not really, but let's talk about it."

Silhouette Intimate Moments

COMING NEXT MONTH
Four New Authors,
Four Exciting New Romances

SACRED PLACES—Nancy Morse

When the Indian heritage Carly sought to protect was threatened by Jesse's plans, she struggled to preserve it. But when Jesse wanted her heart as well, she didn't know how to resist....

WITHIN REACH—Marilyn Pappano

Rafael was a Border Patrol agent who wanted nothing to interfere with his job, especially not the daughter of a suspected drug smuggler. Krista was the pawn in a dangerous game where the stakes were her life—and Rafael's love.

BEAUTIFUL DREAMER—Paula Detmer Riggs

They had been separated once by his father's wealth and power. Ten years later Trey came back, and Lisi felt that nothing had changed. She still loved her ex-husband, but was Trey still his father's son?

SEPTEMBER RAINBOW—Sibylle Garrett

Caught in a web of international intrigue, Jessica faced death, betrayal—and romance. Damon was a businessman with a mysterious background. She couldn't trust him, but she loved him anyway.

AVAILABLE THIS MONTH:

Silhouette Intimate Moments

MARCH MADNESS!

Get Intimate with
Four Very Special Authors

Silhouette Intimate Moments has chosen March as the month to launch the careers of three new authors—Marilyn Pappano, Paula Detmer Riggs and Sibylle Garrett—and to welcome top-selling historical romance author Nancy Morse to the world of contemporary romance.

For years Silhouette Intimate Moments has brought you the biggest names in romance. Join us now and let four exciting new talents take you from the desert of New Mexico to the backlots of Hollywood, from an Indian reservation in South Dakota to the Khyber Pass of Afghanistan.

CLAIM THE Crown

Carla Neggers

The complications only begin when they mysteriously inherit a family fortune.

Ashley and David. The sister and brother are satisfied that their anonymous gift is legitimate until someone else becomes interested in it, and they soon discover a past they didn't know existed.